For Mal,
Love

May this your whelming heart always lead you through loving moments

Bottomless Dreams

25 stories

RYAN POWER

CAUTION:

No Holds Barred Fiction

 **FriesenPress**

Suite 300 - 990 Fort St
Victoria, BC, Canada, V8V 3K2
www.friesenpress.com

ISBN
978-1-4602-5925-2 (Hardcover)
978-1-4602-5926-9 (Paperback)
978-1-4602-5927-6 (eBook)

1. *Fiction, Short Stories (single author)*

Distributed to the trade by The Ingram Book Company

Stories for
Bumblebees and Cyborgs

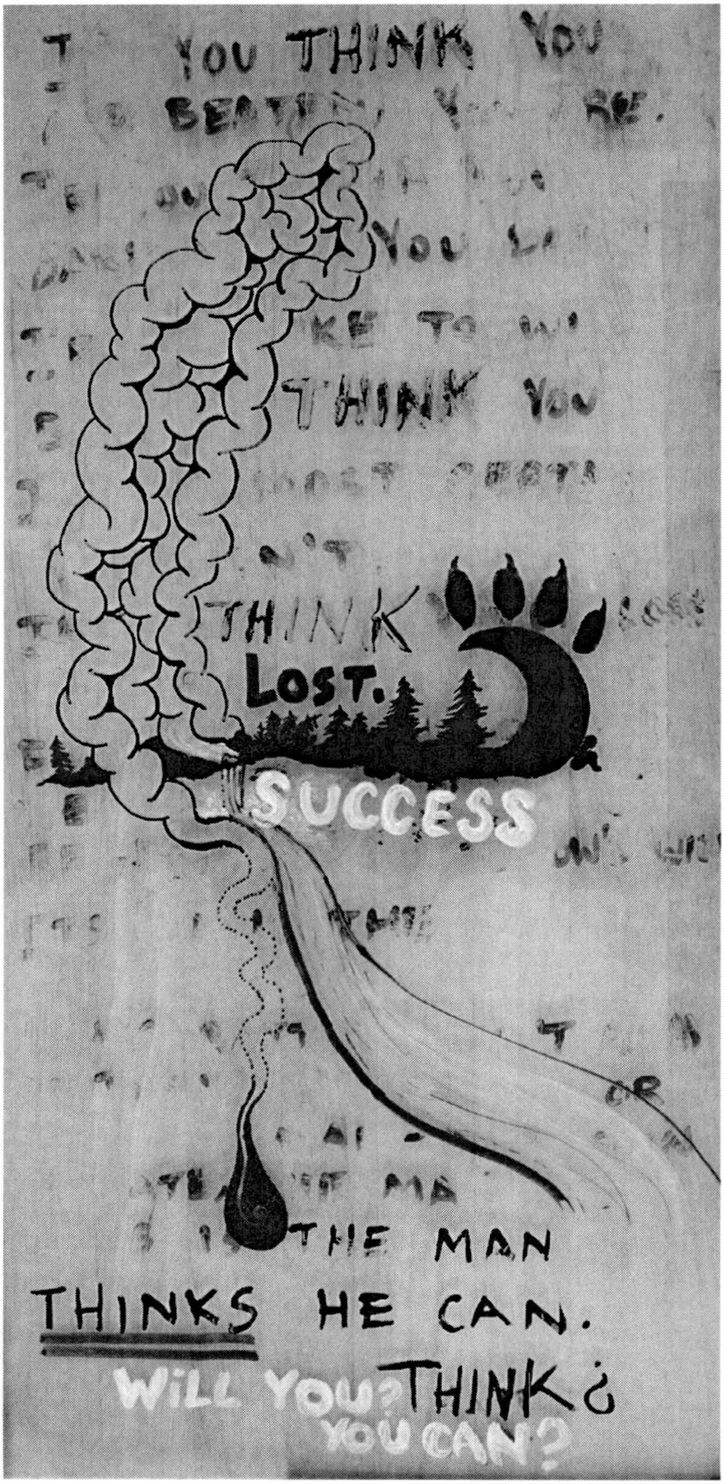
YOU THINK YOU
BEATEN
THINK YOU
THINK
LOST.
SUCCESS
THE MAN
THINKS HE CAN.
WILL YOU? THINK ¿
YOU CAN?

1

LOST

2:34 PM

The forest is ceilinged by gnarled branches, twisting and touching, as if the trees hold hands as they reach towards the light. One lone sunbeam, illuminating the dust as it swirls in the pine-scented air, shines through to the forest floor.

Philip sits in the beam of light, hunched on a rock, naked and alone, his smooth face pressed into his callused hands. His wiry frame is birdlike in its thinness, with its protruding Adam's apple and knobby knees. He shivers as his breath puffs from his mouth and hangs in the crisp air. A cross dangles from his fingers on a silver chain. Dust from the cement factory is crusted under his nails.

Goosebumps cover his pink flesh, rippling the boxing-glove tattoo on his right shoulder blade. Below that lie the words, "I'll die fighting before I live on my knees". His jeans and hoodie hang drying in the sun. He flicks his lighter, but it's too damp to start so he rests it on the rock next to three soggy cigarettes. He knows he should wait for the lighter to dry so he can start a fire, but the need to find Shyan and make things right gnaws at him from within like a blood-borne parasite, making it nearly impossible to sit still.

He stands, the movement stirring the mist, and he searches the ground for firewood. Since well before the roar of chainsaws or thunder of guns pierced the forest, a conversation of sorts has been unfolding in this untamed refuge. It's not a language of word or tongue, but of instinct and cunning, one that is felt and seen as well as heard, where every broken branch and turned stone tells a story. It is a language as old as the forest itself, spoken by plants and animals, but forgotten by man. It now warns of a danger lurking in the woods, but Philip is too distracted to hear its counsel. His mind is a raging bull in an arena, taunted, prodded, slapped on the ass, trying to buck off the weight of life on its back. Hooves kick the inside of Philip's skull, making his head throb.

He curses the forest for appearing to be the same in all directions, playing some sort of evil trick on him, leading him in circles farther and farther from the road. He wishes he hadn't cried, the embarrassment of his tears driving him from the path in search of complete isolation, and causing him to lose his way. What kind of man cries? He wishes he hadn't slipped on a patch of mud on the river's edge—the water, a thousand frozen daggers sweeping him even further from the road. He wishes he could remember the way back to his truck. But none of these things are what's making him want to scream and tear himself out of his own skin.

Craving warmth and fearing that his lighter might be broken for good, Phillip picks up a smooth stick. He lays a piece of bark flat, then stands the stick on end, pushing the tip into the bark as he spins the stick in his hands. He presses his weight into the stick as he spins it, hoping a flame will jump to life. He spins and spins the stick until his hands hurt, but there's no sign of fire. A voice in his head whispers that he deserves this fate, telling him that he is a monster—a fiend sucking the life-force from the one he loves. Earlier that morning, he had unleashed a cowardly rage upon his girlfriend, the only girl who has ever attempted to know him—the complete him, with all his inner complexities, good and ugly. Usually he'd blame his juvenile reaction to her unsettling news on any number of past events, primarily his abusive father, but he wouldn't let himself do that anymore. He's simply a monster. There's no other explanation.

~

"This is your fault," he had yelled at Shyan across the pile of dishes that were cluttering their basement-suite kitchen. "This is why I told you to take the pill. How could you let this happen?" And there it was again, blame, the little demon that reared its ugly head whenever something went wrong. As soon as the words had left his mouth he despised himself for saying them. But he hadn't been able to stop, even though he'd known he should. It was as if he'd been possessed. Not by some devil, but by some previously unknown part of himself that was unleashed by his panic.

Shyan had stood in stunned silence as Philip felt himself morph from her usual pliable teddy bear into an uncontrollable beast, spitting venom-soaked words. At first, her tears had escaped silently as he feverishly ranted, "I'm too young for this. We can't keep it." But then the flood gates broke.

"Go," she'd cried. "If you wanna run away like your father did, then get out of my sight."

So Philip had left, slamming the door to emphasize his anger—as if transferring his inner torment into a violent action somehow justified his response.

~

Now, he sits alone and in the throes of a self-inflicted emotional beating. *If only life had a rewind button*, he broods, wondering why his anger had held sway over his rational mind. What had made him crumble? Is he that afraid of responsibility, or is there more to it? He knows he needs to develop patience, but doesn't know how. If only there was a guide book—*Manning Up for Dummies*.

The wind picks up, rustling branches, and Philip hugs his knees for warmth. He longs to hold Shyan and tell her that he's sorry. He wants to tell her that he loves her and that he'll be there for her, but apprehension washes over him. How is someone supposed to know that the person they're with is truly 'the one'?—or if 'the one' is even a real thing?

What would he even say if she were to miraculously appear through the bushes at this moment?—*You see? This is all I am without you! A naked idiot who can't even find his way out of the woods.*

Philip is fearless on his dirt-bike, and he never backs down from a brawl, but the responsibility of loving another person scares the romantic right out of him—the commitment too akin to a loss of freedom. So, instead of cuddling Shyan by the fire and celebrating the creation of a new life, he sits on a rock, shivering, unaware of the twelve-hundred-pound grizzly using paws the size of baseball mitts to scoop fish from the river less than fifty feet away.

8:06 PM

The sun is down, having caught Philip off guard in its quick descent. A blanket of cloud hovers above the forest, blocking the moonlight. Philip's clothes are still damp, but he wears them anyway as he navigates the forest by the glow of his lighter. Hunger pangs jab him below his ribs, making him all the more frantic. Fear creeps into his mind, swelling, grabbing hold and tearing into him, spurring him forward in a crazed hunt for the road. He picks up another branch in an attempt at lighting a torch, but the wood is too damp and his patience too fleeting.

He walks, deeper into the forest, deeper into the darkness, and deeper into himself, praying for salvation. *Please God, get me outta here. I'm cold and hungry and wet. I've learned my lesson. If you help me out, I'll go back to church. I'll never question my faith again. I'll be better, promise.* But the words are empty, the intention is selfish, and the only response is a chilling silence.

Leaning against a tree, Philip lets the lighter go out and sucks his thumb where the glowing red metal has left a crescent-shaped blister. He blows hot breath into his cupped hands, rubbing them together. The warmth engulfs them and momentarily relieves the sharp pain radiating up from his fingers. Cold air bites the exposed skin of his face and neck. He pulls the strings of his hood, scrunching it up around his face, and licks his lip where it has split. He tastes blood.

His knuckles are white as he grips the lighter, trying to spark a flame. His fingers have lost all strength. They've stopped answering his brain. They're on strike, refusing to work until they're given warmth. He uses two hands, attempting to will the flame to life. He needs this fire—the primal element—the force that brings heat and strikes back the darkness.

The flame jumps to life and Philip is momentarily relieved. But the haunting feeling slinks back in as he looks around, aware that the forest has ceased to be a place of stillness and tranquility—no longer the refuge he'd sought to soothe his burdened mind. The forest has been swallowed by darkness and swamped with the unknown. His mind plays tricks. Branches resemble the arms of skeletons, grasping with bony fingers. Stumps look like wolves, poised for attack. The wind sounds like the distant cry of a witch.

Philip is not prepared to even think about death, certainly not to confront it. He tries to push the fear from his mind, thinking instead about his unborn child and imagining looking into its eyes. Would they be brown like his, or green like Shyan's? What would it feel like to hold the life that he had helped create? To play with it and give it the love that he rarely got?—a pure spirit, innocent, ready to absorb what Philip can share. He's not ready to be a father. But is anyone ever really ready? He thinks of Shyan. The thought of how he had treated her fills him with renewed shame, the filth of his words clinging to his conscience like a hungry tick.

Philip remembers their first date. They'd gone to the Frontier's Man pub to watch a Rolling Stones cover band. She'd told him of her dream to one day go to Nepal, her eyes blazing with excitement as she spoke. He'd listened patiently, wondering why on earth someone would want to carry a heavy backpack around the humid streets of Kathmandu or up the slope of a mountain, when they could be relaxing on the beach with a Corona. She had asked him to dance. He'd been embarrassed but danced anyway because she'd let him put his hands on her hips and it felt right.

They'd left the bar hand in hand, walking to the baseball field on the edge of town where they had lain in each other's arms stargazing. He remembers hearing her laugh for the first time, how the sound had roared out unabashed, staking claim to the moment—a laugh that rumbled up from her depths, filling the air and drawing him in. That laugh and those kind, crescent eyes, had made it easy to open to her, sparking in Philip a natural self-assurance that he rarely felt in the presence of others.

In the forest, the lighter flickers out and Philip fumbles to re-ignite it. For a moment the air is still. He hears rustling in front of him. He breathes deep, ashamed of his fear. *You're not afraid of the dark,* he thinks. *You're a badass. Anything out here should fear you.* Clenching his hands into fists, he throws a quick, jab-cross combo, imagining the satisfying thud of knuckle on heavy bag. The action soothes his fear, so he continues with the lighter.

The light flicks on. There's a rustling in the bush in front of him as a bear cub peeks out. It looks up, startled by the glow, and Philip finds himself staring into the cub's curious eyes. His initial reaction is one of awe. He wants to pick up the adorable creature and rub its velvety fur. It grunts. He steps toward it, then notices the massive head above the cub turning to face him. The mother-bear's gaze is a stun-gun, freezing Philip mid-breath as the beast steps in front of her child.

Terror surges through him like an electric jolt, stretching time. Adrenaline floods his bloodstream. Every hair on his body rises as he looks at the tremendous beast. Its lips curl back like an angry dog. Saliva glistens on its teeth. Muscles ripple under its brown fur, and fearless eyes state its place as the ruler of this forest.

Philip's muscles clench, waiting for his brain to send a signal for action. The grizzly swipes at the ground, tossing aside a moss-covered log. It growls, guttural and harsh, filling the air with the stench of fish.

The beast rises onto its hind legs, seeming to grow to immeasurable proportions. Philip eyes the claws sprouting from the creature's burly paws—three inches of razor-sharp nail capable of tearing a man open in a single swipe.

Then the last drop of butane in the lighter burns up, and the light flickers out.

Silence hangs in the darkness. Then there's a grunt, followed by the snapping of a twig. Philip's brain kicks into gear. He hears the thump of the grizzly's feet on the ground. He turns and takes four strides before catching his forehead on a branch. There's a flash of light behind his eyelids as his body flies through the air.

6:42 AM

When Philip wakes, he is buried under a foot of dirt and moss. The grizzly, stomach full of fish, had buried its catch for later, covering Philip with a blanket of dirt and moss and inadvertently protecting him from the cold.

Philip digs himself out—re-birthed from the earth. His arm throbs. His shirt is torn, exposing dirty puncture wounds where the bear's jaw had clamped onto his arm as it dragged him to the hole.

Feeling nauseated, he looks around, jaw chattering. The cold has sunk deep into his bones. The bear is gone, but for how long? It could come back any moment, ready for breakfast. Terror claws its way back to the forefront of his mind, impelling him to run. He flees his burial spot, crashing through a tangled web of bush and branch.

A mile away, gasping for breath, he collapses at the base of a tall cedar. The sun illuminates the mist swirling upward from the forest floor. Pain radiates up his arm, shooting into his shoulder. The flesh around the bite is purple and yellow, but the blood has clotted. Closing his eyes, Philip remembers what his boxing coach had taught him about pain. It exists whether you like it or not. Focusing on it—revolting against it—is what amplifies it to intolerable proportions. Focusing on his breath instead, he tries to calm himself, tries to reach a state of harmony with the throbbing in his arm, but fear keeps sending his mind on a spiral of doubt: fear of the bear, fear of being alone, fear of responsibility, fear of failing as a man.

Sitting, observing his breath, in and out, in and out, he thinks about life and the untameable current that has led him on paths he had never wanted to walk. He feels victimized, slapped by the hand of fate, instead of guided.

After a few minutes, his pulse slows and he falls into the rhythm of his breath. Maybe it's the loss of blood, maybe the hunger, maybe the concussion, maybe his brush with death, but he feels different, light-headed yet contemplative, almost as though he's entering a trance. The pain in his arm makes him think about his body, his identity, his mortality. He wonders who he is—a collection of bones and flesh housing a nervous system that generates conscious thought? Is he the body feeling the pain, or the mind observing it?—or both?—or maybe something else entirely?—perhaps his body is simply a vehicle for something else, the real him, the soul. But if so, who is Philip?—the name is attached to his body. Will his identity as Philip live on after his body dies?

He stumbles through questions as old as humanity—questions he had previously avoided, thinking them irrelevant. But now, in his near-death state of mind, the questions grow to colossal proportions, becoming primeval, universal, essential for the unfolding of his consciousness. These are the questions that have helped shape human existence. They are questions without answers, and, Philip suddenly realizes, that it is the questions without answers that define the limits of human thought. A question with no answer acts like a wall at the end of a tunnel. It is the farthest probe in that direction of understanding—the end of the verifiable line. Such questions set the temporary limits of human possibility, erecting the metaphorical fence around human knowledge.

As Philip emerges from his reverie, he hears the river's gentle voice. He gets up and walks to it. Shivering, he envies the bear, built for survival with its fur and claws. An ancient knowledge, primordial and vast, lives deep in the bear's cells, communicating to it via instinct. Suddenly humbled, Philip realizes that he's completely out of touch with his natural self—unable to survive in the environment his species has lived in for hundreds-of-thousands of years. He is human, the supposed ruler of all domains, but the reality is, he is helpless without his tools.

Phillip notices a fish in the river and wonders if it has come to spawn. A squirrel climbs a tree with an acorn in its mouth. He observes the plants and animals living in accordance with the laws of nature. It's a complete contrast to society, where people rebel against the natural order, desiring total mastery over it. But total control over the world around is impossible. No matter how hard we try, life hits us with unwelcome situations.

The reason for his suffering dawns on him. Every time the path of his life veers from the path he has envisioned, he resists, feeling he has been served a plate of injustice. And the more he rebels against the reality he is faced with, the more he suffers. He realizes, finally, that mental pain is akin to physical pain, amplified exponentially when dwelt upon. Pain, he realizes, really begins the moment you wish it wasn't there.

Philip follows the river. He gets frustrated by the way it meanders in one direction then another. Why can't it just flow straight to town? Is it even going in the right direction? Thirsty, he lowers himself to his hands and knees, and drinks directly from the stream. He feels the cold water in his chest, and realizes that the river is the life-blood of the forest. The flow of life is like the flow of the river, he thinks. You can't control it. It has its own path. Rivers do what rivers do, sometimes raging sometimes calm. It is not up to the river to bring us to happiness. How can it? The river is just a river. What brings us joy or sorrow is not what the river is doing, but rather how we react to it. You can hate the sharp corners and fear the drops, a victim thrashed about in the river of life, always fighting the current, or you can swim with it and enjoy it, thrilled by the unexpected turns. The bear could have killed him, but it didn't. Instead it warned him, it showed him how precious life is.

He thinks of Shyan curled on the couch with a book. He loves their cozy Sunday mornings. Their argument seems so trivial in light of everything he's recently been through. He could die out here. Then what? She would never know how he feels.

He vows to find his way home, wrap her in his arms, and tell her all the things he'd been too scared to say, finally saying the right thing. His words will tumble freely from his heart. Something like— *Remember the waterfall we hiked to last summer? Where we made love—first in the cave, and then in the sunshine with the mist cooling our skin. You told me that I'm like a watermelon, tough on the outside but sweet and juicy inside. Then, for the first time ever, you told me you loved me. Your words traveled deep into my psyche, drilling an opening that allowed a well of emotion to fill inside me, swelling me with love. That day, the best of my life, we walked through the woods until we came across a giant fir tree. You were awed, saying that it's so old it must have stood tall back when the Natives ruled this land. We noticed the huge roots twisting into the ground and thought about how enormous the root structure has to be in order to support the tree and bring it water and nutrients.*

I know now that my love for you is like that root structure. It runs deep and wide to help support you and bring you what you need to grow into a giant, reaching for the light. I will be there for you and our child.

The wave of love washing over him clears the junk out of his mind. He sees clearly, realizing that his life isn't the only one on the line. He has to get out of the forest, not for himself alone, but also so his child doesn't grow up fatherless, so Shyan doesn't have to be a single mom, so his mother doesn't lose a child. These thoughts fill him with determination. Survival is no longer the force driving him forward, it's love.

Looking around, Philip sees that the forest has changed again. For the first time he notices life bursting forth, surrounding him, above and below. The trees are living and breathing. Mushrooms sprout up from the forest floor. A chipmunk squeaks as it makes a cache. Even the moss is alive. Inside him, billions of microscopic life-forms exist in harmony with his body. He understands himself as part of it all—connected to the universal flow of life. He is on the ultimate ride—the journey that is the human experience. Heightened senses take everything in: the gentle rustle of falling leaves, the morning birdsong, the breeze as it dances in his hair.

Standing at the edge of the clearing, he looks into the sky. Orange and red burst forth, twisting into each other, becoming one, pouring over the horizon and streaking the sky, setting ablaze the few lonely clouds. It's as if the sky has been torn open and he's looking directly into Heaven.

He feels like he's dreaming—caught in an ancient land reaching beyond the confines of our modern age.

Reaching down, he digs his fingers into the dirt, setting imaginary roots, sensing that the earth is one immense organism. He is part of it, just as the bacteria in his body are part of him.

He thinks about his unborn child, excited to meet it. He walks along the river, the sun on his back. The mark of the bear glistens red in the light. It is the mark that shows he has faced death and remains alive, gifted a second chance. A smile falls across his lips as he walks, aware that a new part of himself has surfaced—a precious yet defining part. He will nurture it, like a little seed, growing tall and straight like the mighty trees around him.

He looks around and knows that he had been wrong. The forest had never been playing tricks on him. It had been guiding him this entire time.

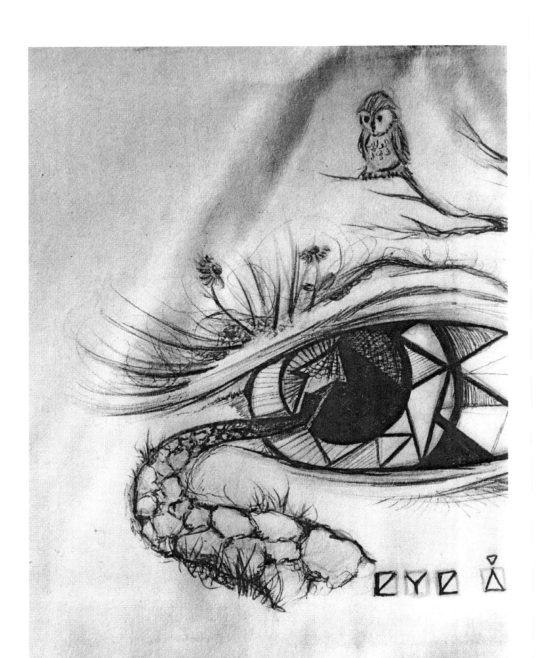

N THE WINDOW

2

EYE IN THE WINDOW

"My obsession was born about a year ago. At first it was that old house. I thought it was abandoned. It certainly looked that way: overgrown yard, cracked paint, rotten steps, moss crawling up the tower like a living carpet, creeping ever closer to the lonely window perched above the neighborhood. Sometimes I think about how peaceful my life would have been if I'd never moved into that neighborhood. How normal I'd be. How happy—if it wasn't for that damned house with its damned window. But I guess there's no point thinking about what could have been, rather than what was.

The curiosity awoke in me the moment I realized that the blinds moved when I looked at them. I had just come home from a long day at the office—I'm an accountant, but I guess you already know that. There were no lights on in the house even though it was dark.

There were no signs of life at all. There never were, until that day. No cars. No sounds. No animals on the property. Just that ancient house, rising out of the hill, left to rot. I thought it a shame that such a statuesque house had been abandoned. I'd never have imagined that somebody lived in that majestic dump. But then the blinds moved, the white slats jerking to the side as if someone had knocked into them. I rubbed my eyes and looked a second time. The blinds moved again. I closed my eyes and opened them, again the blinds moved. I looked away and then back, same result. And they seemed to be moving faster, as if someone was playing with me.

I told myself the wind must be getting in the window and rustling the blinds. I put the house out of my mind and went to bed. But I didn't sleep well. My thoughts kept returning to that old house on the hill.

For months this continued, blinds rustling, my inquisitiveness slowly building, but it was really nothing more than a mild curiosity. Until, of course, I saw the eye staring at me through the blinds. The eye locked onto me. I froze, heart churning. The eye was only there a split second, but that was enough—I knew that it wasn't the wind moving the blinds.

Seeing the eye birthed an insidious gnawing at my core, questions festering in me like a knot of maggots. Who lives in the house? Who watches me from high in that window? Why do they stay hidden?

After that day, my eyes turned to the window every chance they got, each glance stoking my obsession. At first the eye rarely appeared, but over time it began appearing more frequently. I grew to know it well. I could picture it in my mind. It came to me in my dreams. It was the eye of a woman. Of that I was certain. The iris was dark, almost black, although the skin around the eye was pale. The focus was sharp, intelligent, sad. Very sad.

I can't pinpoint the exact moment when my curiosity blossomed into a full fledged obsession. It snuck up on me gradually, creeping into my thoughts. I'd lay awake at night plagued by my macabre speculations. I spent my free time sitting on my porch, staring at the window, waiting for a glimpse of the eye. I daydreamed about meeting the woman. Who was she? An old woman perhaps, no family left alive, too scared to go outside. Maybe a young beauty, locked in the tower by a sadistic man. Or a fugitive, so recognizable she couldn't show her face. Maybe she was a mutant, locked away by ashamed parents. Whoever she was, I felt I had to know her. I felt connected to her in an unexplainable way, like our paths were destined to cross.

I alienated most of my friends with talk of the eye. Nobody but me grasped the depth of what it might mean, an entire existence confined to the solitude of that house. Time passed. Seasons changed. Leaves fell. My girlfriend dumped me. The snow came and went. Flowers bloomed. And through it all, the eye watched me, unraveling my mind with its penetrating glances. I carried it with me everywhere I went, in the back of my mind, haunting me. My mind began playing tricks on me. At times I thought I saw the eye in town, in the window of a moving bus or belonging to the teller at the bank. I'd get anxious and investigate, but, of course, it was never the same eye. I began wondering if what I'd seen in the window was a creation of my imagination. Doubt crept into my thoughts. Could I be losing my sanity? Was the eye even real?

Then, one humid summer day, as I sat staring up at the window, the eye appeared. Only this time the eye didn't look away. It stared at me, unblinking, cold and hollow, like the eye of an assault rifle. I stared back, defenceless—a slave at the mercy of his master. It could've been ten minutes, an hour, I don't know; I was so transfixed that my sense of time vanished. I couldn't have moved even if I had wanted to. When the eye finally disappeared, I stayed on the porch for hours before finally going to bed. But I couldn't sleep a wink. I had reached a breaking point, gone over the edge so to speak. Nothing else mattered but the eye. I had to know who was in that house.

The next morning was devastatingly hot. Upon waking, I peeled myself from sweat-soaked sheets. It was a thick, sloppy heat, wrapping me in a grip so tight I could barely breathe. Sweat dripped from my forehead and nose, soaked through my clothes. The eye called to me, like the full moon to a werewolf, primal and undeniable. I called in sick for work, sat on the porch all day, and watched the window. I rocked in my chair, cigarette after cigarette burning my fingers. But the eye didn't emerge. My eyes itched, but I refused to blink unless absolutely necessary. I forgot to eat, the need for food nothing compared to my obsession. Dusk came, but the heat clung to the darkness, pressing me down. The moon peeked over the horizon, full and ominous. Thirst clutched at my throat; I ignored it until, finally, after hours upon hours manning my post, I gave in and went to my fridge for a coke.

When I returned, her blinds were up.

My entire body was suddenly jittery, as if I had drunk too much coffee. My heart raced. My hands trembled. The room was dark, apart from a faint glimmer cast by a streetlight some forty or so feet away. I couldn't see any furniture or decoration in the room, just shadows. Then, just for a second or two, she appeared at the window. Naked. Soaked in blood. Smiling. Hauntingly beautiful. Skin pale as porcelain. Long black hair wild and unkempt. Her lean body arching up, blood running down, dripping from her hands and breasts. A tattoo spiraled up her right arm, circling it like a double helix from wrist to shoulder. I was immediately drunk with lust. Then she was gone. The blinds closed.

I flung myself backward, slamming into the porch wall, gasping, hands on my knees. What the hell was that? Blood? Why was I so aroused? Sweat streaked down my forehead, stinging my eyes. I wobbled on my feet, falling forward, steadying myself on my porch railing. The absurdity of what I'd seen burned in my mind, igniting an inextinguishable blaze of questions that shattered the last of my rationality.

I was unaware that I had left my porch until I found myself standing in her yard. I paused on her steps, failing to talk myself out of knocking. I climbed the groaning steps, crossed the porch, and gripped the brass knocker, clanking it against the door three times. The door swung open.

The front entrance was empty, the air dank. It smelled of old incense and mold. Dust swirled out of the house, unfurling into the night air and clinging to my sweaty skin. A rat scampered into a hole in the wall. A hallway led into darkness.

I called out, "Hello?" No answer. "Are you OK?" Still no answer. A gentle glow lit the end of the hall, calling me... welcoming me... summoning me. I stepped inside the house without realizing I was doing it. A chandelier hung in the entrance. Cobwebs stretched to the floor. I pushed them aside and stepped deeper into the house. Suddenly the door closed behind me, shutting out the streetlight with a bang. I fumbled for the handle in the dark and tried it, but it spun uselessly in the socket.

I was trapped.

Scared, unsure what to do, I started down the hall towards the faint glow. The floor boards creaked with each step. I called out again, but still no response. I came to a large room with hardwood floors and a stone fireplace—the only furniture an antique wooden bookshelf. The light came from a single candle on the top shelf. It made visible the blanket of dust covering the room. One book stood alone on the empty shelves. I picked it up and blew the dust off to examine the book in the candlelight. It was bound in leather and intricately branded with geometrical patterns, which appeared almost three dimensional in the candlelight. In the center was an upside-down pentagram, and in the center of that, an eye. Her eye.

I opened the book to the middle. It had been penned by quill in what looked to be blood. I didn't recognize the language. Some of the characters were from foreign alphabets. But the drawings were clear.

A man with a wolf's head. A mask. A sacred knife. A circle of fire. It was organized sequentially, like a recipe.

A board creaked upstairs, coming from the tower. I replaced the book and picked up the candle, starting up the stairs. "Hello?" No response. I had made a mistake. I shouldn't be here. But it was too late. My legs were ascending the stairs, my mind helpless against their movement. My hands balled tightly. I felt chilled despite the summer heat. A drop hit my forehead and I wiped it on my forearm. Blood.

I reached her room, frantic and out of breath. The door was open, so I entered. The blinds were down. The room was bare, except for a desk next to the window. On the desk sat a typewriter amid a pile of papers. Above the desk was a painting done in blood. The painting was of an eye—my eye. I turned to leave, but the door was shut and locked. I kicked it but it wouldn't budge. I was alone with nowhere to hide. The window was too high to jump out of.

I stood at the desk. It seemed the woman was in the process of writing a novel. I picked up the manuscript and began reading:

> *Every day he looks to the window, his blue eyes bright with curiosity. He studies the house. The way it looms over the neighborhood, once grand and full of life, now left to ruin, nature slowly reclaiming the wood frame, vines twisting up the tower to the lone window where she waits patiently. He's a quiet man. His curiosity is amplified by his loneliness. He seldom has visitors, and when they do come, they don't stay long.*

It was about me. Imagine how unnerving that is. I lowered the manuscript and glanced over my shoulder before continuing, growing more and more incredulous as I read. She had documented the last year of my life. She had gotten into my head, putting my thoughts onto the page. She knew me intimately. She knew things I have never shared with another soul. Even my dreams found their way onto those pages. How was it possible? I read page after page, entranced, stopping only to pull the last page from the typewriter. The ink was fresh.

*Peter follows the candle's glow to the bookshelf. He finds the dead Witch's Cookbook, the sacred spells bound in human flesh, inked in the virgin's blood. He's clueless to its power. He opens it to the spell of the man-beast, and the Witch takes it as a sign. He's been chosen by the **Dark Prince**. She makes a noise to divert his attention from the book, to keep him focused, to call him to her. He climbs the stairs. Shadows creep along the walls, playing with his fears. The musty air fills his nostrils. He walks through the darkness like a scared child, unsure of every step, as if the world could fall away at any moment. She watches him from the ceiling, clinging to it like a spider. One single drop of blood falls from her, hitting him in the forehead, but when he looks up she's already gone. He wants out of the house, but it's too late. He belongs to her. The stairway seems to climb endlessly as he runs, desperate to find the light.*

Her room's smaller than he expected, but the streetlight streaming through the closed blinds eases his fear. Her desk waits beside the window, her manuscript on it. It calls to him, drawing him like a moth to a candle flame. He flips through the pages, devouring the words, growing more and more agitated as he reads. Not only has she been watching him, but she's been in his head. She knows the inner workings of his thoughts. This is too much, impossible. He wants to leave but doesn't possess the willpower. He continues to read, coming to the final page. The words dig into his soul, the devil's claws pulling him towards madness. Soon her spell will be complete. He will become her beast and he will avenge her death. The words cripple him with fear, 'her beast'. What does it mean? Then, she appears behind him.

I froze, too scared to turn around, the paper shaking in my hands. I placed the manuscript on the desk, trying to appear calm. When I finally turned, she stood in the shadows, still naked. She walked toward me, leaving footprints of blood. She was tall and thin, yet appeared strong—such power and grace. She appeared not of this world. I couldn't move. My eyes were glued to her as she approached, her thick black hair streaming past her shoulders in shiny waves. A few strands stuck in the blood, which shone bright against her colorless skin. Rivulets flowed from her wrist. From this close, I could tell she was older than me. There were no signs of age on her face, but there was something behind her eyes that made me sense that she'd been around a very long time.

Her lips curled in a frightening smile. Her eyes narrowed as they locked on mine. They blazed, as if some secret power lay beyond them. I tried to call out, but my voice was empty, soundless. I could see her tattoo clearly; words, the same language used in the book downstairs. She raised her hand. Blood dripped from the fingertips. I fell to my knees, powerless. My entire body shook. I wanted to leap from the window, but I was paralyzed. She pressed her palm to my forehead, the blood cold on her hand. A drop snaked down the side of my face. She spoke what sounded like an ancient tongue, her voice resonating through my core. Then the darkness took over.

And that's the last thing I remember. Until you two found me."

~

A fluorescent light dangles from a wire running along the ceiling. Peter feels a bead of sweat trickle down his back. The handcuffs dig into his wrists. How did he get here? He looks across the table to the police officer.

The cop's ass-fat spills over both sides of his chair as he leans his weight on the table, making it groan under his bulk. He's obviously annoyed.

"Come on, Peter. You can't be serious. That's your statement? We find you sleeping next to Mr. Smith's butchered body, covered in blood, the remains of his heart in your mouth, and this is the story you give us. A witch in an abandoned house. We need answers! Real answers. How did you get into Mr. Smith's apartment? How did you get past his guards? Where's the murder weapon?" Officer Jones turns to his partner. "This is ridiculous. What do we do with that?"

The younger officer leans close to his partner and whispers, "I need to talk to you outside."

The officers step out into the privacy of the hallway, leaving Peter handcuffed to the chair. He feels changed. The moon calls to him. And he can smell each object in the room individually—the order each object was last touched, who touched it. The scents weave a story. He can smell the officers outside. He smells their emotions. He smells the city air through the closed window: exhaust, fast food, perfume.

His hearing is so powerful that he can hear the distant traffic. People on the sidewalk laugh. A dog in the distance howls. The urge to howl along almost overpowers him, but he withstands it. Instead, he focuses his hearing on the officers in the hall.

The younger officer's voice is full of concern. He asks, "Does the description of the woman seem familiar to you?"

"No, why? You can't doubt that he did it?" The older officer still sounds annoyed.

"No, of course I don't doubt that he did it. But Mr. Smith's wife died a year ago last night. It was my first suicide case."

"So?"

"I can still picture her naked corpse. Peter described her exactly... the blood, the tattoo, the eyes. I had had this nagging suspicion that Mr. Smith killed her, but I couldn't prove it. The evidence was black and white. Suicide. Case Closed. But something Mr. Smith said stuck with me. Something about having to burn the old Witch's body or she'll be able to use her power from the other side. I thought he was crazy, driven to madness by grief. He demanded cremation, but her will specifically requested burial."

"What are you saying?"

"I don't know. I guess I'm not saying anything. Just... what if?

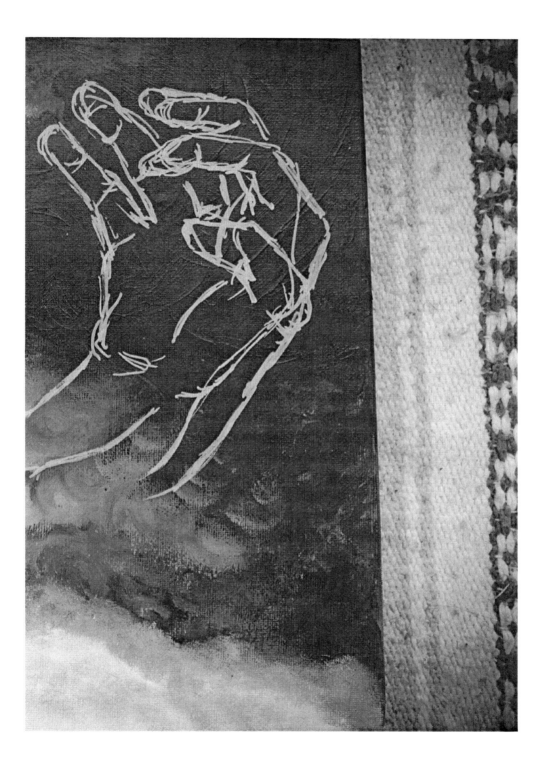

3

RIDING WAVES

Bro, you gotta hear this story. It's wild. It's all about how the shit in my life built to this epic climax and exploded five days ago. I'm still trying to wrap my head around it. It's a good thing I have the psyche of a Holy Man, because a weaker-minded man would completely fall apart. Not me though, I'm solid.

I was surfing the heaviest waves in Central America every day. I had it all, a beach house in Costa Rica, the sexiest chika you ever saw, a job running the booze cruise. But it's all gone now. I got chased outta town by a local rat. What can I say? Life shit all over me. But it's not about what hand you're dealt, it's about how you play it. I can't help it that the universe decided to take a fat, old crap on my life. That's the hand I was dealt. Shit happens. But you know what I'm gonna do? Turn that shit into fertilizer! Just gotta keep faith in myself.

It's like being held down by a massive wave—you panic that you're not gonna get up for air in time, but you just gotta stay calm, conserve air while the wave passes, then float up to the surface. Everybody falls. I've fallen before. The true test of a man's merit is how high he bounces back. I'm like a basket ball; the farther I fall, the higher I bounce. I'm bouncing up to Puerto Escondido. I'm gonna start a new life in Mex. A better life. Sell tours to tourists, maybe. The locals need a friendly face to bring in the tourists, a face they'll trust. My face. The man who makes the sale is king. He's the one who brings what matters—cash. You can have the best product in the world, but if you don't make the sale you got nothing. And if there's one thing I can do, it's sell. I'll sell anything. Anything, as long as it pays for me to stay and surf.

I miss her though—Sasha. Long legs, tight ass, smooth brown skin. Mmmmmm. We lit the strip on fire, rolling side-by-side on our long-boards. Her: an exotic goddess. Me: a chiseled, blue-eyed Apollo with a surfboard for a chariot. Fuck ya. She's more than just looks though. She's a ripper too, on top of that ultra-fine body. She shreds waves almost as good as me. Almost.

I feel bad for her now, man. She had it good with me, liv'n on my dollar. Now she's dancing in that club to pay the rent. It makes me want to puke. The thought of her in that club, almost naked, creepy eyes all over her... it drives me fuck'n mental. I'll crack skulls if she fucks some douche. She deserves better. I emailed her, asked her to come up to Mex, but she hasn't replied. Maybe I'll email her mom, let her know how sorry I am it all played out the way it did. Girls talk to their moms about this kinda shit. Maybe her mom can talk some sense into her. Make her realize what an opportunity she'll be missing if she doesn't follow me to Mex. Guys like me are hard to find. One in a million, bro.

I'm gonna hang around this hostel for a few days anyway, give Sasha a chance to think things through before I take off for Mex. She'll come. I know her, what she needs. She needs a guy who lives this life. Really lives it. Not like one of you guys who's just pass'n though—two weeks, maybe a month or two down here. This is my life, bro, been here three years. This shit's real for me. A girl like Sasha needs a guy with passion, who lives it, breaths it. Plus, she's got no money. She needs a guy who'll pay her way. Girls like that are simple, bro. They need a guy with money and looks, who lives this surf life-style, and who fucks 'em real good. In other words: me.

My hand's fuck'n kill'n me. Look at that gash. You think it's infected? That yellow shit's no good. It's like a fuck'n volcano coming outta my hand. That tight little Brazilian chika I'm fuck'n while I wait for Sasha to calm down told me to take a break from surfing and see a doctor. I think the salt water's good for it though. Cleans it out. I can't stop surfing. She gave me some gauze and polysporin. Fuck, what's her name? Florence? Flowencia? It doesn't matter.

You know what pisses me off? Last night we're down here in the tropics, the Brazilian and I, sharing a tent in ninety-degree weather, and after I bang the shit out of her, she wants to cuddle. All I want to do at that point is get away, crawl to the sea and wash myself. I'm not an asshole, but at that point I'm sweatier than a fat man's ass crack mid jalapeno-eating-competition in the heat of the Texan summer. I've just performed a physical marvel. I'm a wild animal in bed, pure sexual ferocity. Believe it. I blow minds so wide open it's dimension-shifting. I rocked that Brazilian chika so hard she'll never be the same, and with one hand no less.

No kidding, this hand's useless. Look how swollen it is. You think it's broken? Being hurt is the shits, bro. It's fuck'n debilitating. Not the pain, I can handle pain, but the way it hinders my surf. I can barely push on my board when I drop into waves. Surfing injured is like trying to fuck with a limp dick. Not that I know what that's like. My dick's got more muscle than a marathon runner's leg. It's kinda terrifying, too. Not my dick—surfing injured.

A double-overhead wave rolling in and the water's sucking out. You see the reef right there, just below the surface, and you know if you don't make the drop you're gett'n tossed right into the reef. Ten feet of water churning over you, rolling you over and over underwater, slamming and dragging you across the jagged reef. And right as you push your board down to drop into the wave, you get searing pain shooting up your arm. I can handle the pain, bro. I don't care about that. My mind's rock solid, like a Shaolin Monk. What bothers me is that the pain rips my mind out of the moment, away from what I'm doing. And when you're surfing giant waves, that moment can mean life or death, bro. You gotta be in it. Respect.

And I can't sleep properly. I rolled on my hand last night, woke up in agony. Couldn't get back to sleep for an hour. And when I finally did, I had that dream again. The one where I'm suddenly back in California. At first I'm choked; I can't forgive myself for coming back. I can't figure out why I came back. Then I realize my Dad and little brother are there. I don't know why my Dad's there; he left when I was a kid, just sold the business and took off. I haven't seen him since, but he's there, in the dream, yelling at my little bro. He's got his belt in his hand. He goes for my brother. I try to step in to stop him but I can't move. My body feels like mush. There's no power in it. I'm forced to watch as he raises the belt. I call out, but my voice catches in my throat. I panic, try to act, but I can't fuck'n move. I feel the futility through my whole body, like I'm a cartoon character who's eaten a cinder block and is now pinned to the ground. Then the belt comes down on my bro and I wake up with the crack, all sweaty and startled, hand aching, heart kicking like a mule in a snake-pit.

I'd take a bat to that rat who did this to my hand, but I'd get the shit kicked outta me if I stepped foot in Puerto Viejo again. That's why I'm chill'n in San Juan Del Sur. This hostel's not bad. Waves are all right. No Salsa Brava, but good enough for now. And the hostel owner's pissed at me for taking all the girls. I gotta have more respect. That's what I'm learning. Respect. That's what got me into this mess. Life's lessons aren't always easy, bro. Sometimes life's gotta smack you over the head with 'em. Or in this case, the hand. Respect.

It started when I took my board to that rat to fix a crack, and he poured epoxy all over it and burnt the fibreglass. Fuck'n idiot. I told him so, too. Told him if you're gonna advertize that you fix boards, you should learn how. So I took my board and left, refused to pay. He was furious, his rat face snarling out curses as he followed me down the road, yapping at me for the forty dollars for the botched repair job. You know what I did? I grabbed my crotch and told him to suck it. That really pissed him off. He didn't hit me then though. He waited until the next day.

That night I was so choked I ended up getting in a fight with Sasha. She was fuming when I got home, just waiting there with her panties all twisted up, said she saw me flirting with some other girl. She musta been on her rag or something because I didn't do anything to deserve her crazy shit. I might have checked out someone, but I don't even remember, so it couldn't have been that big a deal. She just came at me, spitting her girl venom. As if that's what a man needs after a hard day. I was so tired of her jealousy I snapped—screamed at her. She didn't deserve it. I fucked up, I can admit it. I shouldn't have lost my cool, but fuck, sometimes life gets you so wound up. I'm a passionate man, and sometimes that passion bubbles over. If you love somebody for being passionate, you gotta leave them some room for their passion to fire up and consume them.

Sometimes fire burns things you don't want it to. That's the nature of fire. Don't hate the fire for being fire. Love it for its heat. Respect. It's stupid when people get pissed at their lover for the same things that drew them to them in the first place. It's like a guy with a gorgeous girl getting mad at her every time another guy checks her out. I just want to slap those morons. It's like, bro, you're dating her cuz she's hot. Her sex appeal got your attention. Don't hate because it gets other guys' attention. It's part of the package. You can't date a sexy chika without other guys checking her out. Be proud.

Anyway, I'm sidetracking. Let's get back to the story—this is the good part. The next day I'm watching the waves, getting ready to paddle out. A mother-fucker of a swell's coming in. I'm talking, big old bad-ass ten-foot barrels blowing out the tube, so I'm getting real excited—raging surf-boner excited. Then that local rat comes at me outta nowhere, wielding his skateboard like a bat, and tries to sucker me. But he wasn't ready for my ninja reflexes. I surf the heaviest waves on the planet; I can handle a little rat.

So I block the skateboard with my hand like this. Crack, the trucks hit right here, rip that chunk of flesh outta my hand. Blood starts flowing. It's everywhere, but it only enrages me. I'm like a bull when I see red. Adrenaline is pumping through me. The rat comes at me again. I step in close. Take away the advantage of his skateboard. Bam. I drill him hard in the temple. He drops the board and stumbles back. I grab him. He tries to wrestle free, but I'm way too strong. He's a big guy, 6' 4", thick arms, not an ounce of fat, but that's not enough to handle me. Look at these arms, bro, they're beautiful, carved by a lifetime of surfing. I could throw both a you outta that window before you knew what was happening.

Anyway, I throw the rat on the ground and jump on him, pinning him down. I grab his afro, pull his head back, and come over the top with my fist like this—raw—a motha-fuck'n lion. I hit him with my fucked up hand, but at that point I don't care. I'm an absolute force of nature when I'm mad, bro. Believe it. I drill that bastard right in the face. Bam. Game over. He just whimpers like a little bitch.

I could a bashed him a few more, really taught him who's the boss, but I'm more man than that. I'm not gonna keep on hitting some-body when they're done. I'm a pacifist at heart, bro. I hate fighting. I'll defend myself, but I'm not one of those assholes that'll stomp on somebody's head after they're knocked out. So I get off the rat. I'm standing over him, feeling like a blonde Mike Tyson, when I see a few more locals running toward me. So I hop on the rat's skateboard and take off. I woulda fucked 'em all up, but my hand was already too messed up. I start downhill, their coward feet thundering behind me. I know they can't catch me, so I flip 'em the finger. I hear them yelling—something about what I did to Sasha's eye. As if that was my fault. She started it with her jealousy.

Anyway, I just hope she gets some sense and gets outta that shitty, rat-infested town. She deserves better. She shouldn't be dancing in that club. That Afro-rat is gonna be all over her. He thinks he's so hot because he won the surf comp. Fuck that. It was rigged. I beat his ass in the water just like I did in the street. But judges favor locals. I still got third, which is pretty much first seeing as I'm not local. Once Sasha calms down she'll come back. Always does. She needs a man. We'll head up to Mex together and start a new life. I got some cash saved. We could start a new business. I'll really take care of her.

4

REMEMBERING FUTURES

Slumped on his knees, head bowed, Joseph peered through tangled hair at his father's grave—the tombstone: a hand chiseled rock. The muscles of his back ached from digging, a sensation made familiar by years of working the land. His eyes were hard under his hood, his mind burdened by doubt. He leaned forward, his shirt pulling tight around his pubescent shoulders, and rubbed a calloused thumb across the freshly etched words, *Here rests Patrick Mculla, father of Joseph, husband to Sarah, and founder of the New World.*

Now that his father was gone, the dream of the New World seemed unrealistic. His father's dream of humanity being able to start again, to do it right this time, was destined to fail. Who would lead the village now? Most of the elders had passed away. Adam, the last male elder, was far too old; his body so hunched from working the land that he couldn't look to the sky. Joseph himself was too young, and he had known no other life than the village. He lacked the perspective of the elders, who came from the Old World to start over. And besides, how could the village survive when all the young women had died from either starvation or disease? Who would bear children? If this was truly humanity's last hope, as his father had taught him, then Joseph feared humankind was destined to perish.

They'd been waiting for others to find the village since before Joseph was born. Finally, after a lifetime of waiting in vain, Joseph admitted to himself that no others were coming. He could wait no longer.

After kissing the tombstone, he turned to the village—five log cabins, two now abandoned, a church, and one barn housing the cattle and chickens. A veil of grief lay heavy on the decaying community. The forest reclaimed the land as the population dwindled. No roads came to or left from the village. There was nothing but forest in every direction. The Dark Forest. That's what the elders called it, warning those born after the 'new beginning' never to stray too far into its depths.

Joseph passed the church as he walked home. Above the door, the carved words, *God lives in the heart of Man* were fading, moss encroaching upon the building. The priest, an elder, had passed away a few years back, when Joseph was still a boy. Now the church was more of a library, housing the books of the Old World's greatest teachers.

Peter, the son of the late priest, sat on his porch. He was two years younger than Joseph and hadn't yet sprouted his first facial hair.

Joseph sat next to him, anxiety twisting his features and bringing lines to his normally smooth skin. "Peter", he said, with a pleading tone in his voice, "I fear we cannot stay in the village any longer. We will die here. Come with me into the forest to search for others."

"There are no others. The village is all there is."

"I know they're out there. I can feel them in my heart. We have to find them."

"How can you have such faith? Not one person in the village has seen another survivor. All we know is the village."

"Nobody has seen one because we're all too afraid to leave. Neither of us has ventured more than two-hundred yards into the forest. Today that changes."

"Joseph, you don't know what you're saying. You've heard the warnings of the elders. You know what lurks in the dark forest."

"I'm not afraid."

"If you venture into the forest, they will kill you!"

"Maybe, but at least I'll have died trying. Isn't that what our fathers taught us? To stay strong to the end, even in the face of death. If we stay here, we will all slowly die, then all this was for nothing." Joseph gestured to the village with his hands. "Our fathers' dreams will die in vain."

"Don't go. You're being foolish."

"No. I'm finally seeing clearly."

"What about the others? Your mom? You're her last remaining child. Who'll till the land if you leave?"

"I'll come back. Before the autumn harvest."

"Please, Joe." Peter's eyes were stricken with heartache. "I don't know if I can survive without you."

"Then come."

"And leave Mikey? He's too young."

"We'll come back for him."

"What if we don't make it back?"

"I can't wait. Something's calling me. I'm leaving today, when the sun's at its peak. You coming or not?"

"Your stubbornness will be your death."

"Maybe. Or maybe it'll be what saves us all. If we let our fear dictate our choices, then not only will our bodies die, but our spirits will as well."

Peter sighed, leaning forward and cradling his head. Then, looking up, he said, "Take this." He untied the leather belt holding the steel hunting knife his father had left him. "You're gonna need it." The blade shimmered in the sunlight.

Joseph threw his arms around his friend. "I'll bring it back. I promise."

Joseph's mom sat in the sun less than fifty yards away, spinning wool from the sheep. He loved her deeply, but feared telling her he was leaving, especially so soon after the death of his father. It would be cowardly to leave without saying anything, and his father had taught him to always act with honor. "The things we fear," his father had told him as a boy, "are often the most important for us to do. They are the things that help shape us as humans, the things that set our limits."

Walking toward his mom, Joseph observed her sitting calmly in front of their house. He thought of all the times they had sat together. She'd always been there for him. When the bull had stepped on his foot while plowing the field, she'd been the one who helped nurse him back to health. When he'd fallen out of a tree at the edge of the forest, it was his mom who cooked him soup and read to him every day until he recovered. When their crops had failed, she had gone without so he could eat.

He sat next to her. She looked old and tired, her cheeks sunken and sallow, her eyes hollow. Thirty years ago she'd started the village with his father, the love of her life, truly believing that they were expanding humanity's reach—sixteen pilgrims with dreams as vast as this new land, escaping an Old World evil. But now almost all of them had perished and only a few of their children remained. She'd watched her village slowly dwindle. She'd buried two children, and now her husband.

Joseph put his hand on her shoulder. "How are you?"

"Tired."

The fear of hurting his mom twisted in his chest. He cleared his throat. "I have something to tell you."

"I know."

"What do you mean?"

"I don't blame you for leaving. You must. There's nothing left for you here."

"How—"

"A mother knows these things. I've seen you gazing into the woods. You've always been such a curious boy. I'm not going to stop you. I love you too much to keep you here. Your destiny is out there, beyond the Dark Forest."

Joseph didn't know what to say, so he rested his arm around her. She continued, "Your father thought we were the only ones here, but that can't be. There must be others. You'll find them. You have your father's courage."

Joseph embraced his mother. He could think of no words to convey the emotion rushing through him. He rested his forehead against her temple and took in her scent one last time, allowing it to sink into his memory. Then, he rose and entered the cabin to pack for his journey.

~

That night, deep in the forest, Joseph pressed onward toward an unknown destination. The wind pierced his deerskin cloak and threatened to blow out the torch, his only source of light. Pulling his cloak tight and hugging himself while sheltering the torch, he leaned against a large cedar tree. Moss hung from its branches.

According to legend, the elders had come from a place that lay beyond the mountains. A place where millions had once lived. He wondered what had become of everyone. Maybe the city still existed. Maybe the elders had been wrong about the sky monsters.

A howl echoed around the valley, sending a chill up Joseph's back. Wolves. Collecting sticks into a pile, he used the torch to start a small fire. The light tamed the immediate darkness, easing his fear. He peered into the shadows, wondering what else might be lurking in this unknown forest. Lying on a bed of leaves, he rested his head on the book he had brought, glad that he had chosen one so thick. The fire's glow caused shadows to flicker in the branches above. The light reminded him of a childhood dream that had re-occurred for years. In the dream he was a baby, naked, hovering in a ball of light. That's all. It would last hours, then he'd wake feeling warm and peaceful.

Joseph thought about his mother as he drifted to sleep. He could see her gentle smile in his mind's eye. He missed her. He loved her soft voice, the bedtime stories of his childhood. She had read to him from the book of Greek myths. Jason and the Argonauts was his favorite. He told himself he was a modern day Jason, questing into the world to save his kingdom.

Shuddering, he realized the pressure on him. The emotional burden brought about a hollow feeling in his chest, bringing dark flashes of uncertainty. Why did he have to do this alone?

The loneliness crept in, clawing through his chest. He hugged his knees to feel the warmth of human skin, even though it was only his own. He had never been farther from the village than the reach of his voice. For the first time in his life he was truly alone. No one would come to his aid if he called out.

He thought about God and faith, and what his father had said to him after the death of his sister. "Faith," his father had taught, "is the cornerstone of the emotionally strong. Faith alone can give strength in the absence of all else. We must have hope. Hope is the food of the soul. Without it, the human spirit withers and dies."

Joseph didn't know what he would find, but he was driven to quest. There was no other choice. He closed his eyes, comforted by the fire's warmth, and drifted to sleep; confident that tomorrow would bring the answers he sought.

~

More than a week later, Joseph trekked on, following a river down the slope of a mountain. By this time he had crossed rivers and mountains and valleys and had no idea where he was or how to get back to the village. His body was haggard, his food gone, his spirit crushed. He questioned his choice to leave the village. Was there even a city beyond the mountains? Or was it all a myth? Maybe his father had been right. Maybe the village really was humanity's last stand. If so, he had just abandoned humanity's last hope.

No. He couldn't think like that. He had to carry on. There had to be others. His mother wouldn't have let him go if the city was only a myth. He would find the great city of which the elders spoke. Other survivors would be there. The sky monsters would be gone.

Joseph bent low to quench his thirst in the river. Should he stray from it, this vein in the woods carrying the lifeblood of this forest? As long as he followed the river, he at least had something. If he left it, he'd have nothing, walking aimlessly through this foreign land. The river must eventually lead to the coast, where the great city of the legends supposedly had been.

The land angled steeply up from both edges of the river. Boulders, partially underground and painted yellow with lichen, lay strewn along the river's edge. All around, trees stood over the earth, their thick trunks reaching skyward. Joseph's legs ached from traversing such grueling terrain. A tree grew from the highest point of the hill. Grabbing the lowest branch, Joseph hoisted himself up. The thin bark was soft. Sap stuck to his palms and fingers.

Joseph's hands trembled. The lack of nutrition had weakened him, but he persisted. Nearing the top, he could see beyond the peaks of the surrounding trees. The forest stretched as far as he could see, the emerald landscape rolling away, rising into peaks and disappearing into the horizon. A few clouds floated idly in the distance. Mist clung to the side of a mountain. An eagle soared overhead, its sharp eyes searching for lunch. Joseph's stomach gurgled. He turned around, his eyes following the river as it carved its way through the forest for miles. It emptied into a large body of water that stretched the length of the horizon.

Gasping, he realized that it must be the Ocean the elders had spoken of. His eyes followed the coast, his heart fluttering in his chest. Then he saw them, hugging the coast in the distance, almost too far for his eyes to perceive. The buildings of the great city rose above the forest. The Old World legends were true. His prayers had been answered. He could follow the river to the coast, then the coast to the city. His mind tumbled forward in nervous excitement as he wondered what answers the city would hold.

But, if the legends of the Old World were true, the sky monsters must be real as well. According to the legends, the sky monsters had come from the stars in a flash of light, vengeful and malevolent, slaughtering everyone. Could it be?—he'd always doubted such a fantastical claim, suspecting that the legends were made up to keep the children from venturing from the safety of the village. But, if the legends of the great city were true, then...

He flinched. His eyes shot upward. He saw only blue, but realized how exposed he was in the tree. Were the sky monsters still here, hunting the last humans? His pulse raced as he climbed down to the hidden security of the forest floor, continuing his trek toward the ocean.

~

The next morning Joseph awoke with the first rays of the sun, legs tight from the long trek to the ocean, stomach still full from the previous evening's crab feast. Propping himself on an elbow, he peered at the sunlight shimmering along the ocean's surface and stretching into the horizon where it met with its source. Joseph walked into the water and bathed himself in this strange, salty sea. He marveled at its taste, and let the seaweed pass through his fingers. The water chilled him deeply. The sun's warmth hadn't yet kissed the land, but he wouldn't wait for the day to warm. He could afford no more time at this sanctuary. He reckoned the city was half a day's hike, and he wanted to make it there with plenty of daylight left.

He dried and dressed himself, then filled a satchel around his waist with roasted crabs and seaweed. An odd stone path, painted with lines, white on the outside, yellow in the middle, ran along the edge of the ocean, where the beach met the forest. He touched the path, caressing its smooth surface. He followed the path as it twisted through the woods along the ocean's edge, growing wider as it straightened out. First it was two lanes, then four, then eight. Machines, the cars of the elders' stories, lined the sides of the street, abandoned. He ran his hand along the surface of their rusted metal bodies. Most had been reduced to the frame of their former selves, vines twisting around them, ferns sprouting up through their roofs. A few were more intact. Amazed, he tapped the glass of one. He had never seen glass. A headless skeleton sat in the driver's seat of a roofless car. Joseph shuddered, hurrying by. As he walked, more and more cars lined the path. He got in a well-preserved car and sat behind the wheel, imagining what it must have been like to drive this extraordinary invention. He imagined himself zooming along the path, faster than even a horse could run. It was all so surreal, like meeting a character from one of the Greek myths his mother had read to him.

The path intersected other such paths, rising from the ground on pillars as it passed over them. Now that the day was warming, the path held the sun's heat and radiated it outward. At points, steel poles rose from its edge, displaying signs telling him the name of the great city—Vancouver. Joseph marveled at it all.

Then, coming over a hill, he saw them, the giant buildings of the legends. He couldn't contain his wonder and leapt into the air. He longed to call out, but kept silent, fearful of the sky monsters. He broke into a run, anxious to get to the heart of the city, desperate to find other survivors.

There were so many cars now, the streets were cluttered with them. Joseph wove a path through them, racing toward the buildings. The forsaken city, full of forgotten dreams, stretched skyward, a skeleton of its former self. Joseph stared in wonder at the colossal structures reaching into the sky, tall as mountains. Some connected to other buildings via glass-encased bridges. Each building could have housed thousands of people. How many people once lived in this sea of castles stretching as far as the eye could see? Fifty million? Five hundred million? Above the ground, tracks of various heights wove through the city. Chunks of the tracks were missing, as if torn savagely out. A derailed vehicle, long and segmented, lay on its side in the middle of the road. Massive slabs of rock lay at the bottom of a ruined building. Grass and small shrubs sprouted up through cracks in the stone paths. A family of deer stood in the middle of the street, eating from one of the shrubs.

The absence of human life lay heavy in the air, wrapping around the tired buildings and abandoned streets. Joseph observed the city, which seemed so advanced, yet was the remains of a lost past. His mind filled with thoughts of action. His curiosity rose to nearly crippling levels as he looked around, yearning to find other survivors, trying to imagine where they might be. Stairs led into underground tunnels. Buildings towered all around, cutting off any view of the horizon. The roads webbed out into a vast, multi-level maze. Along with the cars littering the streets, there were smaller vehicles. They had no wheels, and appeared as if they were ridden like flying horses.

The scene overwhelmed him. Where should he begin his search? One building in the distance rose taller than the rest, offering a good vantage point. A cloud hugged its midsection. The building twisted upward into the sky. A bridge, hundreds of feet in the air and encased in glass, connected the building to its neighbor. Joseph sprinted toward the enormous edifice, intuitively feeling the need to get inside it.

He reached the building, frantic and out of breath, and pressed his face to the glass doors, trying to open them. Finding the handle, he burst through the entrance and stumbled into a deserted lobby. A metal desk stood in the middle of the room. Behind it was an entrance to another part of the building. Joseph walked through. Smaller rooms, visible through their glass walls, surrounded the edge of the foyer. Some of the glass was shattered. It all seemed so stale and foreign, so much colder and harder than the wooden homes of the village, especially in this abandoned condition. He wondered if it had been a place of residence or work. He was so curious about the lives of the people of this lost civilization.

Joseph noticed a door with a picture of stairs above it. Wanting to climb to peer at the city from above, he entered the stairwell. The door closed behind him, leaving him in pitch blackness. He shuddered, his death could be lurking, waiting unseen. Breathing deep, he tried to calm his nerves. "Nobody can say with complete certainty whether or not there's an afterlife," his father had taught, "but if there is, how you face your death will surely point which direction you're headed when you leave this world. So face your death with courage and honor. It just may be the most defining moment of your existence—the moment your entire life is leading you towards."

He fumbled through the dark until his feet found the stairs. Then he ascended into the blackness, continuing until his legs burned from the exertion of climbing.

A metal-on-metal shriek startled him as he fumbled blindly in the dark. A few stories above, a door opened, bringing light from outside. The door was open for only a second, but it was enough time for the shadow cast on the wall above to paralyze him with fear. The dark shape bent up the wall, twisting, long and thin with claw-like hands. *Sky Monster,* was the only thought in his mind. The shadow moved, growing larger as the being stepped into the stairwell. Then the door closed and darkness consumed everything once again.

Joseph felt for the wall, frantic yet with as much stealth as he could muster. He fled down the stairs taking them in threes. He tripped, but scrambled to his feet without losing his momentum. A light shone from the being above, illuminating the stairwell as if by some feat of magic. Joseph saw a door below him. He ran to it. the approaching footsteps behind him piercing him with fear. He grabbed at the door handle, hands shaking. He glanced back, temporarily blinded by the approaching light. The sky monster was dangerously close and approaching fast. Joseph's heart kicked like an enraged bull. He couldn't see past the light. He yanked at the door, but it was locked.

He reached for his dagger and turned to face his fate. If today was the day he was going to die, he'd go down fighting. Joseph's fingers tightened around the blade's handle. His knees bent, toes gripping the floor, readying for a fight to the death.

"Shhhhhh, Shhhhhhh, Buddy, do you want the Aliens to hear you?" It was a man's voice.

Joseph's fear was immediately replaced by wonder. He'd been right. There were others. An immense love for the man instantly welled in his heart. His dagger clanked to the ground. He turned, climbing the stairs toward the man, racing toward the connection he had sought for so long, full of the joy experienced when one's dreams become reality.

The light came from a device in the man's hand. The man raised his hands as Joseph approached. "Whoa. Hold on. Not so fa—"

Joseph flung his arms around the man, wrapping him in brotherly affection. The man twisted free, throwing Joseph to the ground. He shone the magic light into Joseph's eyes and pulled out a dagger of his own. "Don't make me use this." The man wasn't big, but he looked hardened, carved by a harsh life full of difficult choices. His eyes were fierce, his hair cropped short. Joseph didn't doubt the threat.

"Friend, please. I'm new here. I came in search of survivors. Forgive my haste. My actions were intended as a sign of love."

The man eyed Joseph, sizing him up. Joseph realized how oddly the man was dressed. His clothes were made from a tightly woven fabric, colorful and refined, and fit snug to his body, unlike Joseph's, which were crudely fashioned from animal hide and draped over his body.

"There's a few of us living underground," the man said. "I'm up here gathering canned goods from the office cupboards."

"Take me to the others. I'm alone. I'm from a village in the woods."

"Sshhhh." The man raised a finger to his lips. "Shut up, or the Morgatark will hear you?"

"Who?"

"The Morgatark. The Aliens, that's what they call themselves. Most of them have left, but a few remain, searching for the last humans."

"The sky monsters."

"Yeah, whatever you want to call them."

"Please take me to the others."

The man's eyes narrowed as he studied Joseph. "Ok, but first we fill our bags with food."

Joseph smiled, extending his hand. "My name's Joseph."

"Felix."

The two shook hands.

~

Once his bag was full of cans, Joseph slung it over his shoulder and stood. "Ok, let's go." He was anxious to meet the others.

Felix nodded. "We'll take the stairs underground. Under no circumstance step into plain view on the street."

"Why?"

"The Aliens patrol the air."

"I came here by street."

"Then you are a lucky fool. You should be dead."

The men walked from an office into the stairwell, following it underground. Once in the basement, Felix removed a grate from the floor and slipped into an underground tunnel system. Joseph followed.

Felix spoke softly as he shone his light down the concrete tunnel. They walked along a path following a polluted manmade river. "For thirty years we've been living down here, catching the odd animal, mostly rats, and scavenging what we can from the city. I was just a boy when they came. It was like nothing we'd ever imagined. In an instant the sky above every city in the world was full of them, raining hell down upon us. Our armies were no match. In a matter of days they'd killed ninety-five percent of humanity, reducing the rest of us to scattered scavengers. I have no idea how many of us are left. You're the first newcomer we've seen in over a decade."

"Why did they attack?"

"No one knows. They kill only humans, sparing the animals. Maybe we were becoming too advanced. Maybe they thought to wipe us out before we became a threat. Once we'd mastered fission engines, our space travel was advancing exponentially. We were mining other planets and even comets."

"Where did they come from?" The men turned a corner and Joseph made a mental note so he could remember the way.

"The stars. Nobody knows which one. Some say there's a planet beyond the middle star of Orion's belt. It's invisible to the naked eye. Some say they have been coming to Earth forever."

"Have you spoken to one?"

"No. If you get close enough you're already dead. There're two kinds. The little green ones with the big heads. They're rare. I've only seen one. They fly the ships. I think they're the brains behind the whole operation. But they're not the ones you have to worry about."

"What d'you mean?"

"It's the big ones that hunt us on the ground. The little ones rarely leave the safety of their ships. They fly so fast you can barely see 'em. They'll kill you before you even know they're there. But they don't come into the buildings or tunnels. They leave that to the big ones. Giant insect-like creatures with red eyes and a hard shell. We call them Taladwar."

"Taladwar?"

"The most vicious creature in the universe. Pray that you never see one."

"Have you?"

"Once, it was huge. Seven or eight hundred pounds...maybe a thousand. Covered in an impenetrable exoskeleton. It was so fast. It was everywhere. On the sides of the tunnel, the ceiling, ahead of us. Our weapons were useless against it." Felix shuddered. He stopped walking, consumed by the memory. "It killed my brother right in front of me. Tore him apart."

"I'm sorry."

"It was over twenty years ago. We've all lost our families. But we have a new family now, the Haven."

"The Haven?"

"Where I'm taking you now. There's twenty four of us living below the tunnel."

Felix stopped. He ran his hand along the brick. "Forth brick from the top."

Joseph nodded. Felix removed the brick and slid a lever behind it. A small portion of the brick wall swung in, revealing a hallway. They stepped in and Felix shut the door behind them. They followed the hallway to the end, where it opened into a large room that branched into a few other rooms.

"The Haven." Felix spread his arms.

A small fire lit the room. An elderly woman glanced up from behind a pot of stew, gasping when she saw Joseph. Two men sat on a couch. They rose to greet the newcomer. People emerged from other rooms when they heard the commotion, and Joseph found himself surrounded, shaking hands with more people than he'd ever seen. He noted how pale and scrawny they appeared, as if they had never developed their bodies by working in the sun. Most looked as if they rarely left the safety of the Haven.

A young woman caught his eye, causing his heart to flutter in his chest. She was noticeably younger than the others. She was the first girl he'd ever seen at the height of her sexuality; none of the girls from his village had lived long enough. The sight blazed in his spirit. Her presence drew him toward her with magnetic intensity, seeming to cause the others to fade into the background. His pulse quickened. He shook her hand, barely able to find his voice. Her head was slightly misshapen, almost oblong. He found it irresistibly beautiful in its uniqueness. Her brown hair was in a thick braid. Her body was thin, but healthy nonetheless. Maybe it was her youth, but her pale skin seemed to glow in the firelight. Her eyes were luminous blue, sparkling in the light and so large.

He'd never seen eyes that large, except in the mirror. The skin of her hand was soft. He didn't want to let go. He wanted to hold her hand, pull her close. He wanted to smell her, but he relaxed, dropping her hand and smiling, trying to control the new passions erupting within and consuming his thoughts.

"I'm Mary." She said.

He looked away, suddenly nervous. He noticed the newspaper on the table. He picked it up. "What's this strange book?"

Mary giggled. "It's not a book, silly. It's a newspaper. It's from before the invasion. We keep it around to remind us of the world we once knew…well they once knew." She motioned to the others. "I was born after the invasion."

Joseph noted the date on the paper; July 17th, 2178. The headline on the front page read, *Population of Lunar Colony now over 10,000.*

The savage sound of crumbling bricks echoed down the tunnel into the Haven, driving fear into the heart of the community.

Scuttling footsteps approached, heavy and rapid, coupled with the sound of metal scraping brick.

"NO." Felix shouted. "It can't be."

"Taladwar." Mary shrieked.

Joseph stood stunned as everyone broke into a panic around him, grabbing weapons from a wooden box. Felix shook him by the shoulders. "Arm yourself. It's here. It followed you."

The beast squeezed through the hallway, breaking bricks, and stood to its full height, towering over the humans. A massive, segmented body, similar to an ant's, stretched upward. It stood on six legs, four on the back segment and two on the middle. Two arms, claws snapping at the ends, extended outward from the front of the middle segment. A thick neck held its fierce head. Four red eyes gleamed as they scanned the room. Its face was flat, scrunched and powerful like a pit-bull. Every inch of the beast was covered in a spiked, black shell. Its mouth opened, revealing rows of sharp teeth. It shrieked, the noise piercing Joseph's ears, stabbing through him to his bones.

He stepped back. The creature leapt forward. It was on top of the old woman. It tore her throat open with a barb on one of its forearms. It moved faster than anything Joseph had ever seen. It crawled up the side of the wall, disappearing into the shadows. Then it was on a man, decapitating him with one crunch of its jaws. Another man rushed toward it, sword in hand, but was quickly skewered through the chest by the tip of a leg.

Horror consumed the Haven, destroying hope, clawing at the walls, filling the air with the screams of the dying. People dispersed in wild efforts to escape. The beast leapt on a fleeing man, stabbing him with its sharp claws. Arrows hit the beast, deflecting off its exoskeleton. It seemed to be everywhere at once. On the ceiling, killing another, leaping through the air. The weapons were of no use against it. It seemed unstoppable as it tossed dead bodies aside as if they were weightless.

Mary cried out from a corner as the Taladwar approached her. Two men fled down the tunnel. Joseph ran in front of Mary, shielding her. She cried out, crumpling under the horror. Joseph pulled Peter's dagger from the belt around his cloak. The beast leapt at them and Joseph raised his arm in protection, ready to die. The beast's head snapped down, mouth open, teeth shimmering in the light. The force of the creature drove Joseph back against the wall, pinning him. He remained in that position a few moments, eyes closed, knife raised, frozen by fear, awaiting his death.

Realizing he had been spared, he opened his eyes to see the dagger's handle protruding from the beast's mouth, the blade piercing the roof into its brain. Sparks fluttered out from between its teeth. The glowing red of its eyes flickered off. It was not a beast at all; it was a machine.

The survivors cheered. They pulled Joseph out from under the creature. Mary embraced him. "You saved my life."

Felix grabbed him by the shoulders. "I've never seen anyone slay a Taladwar."

"You're a hero." Another shouted.

Joseph was dazed. He hadn't thought. He'd only reacted, lifted the knife. It was luck, really. The beast had slain itself on his dagger while attempting to bite off his head.

"Joseph, the Taladwar slayer," another cheered.

But the merriment left as quickly as it came. The survivors looked around at the dead bodies littering the room. People cried out as they cradled their loved ones. Grief lay heavy in the room. The Haven was no more, half the family dead.

Felix was the first to speak. "We have to get out of here. They know where we are. There'll be others any minute."

"But where can we go?"

"The woods." Joseph answered.

"The woods?" replied a woman. "Aren't the woods ripe with Morgatark?"

"I have lived in the woods my entire life and I have never seen one until now. There are other survivors. I am from a village where the Sky Monsters have never been. Where we can live in peace. We can start again."

"Ok. Let's go." Felix was anxious. His eyes scanned the tunnel. "Move."

They quickly did a head count as they entered the tunnel. Twelve of them had survived the attack. Four men and eight women.

"We'll take the tunnels to the edge of the city," Felix said, "then flee to the woods, hopefully unseen. Which direction is the village?"

"We follow the coast north to the river, then go east."

~

"Do you think there are more survivors?" Joseph asked, as they neared the end of the tunnel.

"There has to be," Felix said. "The world is huge. If we could survive, others must have survived as well."

Mary walked next to Joseph. "I want to thank you. You could have fled, but you didn't. You protected me."

"It's my fault. If I hadn't come to the city, the Sky Monsters would never have found the Haven."

"It was only a matter of time before they found us. We've talked about fleeing to the woods. Others have gone, but none have reported back, so we had little faith."

"We have to survive." Joseph's eyes were hard, his face cloaked in determination.

They reached the end of the tunnel and Felix ascended the ladder first. Turning back, he whispered, "Ok. I'm going to slide the grate off and take a look. Line up. When I give the go ahead, we all sprint to the forest. Single file on the ladder. Calm and quick."

He slid the grate off and peeked out. Looking back to the others, he said, "Two blocks to the forest. Follow me. Stay close. We rendezvous in the woods and Joseph'll lead us to the village."

With that, Felix sprung from the tunnel and sprinted toward the woods, the others close behind. Joseph stood over the tunnel, helping the others onto the street. When the last was out, Joseph ran toward the woods, bringing up the rear of the human stampede. His heart thundered. The image of the Taladwar in the tunnel was still fresh in his mind, driving fear into his core, spurring him forward in a desperate dash for safety. Out of the corner of his eye, he saw a flash of light. Then the man beside him was gone, vaporized. Nothing remained but a red mist drifting to the ground. Then another flash, and another man gone.

Before Joseph had time to react, an Alien was in front of him. It hovered on a platform much like a hover-skateboard, holding a ray-gun at the end of its long thin arm. Its body was small, almost frail looking, but its head was massive. Its skin was green and scaly, like that of a lizard. And its eyes, large black orbs staring into Joseph.

Do not fear. It spoke to Joseph telepathically. *Death is not the end for you. It brings liberation from your hindering form.* The gun's barrel pointed at Joseph's forehead.

Joseph looked the creature directly in the eyes, refusing to show fear, standing strong in the moment of death, as his father had taught him. Another Alien whizzed by on a hover-board, going after the others.

You are different. The Alien said, leaning close, smelling Joseph. It grabbed Joseph by the face, squishing his cheeks, and pulled him eye level. It had remarkable strength for its size.

The Alien was clearly agitated. It shifted on its platform, flinging Joseph to the ground. *It cannot be.*

"What?" Joseph questioned. "Please. Why?"

"Zarg'ola'mues," the Alien said aloud with obvious frustration. It was the first time Joseph had seen the small mouth move. Above it there was no nose, only two nostrils that pinched shut when it wasn't taking in air. It looked at Joseph long and hard, calculatingly. It spoke telepathically again. *It is your right to know.*

One of our leaders broke orders. He'd lived among humans for centuries, growing too empathetic. He spoke of another way. A way that would keep humanity's genetic code from dying out. Now I know what he did, but it is too late. What is done is done. He broke Morgatark law. He implanted our DNA into yours. You are no longer human. You have mutated, evolved. I can no longer kill you. My orders are only to kill humans.

It turned to leave, but Joseph called out, "Wait." The creature turned back, so Joseph continued. "Why? Why kill humans? It makes no sense."

It was the only way. Believe me, we didn't want to. There were great debates on our planet, but time had run out for humans. We were left no other choice.

"Why?"

For thousands of years we came to you, taking the role of gods, known only to most in your myths and legends. We loved you. We nurtured you. We tried to help you evolve. We brought plants and fungi from our planet and gave them to you to help expand your mind and raise your consciousness, but still your greed prevailed.

We loved humans in many ways. I have seen works of art created with heartrending richness. I've heard recordings of music whose vibrations caused me to swell with emotion, and I've read books brimming with knowledge. I have witnessed deep bonds of love between individuals. But alas, in spite of all this, humans were mere weeks away from damaging the earth so drastically that you would have killed all life on it. You were a parasite and you were killing your host. We simply couldn't allow it.

Joseph was shocked. A parasite? The Alien disappeared in a flash, leaving Joseph alone and confused. He ran towards the woods in search of the others. Once in the woods, he called out in a frantic voice. Hearing a woman, he ran to her. It was Mary. He embraced her.

"Th... The others," she stammered. "Th... they're all d... d... dead."

He held her tight. He didn't know what to say, so he just hugged her, tried to radiate his love into her.

"Why?" She asked. "Why not kill us?"

Joseph kissed her large head. He cradled it in his hands. He looked into her giant eyes, and he knew the answer to her question. "When you were a child," he asked, "did you dream about floating in the light?"

"H... how did you know?" Her body trembled in his arms as she spoke. She looked up questioningly.

"Because you and I are different. We are no longer human. That's why the Aliens spared us."

"What?"

"Humanity had to die out in order to leave room for the next step in evolution. That's what we are." Joseph cradled Mary in his arms, feeling an immense love swelling inside. "A god has come to me. Spoken the master plan." He wiped a tear from her cheek. "We are to become the parents of the New World. Mother and Father to the Children of the Light."

the Sexiest Camel in the desert.

5

THE SEXIEST CAMEL IN THE DESERT

Roused by the gentle caress of the rising sun, I sit up, rubbing the sand-filled sleep from my tired eyes. My throat feels like sandpaper, raw from singing around the campfire and smoking beedies (Indian leaf-rolled tobacco). Dung beetles snuggle under me for warmth, each black shell roughly the size of a quarter. They wake, crawling into my armpits and other bodily crevasses. I brush them from the folds of my loose clothes as I stand, searching for my bottle of water. At the bottom of the sand dune, Hakim (camel driver extraordinaire) crouches over a small fire, cooking chapattis and brewing chai. Smoke from the smoldering sticks curves upwards—a grey serpent slithering into the vast blue ceiling above India's Great Thar Desert.

"Smells good, my friend," I call out as I walk down the sandy slope.

"Small problem." Hakim's thick moustache dances above his lips as he speaks. "Magu gone. You find. I cook." He smiles wide, flashing teeth stained by tobacco.

"I'm on it."

The ground at the edge of the dunes turns from soft sand to hard baked earth, beige and cracked. A peacock roams in the distance. Overhead, a falcon soars, looking for breakfast. As I walk, I imagine myself as a bird, riding the currents of wind, looking across the desert at the green patches of life sprouting from the fractured earth.

I find Magu a couple hundred meters from camp, lingering over a shrub. His front legs have been tied together so he can't wander too far—a necessary precaution during mating season. Female camel pheromones have the power to turn a hard-working male camel into an uncontrollable fiend, consumed by lust and the unquenchable thirst to breed—an act that takes upwards of three hours, time that we do not have if we are to make it to the village by nightfall and relieve my backpack of the toothbrushes, paper, and pens I'm taking to the children.

Magu stands nonchalantly, making a *shlaup shlaup* sound as he chews sideways, stained teeth poking through the gap between his lips. Large dark eyes framed by long lashes beg me to not take him away from his breakfast. I let him munch, happy to observe him. The single-humped camel that roams the deserts of western India is a funny creature—tall, smart, peculiar, self aware, and with an ass like a cannon perched head height on legs so scrawny they look like they'll break under the camel's weight.

After a few minutes, I untie Magu's legs and lead him back to the campsite. Hakim and I use chapattis to sop up the mouth-orgasmic curry he's cooked for breakfast. The flavor explodes in my mouth like a firecracker. Like me, Hakim is in his early twenties. His face, however, is already creased, weathered by the rugged desert life. Warming his fingers with a cup of steaming chai, Hakim explains how he is saving for a dowry. He speaks of his imagined future bride, his eyes twinkling as he contemplates his vision of matrimonial bliss.

After Hakim and I finish breakfast, I grab Magu's reins and he drops to his knees. I climb aboard and he rises awkwardly. I hold on tight as I lean back. My body jerks with the camel's motion. My inner thighs are still bruised and raw from yesterday's journey, but it doesn't bother me much—it's all part of the adventure.

Hakim leads the way, laughing and singing the haunting melodies of his desert songs. Periodically, I play my bamboo flute or harmonica and he claps in time; but mostly I ride in silence, enjoying the scenery, feeling as if I've been transported through time. Other than the presence of a transplanted foreigner, it seems nothing has changed in this land for a thousand years. In the distance, a young boy runs with a stick in his hands, laughing as he herds a flock of sheep and goats. The sun is high, and I'm thankful for the loose, flowing clothes that protect my delicate Canadian skin.

I close my eyes, feeling the rhythm of the desert in Magu's stride. The desert is silent, yet it is in the silence that I hear the song of all those who've journeyed before me across this unexpectedly effervescent land.

I rub the coarse hair on Magu's neck, happy to have his friendship on this journey. We are similar creatures. We both enjoy eating, freedom, the outdoors, nature walks, and especially the ladies—his love of whom suddenly becomes evident when he bursts into an unstoppable run towards a female camel on the eastern horizon. Startled, I call out to Hakim, but my voice is lost on the breeze and he's too focused on reading the landscape ahead.

Entranced by the humped beauty on the horizon, Magu pays no heed to my pulling on his reins. I'm hesitant to pull too hard because I don't want to hurt his pierced nose. Plus, deep down I wouldn't mind if Magu got laid—he's my friend and it goes against a personal moral code to cock-block my buddies.

Knowing he's in control, Magu performs the camel's mating call—which on many levels is staggeringly akin to the muscle-flexing mating call of the cologne-soaked homo-sapiens commonly found in North American top-forty dance clubs.

Magu's lumpy head rears back as he burps up pheromones from the depths of his foul stomach. The pink flubber of his giant tongue flops from the side of his mouth as he vomits white froth. Swinging his head from side to side, he flings the putrid foam from his mouth, coating his face, neck, and my legs. I recoil at the slimy texture as it oozes down my shin towards my bare foot. The scent hangs thick in the air with a lascivious tang—the camel equivalent of Axe body spray. Nothing makes me want to vomit as much as vomit. Not wanting to stand in the way of your friend's phallic destiny is one thing, but getting their pheromone-infused puke on you pushes the boundaries of friendship.

Magu continues his wild exhibition of raw manliness by lifting his tail and trumpeting a melody of succulent farts—Tom Jones to the female camel's ears. I hold my breath as the smell fills the air, clawing its way up my nostrils, imprisoning my reality like a bad dream.

Upon seeing Magu's hormone-driven-sexual-showcase, the female camel's pulse quickens and she runs toward us, more excited than a schoolgirl at a Justin Bieber concert—as if Magu is the Don Juan of camels. He breaks into a full run. I turn, screaming to Hakim for help. The rocky ground blurs beneath me as I consider jumping to safety. The blisteringly hot ground is a long way down, and I'm struck by a vision of myself in the desert, hobbling on a sprained ankle, miles from civilization. I should have worn shoes. I hold on to the reins and await a better opportunity to escape.

Twenty feet from us, the female camel turns, thrusting her backside in the air and lifting her tail in a flaunting gesture that increases Magu's desire tenfold. My mind whirls, trying to figure out what to do. I feel like I'm stuck in an X-rated episode from the nature channel—saddled to an uncontrollable sexual lunatic, enveloped in the primal funk of his animalistic mating dance, and all the while crying out for rescue.

Meanwhile, Hakim has noticed the unfolding scene and has his camel in a full sprint, knowing that if Magu mounts the female, we won't be able to get them apart for hours—a fact I'm simultaneously impressed by and jealous of. Hakim rides as fast as he can. I scream at him to hurry, petrified by the thought of becoming the third wheel in a camel sex marathon.

Magu reaches his prize, rubbing his froth all over her backside, lubricating her. She moans in anticipation. Pheromones hover in the air, making me dizzy, blurring the air like heat waves. I leap from Magu's back, landing hard, feeling the impact up my ankles and into my knees. I flee, gasping for breath.

Magu's front legs lift onto the female's hump. His long, pencil-thin penis curves upward in bestial enthusiasm, inches away from its sought oasis. I stare in grotesque fascination, mesmerized, unable to avert my eyes as I anxiously await the moment of penetration. Then, seconds before the point of no return, Hakim rides up fearlessly and takes the reins.

Part of me is deeply saddened for Magu as he's yanked away, crying out and resisting like a child being dragged away from the gates of Disneyland. The tortured drone of his wail rips into me. I remember my teenage acne-covered-face and understand his sexual frustration, knowing the torment that comes with overly-ripe testicles.

That night, as the village sleeps, I creep up to Magu, overwhelmed by the injustice of his defeated sexcapade. In my mind, his loss symbolizes all the lovers who have been separated by the overbearing will of others. His sad eyes stare longingly at the edge of the village, where his lost love awaits her prince. What harm could come from them coming together in a night of love? What right do we humans have to control these animals' sexual behavior, to manipulate the natural process of reproduction? Is dominion over the animal kingdom and Earth really humanity's God-given right as we so often believe, or is that concept merely generated from the grossly inflated human ego?

I consider releasing Magu from his bonds of chastity. I could awake before the rest of the village and retrieve him before anyone finds out. He nods at me knowingly, pleadingly.

I untie his legs.

As he disappears into the dark of the night, I whisper, "Go Magu. Run to your woman. Do it for all the lovers torn apart by distance or war, do it for love, for Romeo and Juliet, for freedom. For all the pent up teenagers with testicles the size of tennis balls, unleash your animalistic passion." Then, I walk to my camp and drift asleep to the satisfied moans of two camels in the distance. I am happy, because for tonight at least, love wins.

6

CASEY JUMPS SHIP

—AN INTERGALACTIC FABLE FOR THE 21ST CENTURY—

1903, en route to the North Pole.

Casey tucked his bearded chin behind his seal-fur-hood to protect his face from the wind's icy kiss. Icicles dangled from his moustache like frozen fingers. He could tell from the throbbing in his left knee that a storm was coming, and he feared getting caught without shelter. He and the other explorers had left the ship for the North Pole five days prior, and were already down to just three sled dogs—enough to pull some supplies, but not enough to pull a man if one of them fell ill. Food shortages during the sea voyage had forced the explorers to kill one of the dogs for its meat. Then, two long and grueling days ago, they lost three others in a night storm.

Ever since the storm, Casey had let the surviving dogs share his tent. The warmth of other lives comforted him in this harsh environment. Even their caustic breath, which smelled of dried meat and normally caused him to turn his face away, helped him feel protected from the hostile wind that had stolen the lives of the other dogs. In the vast loneliness of the arctic, even the most repellent functions of life were moments with value.

Going down in history as the first men to reach the North Pole wasn't worth dying for. The Captain however, didn't share Casey's outlook.

Looking back at the three explorers trudging across the flat expanse of crusted snow, Casey felt a strong love for the men he had journeyed so far with—the men he had slept and eaten with for over six months. They were his brothers, and the ship was their home. Together they'd faced freezing temperatures and starvation. He trusted them with his inner thoughts, telling them at length about Harriet, the woman he hoped to court when they returned home as heroes. They'd teased him when he had compared the unquenchable love inside his heart to an eagle soaring above all else, but the teasing had been in brotherly fun and he'd teased them back when their turns came. None had judged him for coming from a poor family. Rather, they'd welcomed him warmly, respecting the hard work that had earned him a spot on the boat. They valued his keen intellect and determination. This respect had brought with it a feeling of validity, allowing Casey to easily open to the others.

Trudging through the snow, Casey slowed his pace to let the Captain catch up to him. His legs ached. Breaking trail through the snow used a considerable amount more energy than following did. But, like so many of the difficult tasks faced throughout the voyage, Casey accepted the burden, wanting to ease the load on the others. "Captain, there's a storm on the way. I think we should set up camp before it arrives." He nodded his head toward the dark clouds dragging their swollen bellies across the horizon.

"No. We're not far from the pole. We can make it there, plant our flag, and set up camp before the storm hits." The Captain's voice puffed from his mouth, barely audible over the sharp wind.

"But the risk—"

"We won't get another chance like this. No one has ever been this close to the pole."

"Let's set up camp here, wait out the storm."

"The ice receding this far is unheard of. If it shifts, we'll have days further to trek. We'll run out of supplies and have to kill another dog for its meat."

Casey nodded his head in respect. For the duration of the five-thousand mile voyage, the Captain had been the epitome of courage, his leadership both authoritative and brilliant.

The wind picked up and the men bowed their heads to avoid the snow blowing upward from the giant sheet of ice they were walking across. The ice whined and moaned as it shifted underfoot. Casey shivered, tightened his hood, and then began moving his fingertips to stimulate his circulation. Thinking about the ship, he imagined himself sitting onboard, under the cover of a blanket, his mind lost in a book as his icy fingers wrapped around a steaming mug of tea.

He looked up at the sun, thankful that the clouds hadn't yet blocked out its glowing reassurance. *At least I can still feel my toes*, he thought, as he wiped the fog from the outside of his goggles. His legs were heavy from cutting the path through the snow, so he let himself fall to the back of the line. He could hear the dogs grunting, straining their exhausted muscles as they dragged the heavy sled through the snow. He felt their pain, three doing the work of eight.

The sun reflected sharply off the snow, causing Casey to squint against the glare. As he watched the grey bodies wading through the white powder, he saw the Captain hesitate at the front of the line. The ice groaned. The Captain turned to yell, but his voice was lost in the wind. As he strained to hear, Casey felt the ice shift below his feet. It squealed as small fractures in the ice rubbed below the snow. The dogs whined at the sudden movement beneath them. The ice rose and then fell as the Arctic Ocean rolled underneath. Casey spread his stance for balance, breathing deep, yet slow, the Arctic air stinging his sinuses and lungs.

A crack opened between Casey and the others, filling the air with the sound of shattering ice. Snow disappeared into the crack as it widened. The others turned to run, knowing that if they got trapped on the far side of the gap, they would be unable to make it back to the ship. Their movements were slow, weighed down by the snow they pushed through. The dogs were on the ship side of the crack with Casey, still harnessed and dragging the supplies. They stopped pulling and began barking wildly, their cries swept away by the wind. As the men ran toward Casey, the water rolled below them, lifting the ice and spilling up through the crack. Casey stared as the others ran towards the rapidly widening gap.

They're not going to make it, he thought. The fear surged through him, lonely and sour. The vision of himself losing his friends, left in a frozen loneliness at the end of the world and unable to survive on his own, flashed in his mind's eye. Then, suddenly aware that he was in the throes of a futile and self-absorbed emotion, he snapped to attention.

Grabbing the pickaxe from his backpack, he sank the pick into the ice on the far side of the crack and struggled to hold the ice together. The first man leapt across, landing in the powder. The crack continued to spread and Casey's body and arms were stretched to their limit—feet on one side of the crack, pickaxe on the other. His boots slid across the surface of the ice, piling the snow forward until his toes gripped a jagged protrusion in the ice. He held tight to the pickaxe, his resolve fueled by his love for his friends.

His muscles rippled under layers of clothes as he tried to stop the crack from spreading. His comrade grabbed Casey's feet for support.

The frigid water churned below. The darkness brought with it a cavernous horror, but Casey refused to give in to it, using the love he felt for his mates to rise above the fear. His shoulders and abdominal muscles burned. His arms ached and he felt the tension in his tendons and joints. His shoulders felt as though they were being pulled from the sockets, but he wouldn't let go. He wouldn't fail his brothers when they needed him most. The second explorer jumped the crack and barely landed on the other side.

The crack grew and Casey held on, his feet slipping from the grip they had on the icy lip and dragging toward the edge. Each explorer who had made the leap held one of Casey's feet, keeping him from slipping into the gap. Another wave lifted the ice as the Captain approached the gap. Casey groaned, fierce and guttural, muscles tightening, trying to keep the crack together long enough for the Captain to make it across. Water rushed up, soaking Casey's coat.

The Captain leapt into the air, a grey streak of fur soaring toward his men. Falling short, he hit the edge of the crack with his chest. His legs dangled as his arms frantically swept the surface of the ice, searching for a hold, sliding toward the water. The explorers let go of Casey's ankles in order to help the Captain.

The ice shifted again, water surging underneath, and Casey was pulled away from the others as he reflexively held on to his pickaxe. Stuck on the far side, he dangled into the crack as he held on. He craned his neck to look across the gap at the others, his wind-burnt skin wrinkling with horror as he called out for help.

The Captain rolled onto his knees and flung his backpack to the ground, quickly pulling out a rope. He tossed one end to Casey. It landed a few feet away, draped over the edge of the crack. Casey let go of the pickaxe with one hand in order to reach for the rope. The ice shifted again, shaking him loose, sending him sliding toward the turbulent water.

He grabbed the pickaxe again. He hung from an outstretched arm as the water churned below, soaking his legs as they frantically scraped at the side of the ice. Momentarily closing his eyes, he was struck by visions of himself losing his grip and being sucked into the dark water under the ice, lost forever. The desire to live, elemental and all-consuming, flooded over him as he held tight to the pickaxe—his anchor to safety.

A wave pounded up, the force of the water thrust him upward, enabling him to pull himself over the edge. He laid bent at the waist with his chest on the ice and his legs dangling. The cold water soaked through his clothes, biting into him and draining his energy. He was exhausted, but feared another wave would reach up and suck him under. Reaching into his depths for his last remnants of strength, he rolled himself up and over the ledge and fully onto the ice.

He lay on his back, wet clothes clinging to his shivering skin as he looked across to the others, now separated by more than ten feet of freezing water. Realizing he would surely die if he lay still any longer, he stood and ran up and down the length of the watery barrier. He cried out to God for a way across, but the gap in the ice stretched as far as he could see in both directions. Waterlogged clothes hung heavily from his tired limbs. His chest heaved, each gulp of air bringing screaming pain to his throat and lungs.

He ran the length of the fast-growing fissure until his legs could carry him no further and buckled under him. The cold burned his flesh. His hands and knees sunk into the snow. He lifted his head, the air stinging his lungs and eyes. The Captain approached on the far side of the gap. Casey motioned for them to get back to shelter before the storm hit. He knew there was no point in trying to fool himself. His strength was all but gone, stolen by the insurmountable cold. He was going to die.

The Captain hesitated, then nodded in respect, knowing that there was no way for Casey to cross the gap. The two men locked eyes as they drifted apart. The Captain raised his right hand to his heart as he stared painfully at his friend, then he turned and walked into the white abyss.

Casey didn't blame him. What other choice was there? Dark clouds were rolling in fast, and there were three more lives at stake. A prayer left his lips, carried away on the wind as his friends hurried towards the ship. Facing his cold and bitter death, Casey didn't regret his actions, and knew that if faced with the choice again, he wouldn't hesitate to risk his life for the lives of his three friends.

Casey lay on his back and looked at the sun, observing the last of its rays as the clouds drifted in front of it. His body convulsed, shivering, rattling his teeth in a feverish rhythm—the soundtrack to his death. The cold air cut like razors. He couldn't calm his breathing. Snowflakes began to drift down, small and spread out at first, then in monstrous gusts, accompanied by the raging wind's dirge.

Pain bit into his extremities as his body lost its battle to stay warm. His nose and ears burned in frozen torment, and he lost the ability to wiggle his fingers and toes. Each desperate breath was an icy dagger in his chest.

As he lay staring into the grey and white expanse above, a calm feeling fell over Casey. He accepted his fate with resignation and courage. His perception of time became faded, stretched, and, finally, lost. Snow piled around him, pure and white. He knew he was cold, but the pain ceased. He felt at peace. "Thank you," he thought as he gazed at the sky. "Thank you for this life. It's been beautiful, every moment, even now. Please help my friends make it home safely."

And with that last thought his heart stopped.

Warmth rushed in and his vision blurred. The sun's luminosity swelled behind the clouds. So, this is death, he pondered, realizing it is the ultimate journey into the unknown. Fear faded, giving way to childlike curiosity. Death took on an adventuresome quality as he suddenly knew that it is not the end of life, but rather a reunion with the source—a date with God. He felt a sudden excitement for this new adventure.

His brain, still full of blood, remained active, in a dream state, even though his heart had stopped. The light grew in intensity until his eyes held nothing else. He felt as if he was being pulled upward by an invisible harness. He had the distinct feeling of moving quickly. Colors streaked the light, twisting and turning, rushing all around him—even inside him, as if he was travelling through a kaleidoscope. He felt his body disintegrate. He was no longer connected to his earthbound form. He became light.

Time and space ceased to exist, Earthly reality melted into a vague concept, and Casey journeyed through a novel dimension at mind-melting speeds. All of eternity happened in an instant, and he faced his life. His brain brought up every choice he'd made, every thought he'd had, and every feeling he'd felt, and immersed him in all of it—at once and forever. Then, six minutes later, his brain shut down.

Casey Caldwell was no more.

~

1,768,584 light-years across the universe on a small, earth-like planet known as Timballa, a female was being born amidst a great celebration. The mother lay on a bed of fuzzy leaves in the center of a large circle, as the community danced around—a sea of bodies, arms raised, chanting and singing praises to the creator. Birds circled above, bestowing their blessings. A group of musicians sang praise—drummers beat primal rhythms, lute players strummed their strings, and a horn section blew melodies through loops of the finest metals. The music filled the air with the splendor and excitement that accompanies the entrance of new life into the world, calling forth the powers of love to surround the newborn.

It was a beautiful day for a birthing. The sun shone high, two of the three moons were visible, a breeze blew through the forest, and Necritone, the closest planet, was directly overhead—a very good omen.

An old medicine woman held a masterfully carved wooden staff, pointing its crystal top at the sun. She wiped the exhausted mother's forehead with a wet sponge from the holy lake. In a tender voice, she spoke words of encouragement. The mother pushed, letting out a tortured groan. The medicine woman took the mother's green hand and spoke a prayer to the heavens. Her eyes rolled back, revealing the whites as she chanted in the sacred language of the ancestors. The mother grunted, breathing deep and hard. Sweat covered her naked flesh. Her hands shook as they balled into fists. She pushed, groaning, eyes wide, muscles clenched. Her hand slapped the ground, fingers digging into the soil. Her chest heaved as she pushed, screaming. Her back arched upward. Her birth canal stretched, and a large blob of green slime squirted out, landing on the forest floor with a splat. The mother collapsed back onto the leaves, exhausted. The medicine woman reached her hands into the sac of slime and pulled out the newborn, wiping the slime from it with a cloth. The baby's head appeared, followed by the shoulders, then the arms, then the wings, the waist, and finally the legs.

The medicine woman wiped the goo from the newborn's face and placed her in her mother's arms for the first time. The family looked the baby over. She was perfect—webbed toes for swimming, gills on her neck, and strong double wings similar to those of a dragonfly for swift, focused flying. The baby girl held up her green head, opened her bright eyes to look at her world for the first time, and then let out a small cry.

The mother held her daughter next to her hearts. She looked into her daughter's eyes and then emptied all thoughts from her mind so that she could allow the name to come to her. The mother closed her eyes, and then when her mind was fully clear, she spoke the name 'Ghianna', and held her daughter high in the air. The community burst into a frenzy of cheers and began chanting the newborn's name.

~

As the years passed, Ghianna's life on Timballa progressed in a rather ordinary manner. She lived in a modest clay house with her mother, father, sister, and two brothers. The small community where she was raised existed in harmony with the environment, and Ghianna was taught that every inch of Timballa was sacred—all of it given by the creator so that they could experience the gift of life. She attended school, where she learned to read, to write, to play the lute, to dance the sacred dances, to swim and catch fish, to fly, to grow vegetables, to make clay houses, and to travel through the dream dimensions. She studied the great philosophers of Timballa, and when she was old enough, she flew to the temple in the sky where she studied the art of meditation with the great priestess.

Among the millions of species on Timballa, there were three highly intelligent types that could communicate with each other. There were the Maundil (of which Ghianna belonged), the Shepfins (who lived only in the sea and built magnificent cities along the bottom of the oceans), and the Diadolites (who were gigantic, covered in white hair, and lived primarily in the far north where it was always winter).

The Maundil had two hearts, of which it was said that one beat for themselves and one beat for others.

The concept of greed had never existed on Timballa. Everyone shared what they had, understanding that the greatest crime was to take more for yourself than you needed, because that would throw off nature's balance, leaving someone somewhere else without enough. It was common knowledge that all life was connected, and that beyond the perceptual limitations of the senses, there existed an interwoven dimension of the spirit, in which all shared the same source.

Ghianna had an adventurous spirit. While in school, she dreamed of travelling around the vastness of Timballa, seeing all the various landscapes. She wanted to swim to the bottom of the Great Thar Ocean to see the city of Olexis—the largest city on all of Timballa, home to almost ten-thousand Shepfins. She wanted to fly to all the sky temples to learn from the priestesses. She wanted to climb the great mountains and journey down through the volcanoes into the underground and see the Gaven, fuzzy little creatures that secreted goo which instantly healed wounds.

When she was fully grown, and the high priestess ordained that she was ready, Ghianna left her town in search of adventure and knowledge. She became a scribe, understanding that sharing knowledge between species was crucial for the evolution of life on Timballa. She met Maundil, Shepfins, and Diadolites, learning along the way, and writing scrolls which she shared with all.

Ghianna lived this way for many years—until her hair turned from pink to yellow, her green skin began to crease around her mouth and eyes, and she began to feel like she was ready to settle in one place. Her longing for a permanent home came surprisingly suddenly, biological in its urgency.

She had been visiting a tree-house village in the jungle to celebrate a double lunar eclipse. A family had given her a place to rest in their home. The love shared there made her realize that she wanted a family of her own. She'd had lovers in the past, but her time with them had been fleeting, the romance passionate and complete, but short-lived. Her nomadic lifestyle hadn't lent itself easily to lasting relationships.

The problem that plagued her mind when thinking of settling down, was that she couldn't decide where she most wanted to live. Her parents had died a few years back, and all her siblings were off on their own adventures. No political borders existed on Timballa, leaving its inhabitants free to live anywhere on the planet that felt right to them. Ghianna had been to every corner of every continent, and she loved each place equally, but for different reasons. It was with this dilemma in mind that she walked alone into the great forest of the Nagul to sit and contemplate.

The forest floor spread out before her, blanketed in a yellow moss, which gently cushioned each footstep. Translucent fungi sprouted in large disks from the base of a tree, giving off a faint blue shine. Glowing insects sat in a jomiberry bush, singing their love songs. Ghianna thought about eating a jomiberry, but decided against it. She loved the energy and euphoria they gave her, but wanted to stay clear-headed while she made her decision.

She gathered some nuts from the bottom of a giant blue-needle tree and sat on a log to eat them. As she ate, she thought about her world. She loved all the creatures and the harmony shared, but deep in her heart she wanted more. It was an unconscious longing to be challenged, to be given the opportunity to rise against challenges and become a hero. But she knew it was impossible in a perfect world. In Utopia, there is no greed or wrath, yet she sensed that it is through confronting and overcoming life's negativities that the greatest opportunities for personal growth occur.

Deep in her cells lived vague, unfocused memories of good and evil and heroes and heroic deeds. Looking into the sky, Ghianna wondered if there were other worlds out there, worlds whose inhabitants were still driven by greed, worlds that needed heroes to rise up and light the darkness.

When she finished eating, she stretched out her naked body and lay on a pile of large leaves, looking up at the layers of flora and fauna twisting skyward in vibrant exhibits of life. Her lean legs lay out, taut from a lifetime of activity. She'd never worn clothes. except when she'd journeyed into the far north to see the Diadolites. Nobody on Timballa wore them. The idea seemed absurd. Why block the skin from breathing when it felt so much better to feel the wind's kiss?

Thirsty from eating the nuts, Ghianna walked through the ancient forest in search of a drink. She came across a red Ochano flower and pinched a little of the powder from the stamen, thanking the flower for its gift as she rubbed the powder onto her neck to make herself smell nice. A friendly breeze embraced her. Smiling, she felt that the breeze was the forest's way of giving her a hug, approving of her flowery scent.

After a short walk, she came to a lake that stretched as far as she could see. Letting out a whooping cry, she ran into the water and dove in, exhilarated by its gentle chill.

She dove deep, breathing through her gills. It had been days since she had swum, and the sensation made her feel like a child again. She loved to feel the touch of nature's magic as she floated on her back, letting the sun's peaceful rays warm her. Then, diving deep, where the sun barely penetrated, she frolicked for a while with a school of brightly-colored fish. When she had had enough, Ghianna swam as fast as she could toward the surface, webbed feet thrusting her onward. Bursting through the surface of the lake, she soared into the air, shook the water from her wings, spread them, and took flight.

With an audible buzzing, much like that of a giant bee, she took to the sky, zigzagging and flying in excited loops. The trees on the edge of the lake reached to the clouds. She flew to the top of the tallest tree and alit on a branch with a view over the forest. She could see a large crater in the distance that had been created by a meteor thousands of years before. This inspired thoughts about the planet's existence, how it lasts, stable yet dynamic as living residents come and go, full of all the passions and trials that accompany being alive. In its own way, the planet is itself alive and sharing in the experiences of its children, giving itself to the lives that inhabit it. It too evolves, just as the life-forms populating it evolve.

She turned her thoughts back to considering where she should build her home.

~

Meanwhile, in another part of the universe, Earth had made one-hundred-and-thirty-one circles around its sun since Casey Caldwell had frozen in his icy tomb. Many things had changed. Humans had fallen even further away from their connection with nature, increasingly developing and becoming dependent upon technology. They had become more and more enamored with the concept of time and lived their lives according to strict schedules. They invented cars to get around their giant cities, and airplanes so they could fly around their world. They had little phones that they carried around in their pockets so they could talk to their friends and play video games whenever they wanted. And they spent the majority of their day either working in offices or sitting in front of a screen in their house watching other people live make-believe lives. All of their great technological inventions needed energy to run, so the earthlings spent much time and money drilling for a highly combustible black substance called oil.

It was on one of these oil-drilling missions in the Arctic that Casey Caldwell's body was discovered, perfectly preserved in a block of ice. Sensing its scientific value, the oil drillers kept the body frozen and shipped it back to Boston, where scientists could examine it.

~

Dr. Wahaki's lips stretched in a wide smile as he treated the final small patch of tissue damage on Casey's body. The doctor's grey hair surrounded a face wrinkled from a lifetime of study and a lack of exercise. His small frame hunched over the thawed body as he checked Casey's IV. The sticky pads of the cardioelectro-dynamism-generator were placed on Casey's chest, abdomen, and limbs. Wires ran from each pad to a large machine in the corner of the room. The doctor picked up the defibrillator and turned to the others, "Hurry. We've got to start the heart before the body goes into rigor mortis."

He rubbed the defibrillator's metal paddles together then touched them to the chest of the body. "Charge."

The body heaved upward with the electric jolt, and then fell limply onto the bed.

"Again," the Doctor ordered.

The electric pulse was conducted through Casey's flesh to his heart, causing the muscle to contract and the blood to flow. The blood pumped through his veins to his lungs, which were now full of oxygen. The body lay still.

"Again."

Casey's body arched upwards and his lungs expanded, sucking in air as his heart began to beat on its own.

The doctors cheered.

~

In the forest of Nagul on the far away planet of Timballa, Ghianna's body fell into a coma. Her soul was sucked from her body and thrust through an inter-dimensional wormhole back into the body of her past life, Casey Caldwell.

~

Casey sat up on the hospital bed, mind rattled with confusion. He looked around the strange room. Was this a dream? Where was he? His vision was blurred and the florescent light burned his eyes. His muscles twitched as they awoke. Nausea caused him to wobble in his seat and he scrunched his eyes to combat it. Invasive tubes and wires jutted from his body. He wanted to tear them out, but was too weak. His head throbbed. Sickness came in waves, lessening with each passing assault. Slowly, as he breathed, a hint of strength seeped back in. His vision came slowly into focus, revealing the forms of the doctors surrounding him, staring.

They looked alien, all wearing white masks over their mouths, gloves up to their elbows, and the same blue clothes. He wanted to leap from the bed and run, be free from this dreadful place and these strange men, but his limbs felt like dead weight. A stabbing pain in his head slowed his thoughts as he struggled to figure out what was going on. He was overwhelmed by the peculiar phenomenon of sorting out information from two separate lives vying for reign of his head. He vaguely remembered Timballa and the adventures of Ghianna as if it was a fading dream, but was also acutely aware that he was Casey Caldwell, the explorer.

"What's your name?" Dr. Wahaki asked.

Casey eyed him suspiciously. The man had an odd accent that he didn't recognize, but at least he spoke English.

"...Casey Caldwell." Casey's voice felt foreign and small in his throat.

"What were you doing in the Arctic?"

"I... I was on an expedition. We were going to be the first men to reach the North Pole. Where's the Captain? The others, did they make it back?"

"Captain who?"

"Captain Jones."

"I don't know of any Captain Jones."

"You mean Captain Michael Jones?" one of the other doctors asked.

"Yes."

The doctor put his hand to his mouth. "I don't believe it. Captain Michael Jones was the first man to make it to the North Pole. He died over a hundred years ago."

"Wha, what?" Casey's voice cracked through trembling lips.

"I'm sorry."

Casey's head turned slowly, wide eyes observing the stale room. "What year is it?"

"It's July 27th, 2034."

Casey stared mutely, the impact of what he'd just been told drilling into his conscious mind. Looking around, he began to notice the unfamiliar machines, lights blinking from their screens. He noted that the tubes coming from his arms and nose were made of a material he didn't recognize. They itched where they entered his body. This place certainly seemed futuristic. Sterile and evil too.

Could his body actually have been preserved in the ice? If it was 2034, he must have been frozen for one-hundred-and-thirty-one years. The news weighed heavy on him, pressing him back down on the bed. Overwhelmed, he closed his eyes, wanting to wake up back on the boat with the Captain and the others. He lay with his eyes closed, but couldn't sleep. The doctors asked him questions, but he ignored them. He wanted to drift into a slumber, away from this depressing place, but the opposite occurred; he began to feel more alert as time passed. His body began to feel lighter, the aches lessening.

One of the doctors left the room and was greeted by a surge of flashes and microphones thrust into his face as a crowd of journalists shot questions at him. Cheers erupted as he told the crowd the news. The doctor spoke of scientific breakthrough, telling the reporters that, through Casey, they would not only be able to learn of the afterlife, but they would also be able to develop a procedure for freezing people and bringing them back in the future.

Except for some frostbite, Casey was unharmed. After the doctors unhooked the tubes and gave him the go ahead, he stood up. His legs, although weak, worked fine. His first steps were shaky, but his strength slowly found its way back. He stretched, working out the stiffness in his joints, finding that movement helped him to feel sensation in his body again. The doctors examined him, poking and prodding him, checking his vitals, noting their findings on clipboards. He gawked at the alien world he found himself in. Medical instruments lay scattered on the counter. He picked up a piece of rubber tube, amazed by its stretchiness. He had held rubber from the Indian rubber trees, but this was different, softer, more stretchy, more sophisticated. He picked up a plastic bag, rubbed the material between his index finger and thumb, and asked what it was called. His inquisitiveness grew along with his strength. Possibilities of what this unknown future might contain stirred his thoughts, lifting his spirit.

He wondered if people had successfully developed flying machines. If they could bring him back from the dead, what else was possible? There was a whole world to discover. The thought of exploring this new world ignited a curious excitement in him. This was a second chance, a miracle. He eyed the door, the gateway to this unknown future. What wonders could the other side hold? Curiosity blazed in his mind. An entirely new realm lay beyond that door. He could hold back no longer. He opened the door and stepped into the hall.

The flashes from the cameras caught him off guard and he jumped back, hitting his back on the wall. The crowd, a verbal firing squad, shot questions.

"What is death like?"

"Did you see God?"

"Were you in heaven?"

"Did Jesus send you back?"

The camera flashes hit him with blinding intensity, the pandemonium wrapping him in hot, nauseating delirium. He swayed on his feet, overwhelmed by the bombardment. Casey's stomach wrenched. A thick stream of yellowish vomit, speckled with partially-digested husky-jerky, projected from his mouth, hitting three camera men in the front row, and splashing others. Casey froze in shocked embarrassment. One of the camera men threw up on the floor. The crowd spread apart.

In the midst of the uproar, Casey stumbled through, escaping into the lobby of the hospital. The doctors followed him, wanting to bring him back to the safety of the operating room. A deep urge to be alone welled up inside Casey. His head ached from all the recent events. He needed to clear it. He could see outside, feeling the open space beckon him. He ran for the outdoors, bouncing off the glass wall like a startled toddler. Rattled, he stood up and shook his head, realizing that the walls were made of glass. Running his fingers along the glass, he walked down the hall, flabbergasted. He'd never seen so much glass in his life. It must have cost a fortune. As he walked, a set of automatic doors opened as if by magic, and he ran through.

Outside, the reporters and doctors tailed him as he walked down the sidewalk. They were curious to see his reaction, but kept a close watch to ensure he stayed out of harm's way. He was worth too much to risk losing. Doctor Wahaki, flanked by two hospital security guards, walked at arm's length behind Casey.

Casey's gaze traced the outlines of the buildings into the sky, his fear giving way to a feeling of wonder. He had never imagined a city of this magnitude, with buildings this sophisticated. The thought of having this new world to discover brought with it a nervous anticipation. His muscles twitched, readying themselves for action as the desire to investigate boiled in his explorer's soul. He walked to a large glass window and pressed his hands to it. Wanting to get a better feel, he pushed his face against it, scrunching his beard. Inside the building, a restaurant full of people turned to stare at the window.

Doctor Wahaki took him by the arm and led him towards the hospital. "You cannot be outside yet. It's not safe. We have tests to run and a procedure to follow. You are the first person who's ever been dead for an extended period of time that we've been able to bring back to life. This is groundbreaking."

The outside air brought strength back into Casey's body, each breath both invigorating and grounding. Casey looked through the double doors into the hospital. Florescent lights shone onto the bleak hallway. Remembrance of the unnatural feeling he'd experienced from the tubes and needles crept up his skin. He couldn't go back into the hospital. The place seemed horrifyingly perverted, haunting him with fears of being the object of immoral experiments, poked and prodded, held against his will. He craved—needed—open spaces and fresh air. He couldn't let himself become a medical slave. Fear surged through him, screaming for him to run. He had no idea who these future people were, what their morals were, or what they were capable of doing to him.

The doctors and reporters stared at him with beady eyes full of cold-blooded greed. He was the object of an experiment to them, not a fellow human to be respected. He twisted out of Dr Wahaki's grip, shoving the older man to the ground and running. His bare feet gripped the sidewalk as he bolted from the hospital grounds. Doctor Wahaki called out as the guards chased after Casey, who disappeared into the river of bodies flowing along the sidewalk, the two security guards close behind.

Fearing for his life in this alien world, Casey ran. Adrenaline pumped through his veins, giving him strength. His legs ached, but the pain didn't slow him; the specter of danger overshadowed any physical sensation. A life dedicated to exploring the harshest places on earth had given him an unwavering resolve, teaching him how to reach into the depths of his being for the strength to rise above physical pain.

He pushed through the crowded street, his terror increasing as the doctors yelled behind him. Halfway down the block, he turned into an alley between two buildings. A tall iron gate blocked the alley's middle section. He leapt halfway up the height of the gate. As he pulled himself over the top, a hand grabbed Casey's ankle, yanking him towards the ground. His body stretched, his fingers clinging to the top of the gate as the guard pulled him. The gate rattled under the strain.

Glancing down at the guard, Casey knew that this man stood in the way of his freedom. The guard was not only pulling Casey towards the ground, he was pulling him towards enslavement. The cold iron dug into Casey's fingers. His shoulders ached under the strain. He felt his fingers opening, losing the battle to hold on. He didn't want to hurt the man, but knew he had no other choice. He kicked his captured leg, catching the security guard in the jaw. The large man fell back, landing hard, yelling for the others to hurry. Two others sprinted down the alley, one in uniform, one in civilian clothes.

Throwing himself over the gate, Casey landed on his side with a thud, then scrambled to his feet. His hip throbbed as he ran, but he ignored it, fear overriding the sting. Looking over his shoulder as he turned onto the street, he saw that the civilian had already clambered over the gate and was sprinting in pursuit. Behind the civilian, the two guards from the hospital were helping each other over the gate.

Panicked, Casey crossed the street blindly, causing cars to swerve and honk. He followed a group of teenagers through a rotating door, and disappeared into a building, hoping his pursuers hadn't seen him. An indoor market filled the building. Casey fled down a wide, well-lit hallway. People sauntered about, seeming to drift between the stores in a daze. Large pictures of people covered the windows of many of the stores.

Casey sprinted down a flight of moving stairs, pushing past people as he ran. At the bottom, he came to a tunnel. People stood on a platform next to a set of train tracks. The tracks curved into the tunnel, vanishing in the darkness.

Casey waited for a few seconds, trying to blend into the crowd as he caught his breath. He thought about waiting for the underground train, but the longer he stayed still, the more his fear increased. Anxiety flooded his mind, tormenting him. Images of the hospital flashed into his consciousness. He envisioned the men running down the alley, chasing him. They could be anywhere—just around the corner, sneaking up on him. Fear sank deep into his mind, controlling his thoughts, spurring him into total panic, making it impossible to stand still any longer.

He fled into the tunnel.

He raced through the darkness, tripping once in the blackest part, frantic that a train would run him down. A light in the distance urged him on, giving him hope. Breathless and sweaty, he arrived at the lit area, realizing it was another platform. He climbed onto it and ascended a set of stairs to another busy street.

Near collapse, Casey stopped, bent at the waist with his hands on his knees. He glanced over his shoulder for anyone in a doctor's or guard's uniform. He saw none.

The civilian pursuing Casey, a young reporter, crept up the stairs behind him. Blending in with the other civilians, the reporter continued his pursuit, eager for the story that would jumpstart his career.

Casey stood, watching the machines travel down the street, wondering what powered them. He had heard about the invention of the automobile before he left on his voyage for the North Pole, but he had never seen one. He hadn't imagined that the invention would spread so pervasively in the future. He observed the people driving, and how the traffic-lights seemed to control the automobiles' starting and stopping. Astonished by the technology, he pondered the highly organized life of these strange people. Crowds filed about like worker ants on a mission. People existed in such proximity to one another, hurrying about, speaking into hand held devices, playing their part in this highly developed civilization.

Curious, Casey tried to open a parked car. Its lights flashed on and a high-pitched, pulsating siren scared him so severely that he bolted into the street and was almost run over. The angry driver rolled down his window, "Get tha fuck outta tha street, ya asshole." He pressed hard on the horn, which made Casey dive back onto the sidewalk, scraping his elbow.

Confused and feeling alone, the car still shrieking behind him, Casey hurried away. The reporter followed close behind. Eventually, Casey came to a small city park and sat in the grass to rest for a minute. He looked at the few trees and felt a kinship—like he and the trees were aliens of an old world trapped in the future. Confusion and loneliness gripped him, weighing him down, heavy in his chest. He cradled his head in his hands. Why was this happening? He wished for his crewmates. He didn't want to be on this adventure alone.

The reporter approached him. "Casey, we must get out of here. Men from the hospital will be here any minute and they'll want to take you back for tests. I can protect you." The reporter glanced furtively over his shoulder.

Casey jumped back. "Who are you? Where will you take me?" He doubted this stranger, eying him suspiciously. The young man couldn't have been more than twenty-five. His cleanly shaven face was smooth and calm. His eyes were full of compassion, not greed. His body was thin yet healthy, full of vitality.

"I'll take you to a place where you can rest. A hotel with a comfortable bed." The reporter waved down a cab. "Hurry."

"Why are you helping me?"

"I'm a journalist. I want exclusive rights to your first interview. This story is huge."

"I don't know."

The young man looked around uneasily. "If you don't come now, those people will take you back to the hospital. You'll be the subject of many experiments. You deserve better. You deserve to choose for yourself."

A taxi pulled up in front of the two men. Casey looked it over, wondering what it might be like to ride inside of it. He couldn't think of any other options than to go with the reporter. "OK. If you really are a journalist, then I have a lot to share." Casey got into the front seat of the cab.

The reporter got into the back. He gave the driver the address of a hotel across town, and then pulled out a notepad, ready to start interviewing Casey.

"You can interview me at the hotel." Casey said, face pressed against the window, taking in the outside world. "I need to rest."

Casey gawked at the skyscrapers reaching higher than any tree he had ever seen. The angst of being chased began to dissipate. Curiosity flowed back in as he observed the world around him through the safety of the car. A large, well-lit billboard hung in a busy intersection, advertising tight patchwork jeans. In the picture, three beautiful women grabbed at a man, lustfully pulling his shirt tight. Reading the name, Calvin Klein, Casey looked at the giant face of the man in the picture and wondered who he was—if he was the king.

As the car entered an impoverished area of town, Casey noticed more and more people wandering the streets in ragged clothes. Some of them pushed metal carts full of items. A man sat on some stairs, eyes darting side to side as he smoked a pipe. Another man lay in an alley wrapped in a blanket, presumably sleeping. Papers littered the streets, blown about by the wind. Amazed at the size of the city and the paucity of nature, Casey wondered how these people grew their food. There were so many mouths to feed, yet no agricultural land in sight. It would take hundreds of miles of agricultural land to feed a city this size. He thought about it, and then vowed to himself that he must visit one of these farms to learn how they can produce so much food.

Once inside the hotel, the reporter led him to a room. Casey felt as if he was inside a giant beehive, each door leading to a little individual chamber. The reporter used a card to beep them into the room. Upon seeing the bed, exhaustion overtook Casey—a lead blanket pressing him towards sleep. He collapsed onto the mattress, muscles aching. He closed his eyes and felt himself slipping into the dream dimension. Then, with an audible exhale, Casey fell into a deep slumber.

Anxious to interview Casey, the reporter sat at the desk. Pulling out his notepad, he began to formulate a list of questions. Then he turned on the TV, flipping to the news to determine the extent of the search going on, thinking that the scientists must be exasperated, having just lost their extraordinarily rare find. The reporter smiled, thrilled by the fame this story was going to bring him.

~

Casey's soul travelled through the dream dimension until it reached Timballa. Ghianna awoke with a start, still perched in the tree.

Confused, she looked around to get her bearings. Her experience of being Casey Caldwell had been too real to dismiss as a dream. The terror of fleeing the hospital clung to her, crawling up her skin. She shook her limbs, trying to rid herself of the feeling, thinking she needed the Priestess' advice. She spread her wings, the sunlight illuminating the translucent turquoise skin as they began to beat the air. Then, she dove out of the tree. The air caught her wings and lifted her high into the sky, taking her in the direction of the nearest priestess.

Flying to a cloud temple was no easy feat, and Ghianna knew that she must not let her determination waver. If the will was not strong enough, the wings could become too tired and the flier would fall from the sky. By the time she was halfway to her destination, her wings burned with exhaustion. She glanced down at Timballa below. A few large trees twisted upward, towering above the top of the forest. At the top of the tallest tree was a Baznile's nest—large flying reptiles that dive-bomb fish from above.

Jagged mountains cut across the skyline in the distance. She saw lights from a village nestled between two peaks. It looked to be a peaceful place to recover some energy for the rest of the flight, but there was no time. She had to get to the Priestess as quickly as possible. The ocean lay just beyond the far side of the mountains. Breathing its salty scent deep into her lungs, she allowed it to fill her with tenacity. She could not stop flying. She looked towards the clouds and inhaled.

Reaching the cloud temple, she collapsed. Lean muscles, swollen with blood, twisted up her back like knotted rope. Ghianna rested on her knees, catching her breath before looking up. From underneath, the temple looked like any ordinary cumulous cloud, but from above, it was miraculous. The crystal temple twisted upwards into the sky in an extraordinary display of architectural genius, every inch of it carved with meticulous care. Sunlight refracted through the crystal, lighting the top of the cloud with colors so brilliant they filled Ghianna with awe. The sight calmed her, encouraging her strength to return. A stairway wrapped around the outside of the temple. Each floor had a hand-carved, diamond-shaped door.

As she caught her breath, Ghianna noticed a hand-woven banner painted with the Priestess' writing that hung over the entrance to the stairs. She read it aloud: "Swan dive into the part of the self where the living spirit dwells. Like the molten rock churning at the center of Timballa, let your living spirit burn. Fuel it with adventure. Fuel it with love. Let it erupt in volcanic passion, coming alive as it burns within, giving life to the body. We are here to live, here to experience, here to be the eyes and hands of the Creative Force that flows through the Universe, giving it form. Let your experience guide you to the light, where once immersed, we awaken to the joy of fully living in this world. As we break through the ancient crust of ego, we realize that we are all part of the same force, experiencing our creation subjectively. And on a level beyond the reach of our senses, beyond the grasp of our minds, we are all connected, we are all one."

Ghianna took the stairs up to the top of the temple. The crystal was warm to the touch, giving off a comforting vibration which seemed to sing. Each of the seven levels was carved to vibrate at a particular frequency, each tuned into one of the seven energy centers of the body. Running up the stairs, Ghianna stopped just long enough on each level to touch her forehead to the floor and send a prayer to the universe. Each stair was etched with a different ancient symbol, each meant to open the heart to an aspect of the true nature of life.

The very top of the temple was shaped like a satellite dish, catching the light from the sun and Timballa's three moons, and reflecting it into a condensed point. The Priestess hovered in a meditative position in the center of the light. A prayer for the well-being of all was etched into the top of the temple, circling around the inside of the bowl, starting in the middle and spiraling out. Ghianna felt her energy grow stronger as she approached the Priestess, who radiated love with such force it was almost visible.

The Priestess' long, jet-black hair was tied up in a large bun. A few wispy strands dangled delicately along the sides of her serene face. Her breath moved deeply, slowly, and purposefully. Her face was radiant yet calm. It carried a wisdom connected with age, even though the skin was flawlessly smooth.

Ghianna sat in front of the Priestess, adopting a meditative position, and the two began to communicate telepathically.

Great Priestess of the crystal palace, something is happening to me. I'm very confused.

Yes, my friend, I know. The body of your past life has been brought back to life and now your soul is torn between two worlds.

I don't know what to do.

Neither body will be able to survive long without your soul being fully present. You must choose one life and let the other body die. Lives must be lived one at a time.

But how can I make such a choice?

You must let your hearts guide you and act out of love. Your destiny is up to you to create. I cannot tell you which world to choose. But I can only tell you about the other world.

Go on.

I've been watching the earthlings evolve over the millennia. They are a beautiful race and create many great works of art. They are capable of immense love; however, many are self-serving. Hunger and war plague their planet needlessly because the earthlings compete with each other over wealth and resources. They have set up a system with something they call money, and they work to accumulate wealth for themselves, rather than to spread love and joy.

But why don't they live to spread love?

It is a planet full of young souls. They still have much to learn. You learned to love unconditionally and sacrificed yourself for others. That is why your soul was born on a more highly evolved planet.

But what if someone went back to teach the earthlings? Could the earth evolve into a place of love?

Yes this is possible. Others have tried. Many years ago the great Priestess from the star temple took a life in the form of a man and attempted to lead the earthlings towards love. Unfortunately the earthlings were not ready and killed him.

Could they be ready now?

It's possible. I cannot know. The future is unwritten.

Maybe I could help to lead them.

This is your choice.

Ghianna slouched, overwhelmed by the gravity of her situation. She let her head fall into her hands. The choices bounced around her brain, as she struggled to come to a decision.

My friend, the Priestess said, *sometimes the brain can be misleading. It is best to make the choice from the hearts. You must turn off your mind in order to fully feel your hearts.*

My mind feels like a tornado. I don't know if I can calm it.

I will sing for you. Dancing will help you release pent up energy and separate the head from the hearts. By completely giving in to your physical body, you may become fully present, enter a trance, and drop the mind.

Thank you.

The Priestess opened her eyes and floated down to the top of the temple. She descended the stairs, then returned a moment later with a drum. Straddling the drum, the Priestess beat a rhythm with her hands. Ghianna began to move her body. Her wings and arms stretched outwards as she breathed in, preparing to give way to the powerful rhythms. The Priestess began to sing, her voice resonating with purity, layering notes into an enchanting melody as she sang her love to the creator. The Priestess' hands beat the skin of the drum, fingers slapping rhythms that rolled forward, building, pulsating with emotion. Energy flared within Ghianna, and her body swayed. The temple's vibrations increased—different floors vibrating at different frequencies, turning the entire temple into an instrument that sang a harmony so powerful it ignited within Ghianna, like a super-nova of the soul.

The music swelled—divine in its purity, primal in its raw expression. Ghianna danced under the three moons with wild abandon. Her arms stretched toward the sky, swaying back and forth. Her feet carried her body to each edge of the temple top, which sang now with heartrending richness, sending vibrations up Ghianna's body through her feet. Her hearts beat to the rhythm of the drum as she turned in circles, smiling with the unrestricted bliss of being fully present. Her breath heaved as her eyes rolled back in her head, passion consuming her. She danced, twirling in bolder and bolder circles, her arms flung freely about as the skin of her feet slapped and stomped the crystal floor in time with the music.

Vibrations pulsed throughout Ghianna's body. She felt as if light poured out of her, coming up through the temple and shooting toward the heavens above. The priestess' voice bellowed out, pure and rich in soulful melody. The drums thundered, each beat inspiring Ghianna to throw herself about—swept around in the fierce waters of an ocean of elation. She was no longer in her body. She was flying across mountains. She was inside the sun, burning with love. She was across the universe. Then she was no longer of physical form at all, no longer connected to this dimension, no longer Ghianna. She was simply vibration—one with the universal consciousness.

Then finally, after the Priestess' song came to a fierce climax, holding a note that was equally as haunting as it was passionate, and Ghianna felt as though she might explode, she collapsed, exhausted.

Ghianna rolled onto her back. "The Earth needs me more than Timballa does. I will let this body die."

~

Casey awoke on the hotel bed. He felt better, more himself. The reporter sat in a chair reading the newspaper. On the cover was a picture of Casey—the headline read, *Does this man know the secrets of life and death?* Upon seeing Casey, the reporter sprung from his seat and came over to interview him.

"Mr. Caldwell, can you tell me about death."

"I will, but not now. I have seen beyond the scope of the human experience, I have known God, and I have the answers to your questions. All I will tell you now is that death is not what you think. Heaven exists, but the afterlife is infinitely more complex than humans think it is. We are eternal beings, constantly learning and growing over the course of countless lifetimes. We are all fingers of God, experiencing our creation subjectively, and we are on a journey to become one with our divine selves."

"Go on."

"Now is not the time. I will give the first of many public speeches tomorrow morning in the park down the street. Could you please write about it in your paper so people know to come?"

"Yes, of course."

"Good, because from what I saw yesterday, we have a lot of work to do if we're going to bring Heaven to Earth. Now, if you'll excuse me, I would like to go for a walk."

"Casey, I'm afraid you don't understand the seriousness of the situation you are in. Authorities all over the city are looking for you. If they catch you, they'll take you in for tests."

"But I need to go outside. I need the fresh air."

"I'll help you, but first let me interview you. You need to intrigue people with your story so they'll come to hear you speak."

"Ok"

Over the next few hours, Casey told the reporter about how he'd died and been frozen. He explained his life on Timballa, including his adventures, his village, and the Priestess. Then, longing to be outdoors, he rose, ready to explore the new world he found himself in.

"You cannot go outside looking like that." The reporter warned. "You are too noticeable. Shave and put some modern clothes on. You must blend in."

Casey obeyed, shaving and putting on the clothes the reporter gave him before venturing outside. The reporter followed at a short distance, keeping a protective eye on Casey, careful not to lose him.

On the sidewalk, Casey took a deep breath of air. He smelled the city smog and wondered what it was. He looked around for a patch of green space to sit in, but except for a few lone trees and small patches of manicured grass, saw none. He walked down the street, observing the people—amazed at how many there were.

Eventually he came upon a boy with a sideways hat and a shirt two sizes too large. The boy stood in an alley, using a spray-can to make art on the side of a building. Casey loved art. He loved all expressions of the heart, so he approached the boy. "Hello, I see you're an artist."

"Yeah, so. You gonna call the cops?"

"No. They would just take me away."

The boy eyed Casey.

Casey continued. "I really like the boat and all the people you're painting, but why is it sinking?"

"It's a metaphor."

"For what?"

"The ship is Earth. There's over ten billion people here. Our planet's dying. Get ready for anarchy."

"So, you think the Earth is doomed?" Casey asked.

"We got too many problems. We're destroying the forests, there's a plastic island half the size of America in the Pacific Ocean, there's almost no glaciers left, lakes are evaporating, and we're running out of clean water to drink. Ya, I'd say shit's fucked."

"Oh. I see. Then we have some work to do. But the Earth is stronger than you think. We will not destroy it. Maybe ourselves, but not Earth."

"You're an idealist, buddy," the boy scoffed, as he sprayed a torn sail on the boat.

"Humans have a lot to learn. We have strayed too far from nature, and forgot one of the most fundamental principles of life."

"And what's that?"

"You see, humans believe that we are the pinnacle of creation. Whether one believes in evolution or creation, we all believe that humans are the grandest creation on Earth, possibly in the universe."

The boy turned from his painting to look at Casey. "Aren't we?"

"No. This belief is the reason why the world is off balance. We believe that the world is here for us, so we take from it and use whatever we choose. We are selfish and greedy, seeing ourselves as separate from the world. We look at the world as though it belongs to us, and look for what we can gain rather than give. But the Earth does not belong to us, we belong to it. We are of it. And it has a finite amount of resources. We cannot take forever without using them up."

"Whoa, dude, get a box and stand on the corner. Preach that shit to somebody who cares."

"I am talking to somebody who cares. Why else would you take the time to create an artistic metaphor?"

The boy looked Casey in the eye, caught off guard by this talkative newcomer. "OK. Go on."

"We are not separate from the world. We are all connected to it, part of it," Casey said. He smiled at the boy. "It has taken billions of years of evolution for humans to emerge on this planet. We now have an advanced intelligence with the ability to make conscious choice. It is our responsibility to our world to allow our evolutionary line to continue. You see, we are not the pinnacle of creation or the end of an evolutionary line as our egos like to believe. Humanity is a stage along the way. There is more to the human story. If we learn to live in harmony with our earth, we will evolve into something even more grand than homo-sapiens. That is our destiny—not to sink like the boat in your painting. But it will take great awareness on the part of our species."

"Yeah? And what will we evolve into?" the boy asked.

"The future is unwritten," Casey smiled. "It is up to us to write it. We create ourselves with our thoughts and actions. Whether consciously or unconsciously, we choose our own evolution, both on the individual level and as a species as a whole."

The boy nodded. "So I am who I am because of my thoughts and actions in the past?"

"Yes. There's a great deal of genetic disposition and cultural influence, but in the end, you are responsible for the creation of you, and we are responsible for the creation of we."

"So I have the power to create my future self?"

Casey smiled. "Yes, but not only your future self. We create ourselves in each moment, so you are creating your present self as we speak."

The boy nodded.

Casey was tired. "I have made a very long journey to get here," he said. "I must rest. If you want to hear more of what I have to say, please come to the park down the road tomorrow morning. I will be giving a public lecture."

"I'll be there, brother." The boy nodded enthusiastically.

Casey smiled and waved over his shoulder as he walked away. He stopped just long enough to call out, "remember, my friend, of all the wonders in the universe, seek foremost to know thy self."

Once Casey had rounded the corner, the boy turned back to his painting. He drew an island in front of the boat. Then he drew a boy on the island. A rope stretched from the painted boy's hand to the boat. The artist stepped back, pleased with the addition to his painting. The boy on the island was pulling the boat to safety.

~

That night, the online newspaper headlines read, *Arctic explorer has been brought back to life after 131 years. He will speak about the afterlife in Thoreau Park at noon tomorrow.* The news spread around the world.

~

The next morning at 11:45, Casey looked out his hotel window. He was three blocks from the park. The crowd was so thick that he knew he'd have trouble manoeuvring through it. People had flown in from all over the world to hear what he had to say, intrigued to hear the perspective of a man who had returned from the dead. Casey sat on the edge of the bed, going over what he wanted to say in the first speech. He adjusted the tie of the suit that the reporter had given him, and tried to use the smart phone, but grew confused and put it back in his pocket. Running his palm over his freshly shaven chin, he stepped into the hallway. It was empty.

As he walked to the elevator, a man in a brown suit stepped out and looked Casey in the eye. The man was Reverend Earl Smith, from the Mississippi Evangelical Church. Casey smiled at him.

"I can't be lett'n ya give that speech." The Reverend was holding a hand gun.

"I'm sorry. The world needs to hear what I have to say."

"Like hell, the world needs to hear ya. We have a Messiah."

"I'm not trying to be a Messiah, but I have a message and I'm going to be late. I'd love to talk to you after my speech."

"The Devil sent you to lead God's children away from Jesus. Well, guess what. I'm God's warrior and I'm not gonna let that happen."

"My friend, your mind is full and therefore not hungry for more knowledge, but there is much more to know. A religion that divides you from others is no expression of God. God is far bigger and grander than you imagine, and can only work to connect you with others, not separate you."

The Reverend crossed his chest with the gun, and then shot Casey twice in the chest.

Casey landed on his back, blood pouring out of the bullet-holes. A crimson stain spread across his new suit. His body began to convulse. He grew cold. As he laid there, he thought about his family on Timballa, he thought about the Captain, he thought about the Priestess, and he thought about love. *Maybe hatred remains on Earth because this is the place where souls come to learn to overcome it*, he thought. Then he thought about the Reverend and whispered, "I forgive you my friend. Do not carry your hatred with you."

And with that, his heart stopped, and Casey journeyed into the light, again.

~

50,983,678 light-years from earth, on a small moon circling the planet Rengdow, a giant sea creature gave birth to a beautiful six-legged water dancer.

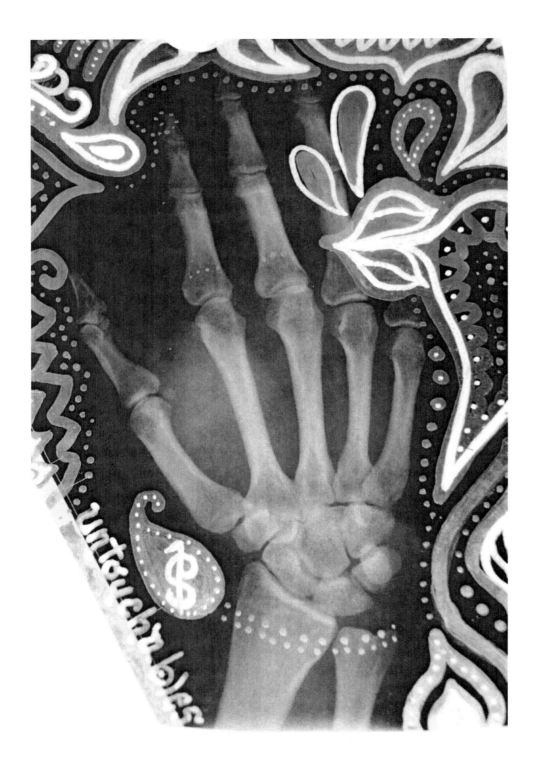

7

UNTOUCHABLES

Following the tourist under forty-five degree sun, bare feet carry you over burning plastic and cow shit—fifteen dusty blocks through the run-down town. The only dress you own, torn at the seam. I see your brown skin stretched over thin ribs, flies stuck to your scabbed legs.

Your fingers, dry and cracked, tug at my shorts as your eyes plead. Your hands, scrawny from starvation, are brought to swollen, snot-crusted lips, begging for rupees. I gape at the tendons and veins squiggling up your neck, and your yellow, Hep C eyes. Warnings run through my head, "Don't give begging children money, it encourages the Beggar-master to buy children for the street." I offer you bananas and crackers. You refuse; your master accepts only cash.

The lumps from your last beating are still fresh, motivation to not give up. You don't. I give in, my heart torn by the claws of compassion. I turn off the voices in my head, reach into my pocket, and hand you ten rupees. Where I'm from this is a quarter, but to you it's a day's wage—quickly hidden deep in your pocket.

Briefly, you smile; tonight you won't be beaten. Then you turn and yell out to the others. Your colleagues hear; from the cracks of the city, untouchables creep out. Lepers and amputees of all ages crawl, limp, drag themselves toward me, hands and stumps outstretched.

I walk away, well-fed legs carrying me to safety.

I don't look back.

8

FREEDOM FROM FEAR

Maria flees down the dark deserted road, her white nightgown dirty and torn. Her face, flawlessly beautiful in a naughty angel kind of way, is twisted with terror. Blonde, perfectly-textured locks bounce around her sleek shoulders and down the gentle slope of her back. Above the pine trees, the full moon shines bright. Maria stops, out of breath, chest heaving, the tight fabric of her nightgown hugging her impeccably round breasts. She peers fearfully into the bushes that line the winding country road.

A leaf floats gently to the earth, brushing the silky skin of her arm, startling her. She turns in a single, jerky motion. Mist rises in the autumn air, swirling in the moonlight. Somewhere in the nearby trees, an owl hoots. The noise haunts her, crawling up her skin. Her finger and thumb grip the silver cross around her neck as her plump lips recite the Lord's Prayer.

She continues running. She can't stop; the beast is coming. It's following her scent. She must make it to Sheriff Conway's house. He'll have a gun and a silver bullet.

A low, animalistic grunt reverberates through the woods behind her. She turns slowly, the moonlight illuminating her skin, sparkling in her anxious eyes. The beast steps from a distant shadow. It stands, man-like, on two legs, nose in the air as it sniffs her. The torn remains of suit-pants hug its hips—the only evidence of its human life. It howls at the moon, piercing the air with its tormented affliction. Then, licking its lips, overcome by the scent of its prey, it breaks into a hunched, four-legged run.

Less than thirty feet away, the massive beast races towards her, leaving a black storm of dirt in its wake. Muscles, sinewy and taut, strain under its matted brown fur. Maria screams, continuing her desperate sprint. Now fifteen feet away, the beast's lips curl back. Moonlight glistens across fangs. The beast hurls itself forward with unearthly speed, urged on by the primal lust for blood.

Tears streak down Maria's face as she runs. The beast is now ten feet away. She hears its laborious breath.

Lunging through the air, the werewolf extends its claws for attack. Maria dives to the side and the beast flies past. She rolls to a stop. The werewolf's claws dig into the earth as the frenzied creature scrambles to turn around. Rising on its hind legs, it towers over her—standing at least seven feet tall.

As Maria cowers at the beast's feet, a cloud blocks the moonlight, stealing the werewolf's strength. It drops onto all fours, convulsing as it shrinks. Paws turn into hands, hair into skin. Maria stares in horror. The beast, the killer responsible for the death of her husband, is her brother.

He looks up at her, anguish in his eyes. "Run. Get the silver bullet. Kill me."

She stands stunned, mind unhinged by this shocking development. Then, the clouds part, letting the moonlight through, and turning her brother back into the snarling, hairy, fanged beast.

~

Francis screamed, unable to contain his fear for even one more second. It was the creature's eyes that finally broke him, so horrific, yet so human at the same time. Could werewolves be real? He looked away from the TV, scrunching his eyes shut and covering his ears.

Austin sprang from the couch, slapping a hand over Francis' mouth. "Shut it, you little dweeb, before mom hears." His hand practically wrapped around the smaller boy's entire face.

Too late. They could hear her footsteps coming up the stairs.

"Crap, look what you did. Where's the remote, dick-lick?" Austin demanded as he released his grip on Francis' mouth.

"I don't have it. You turned the movie on." Francis' voice squeaked and trembled like a mouse in a snake pit.

The footsteps were getting louder. Austin shot Francis a look that said, *get me the remote or I'll pin you to the ground with my knees and shove my dirty socks in your mouth.* Francis looked under the couch cushions. His brute of an older brother loomed over him, Islanders jersey hanging loosely over his pajama pants. Footsteps echoed down the hall, thumping anxiety into the boys with every stride.

Austin glared at Francis; his gaze was so menacing it made Francis want to cry. Austin held up his fist. "If mom finds out, you're dead."

The footsteps were right outside the door. Francis dove from the couch, hitting the power button on the TV. The doorknob turned and the door swung open, revealing their mother's lumpy silhouette. She scanned the dark room, relieved that the boys were unhurt.

"What in the world is going on up here?" She wore her blue dental hygienist uniform, her hair was up, a clay mask covered her face, and her eyes were fierce. She hated being taken away from *American Idol.*

Francis cringed at the sight. "Nothing mom, we were just wrestling and Austin stepped on my hand. It's ok though, it doesn't hurt anymore. See." He opened and closed his fingers to demonstrate that his hand was ok.

"Wrestling in the dark?" she questioned.

"Oh yeah, it's fun. That way I have a chance because I can see better in the dark."

She looked at the TV, suspiciously. "Where's the remote?"

"I don't know," Francis answered, honestly.

The woman stepped toward the TV and her foot landed on Francis' toy '57 Chevy. Cursing, she limped to the wall and stubbed her toe on Austin's barbell. "How many times do I have to tell you two to keep this room clean?"

The boys looked around sheepishly. An empty bag of Doritos lay next to the couch, chip-crumbs sinking into the carpet. A Tupperware container sat on its side, spilling Lego in the corner of the room. Austin's Playstation games were spread out in front of the TV. Francis' dinosaurs were bunched all over the room, abandoned mid-battle.

"Now clean it up and get ready for bed. It's a school night."

"Ok, mom" The boys answered in unison, hopeful that she'd forgotten about the TV.

She touched it. It was warm. "Oh, so you're lying to me now. You were watching TV." The boys flinched as the glow filled the room. There on the flat screen was Maria, on the ground, blouse torn open, flawlessly round breasts exposed. The werewolf lunged at her. Both boys stared at the breasts, entranced by their beauty.

Francis had never seen breasts before. It was possibly the greatest discovery of his short life.

"What the hell are you watching?" Their mother screamed. She turned to Austin. "A horror movie? What's wrong with you? Francis is nine years old."

The boys were stunned into silence by their mother's interrogation. She stood, feet planted firmly apart, hands on her hips, with 'the look' on her face—you know the look—the one only mothers get, perfected by years of dealing with misbehaving children, the one that kids all around the world know to fear. The look that says, *listen to what I say, OR ELSE.*

She turned to Francis, "Go to your room. I'll deal with you in a minute."

Francis quickly shuffled out of the room, happy to be temporarily out of the heated situation, and walked down the hall to his bedroom. He undressed and draped his jeans and t-shirt over the chair. A fallen pile of comics sat on the edge of the desk—evidence that he'd been reading them earlier when his mom thought he'd been doing homework. He quickly stuffed them under his bed. He hated when she was mad at him. Austin had said that their mom only got mad when the 'red monster' was around. Francis didn't know what the 'red monster' was, he just knew he didn't want to meet it. He wondered if it was as scary as a werewolf.

He put his Spiderman pajamas on, sat on his racecar-shaped-bed, and closed his eyes. But as soon as his lids touched together and blackness engulfed him, there was the werewolf, snarling and running towards him through the dark. He quickly opened his eyes and looked around his room to make sure it was werewolf free.

Francis' mom knocked on the door as she entered the room. She pulled out the chair from the desk and sat facing Francis. "You OK, kiddo?"

"Yeah, mom."

"You know you shouldn't watch scary movies. Things like that aren't good to put into your mind. They're not good for anyone's mind, especially kids' minds." She rested her hand on Francis' shoulder. As per usual, his brown hair was a tangled mess.

"I know. I wish I never saw it." He looked up at his mom and smiled, wanting to be back on her good side.

"Don't worry; I'm not mad at you for watching the movie," she said, messing up his hair even more. "You didn't know. Austin shouldn't have shown it to you. But Francis,"

"Yeah?"

"You really shouldn't have lied to me. We're a family. That means we're a team. How are we supposed to be a team if we lie to each other? You know better than to lie."

"I know, mom. I'm sorry," Francis said, and hugged his mom.

She wrapped her arms around his small body. "It's OK, honey. Just don't lie to me in the future." She kissed his forehead as she tucked him in, and then got up to leave. "Goodnight."

"Mom?"

She stopped in the door. "Yeah?"

"Are werewolves real?" Francis' blue eyes shone in the light as they searched her face for an answer.

"Oh no, honey. There's no such thing as werewolves. Don't worry your cute little head about that. They're just make-believe." She smiled encouragingly.

He sighed, relieved. "Good, because I don't like them."

"Goodnight." She turned the light off as she closed the door.

"G'night."

Francis pulled the blanket up around his chin. His nightlight shone in the corner of the room, casting shadows that stretched up the wall, taunting him with their sinister shapes. He tried to think of school, the upcoming science fair, his baseball game, anything but the werewolf, but its image kept clawing its way back into his mind.

A scratching noise at the wall startled him and he sat up. The hair on the back of his neck stood on end. *Don't scream, don't scream, don't scream,* he told himself. *It's just a mouse.* The scratching grew louder. It moved down the wall towards the door. It was too loud to be a mouse. *It's just your imagination,* Francis' told himself. *Werewolves aren't real.* Then came the growl, low and guttural, augmented by heavy breathing. Francis leapt from his bed, picking up the baseball-bat from the corner of his room. The door handle jiggled, turning slowly. Francis' breathing was erratic. His lip quivered. He wanted to cry out, but wouldn't; he wasn't a baby. It had taken months for Austin to stop teasing him after Halloween, when Francis had had a nightmare and had to sleep with their mom. He wouldn't go through that ridicule again. The door creaked open, allowing a sliver of light from the hall to penetrate the room. The breathing from behind the door was raspy and strained. The bat shook in Francis' hands. Then the door flew open and a large body leapt into the room.

Horror seized Francis, triggering his reflexes. He swung the bat. Crack.

His brother dropped to the ground, stunned, holding his elbow. "What the hell, Francis." He looked up, face contorted in pain and anger. Grabbing the bat from Francis, he threw the smaller boy on the bed and leapt on him, pinning him down with his knees. He trapped Francis' arms with one hand and used his free hand to lightly poke and slap the helpless boy in the face. "What's the matter dweeb? Scared of the wolfman?"

"Get off."

"Not until you apologize for hitting me."

"No."

"OK then. Have it your way." Austin grabbed a hold of Francis' chest and delivered an unrelenting titty-twister. Francis shrieked, but Austin smothered the noise with a pillow.

Once the pillow was out of his face, Francis resorted to his last defense, spitting. A glob flew from his small lips, catching his brother in the face, where it clung, stretching as it dangled like a liquid silkworm.

"Sick," Austin said, and wiped it off on Francis' cheek.

"Get off, or I'll scream for mom."

"Scream all you want, I'll cover your face with this pillow."

"Fine, get off or I'll tell Jessica that you pooped your pants in Mexico last year."

"That's not fair. I had food poisoning."

"GET OFF." Francis' face turned red from exertion.

The older brother got off the bed and walked to the door, laughing. He unplugged Francis' nightlight. Standing in the door, he turned toward the small boy, "Just so you know, werewolves are real."

"No, they're not. Mom said."

"She just said that so you wouldn't be scared. But everyone knows they're real." He turned to leave, but turned back adding an afterthought. "And they really like to eat little boys, cuz they have the juiciest meat."

"Get laaawsst." Francis tossed a pillow at the door, but Austin quickly shut it, leaving the young boy in pitch blackness.

Francis swiftly turned on his bedside lamp. He walked over and plugged his nightlight in, mumbling under his breath, "there's no such thing as werewolves." Then he lay on his bed, turned off the lamp, and pulled his blanket over his head to shield out the world.

~

The dark forest was thick with the unknown. The wind whirled through branches, calling out in the night like a reclusive witch. Francis stood alone on a dirt path, baffled by the way it wound through the woods, maze-like. Light from the full moon shone into the woods, illuminating patches of the forest floor in a haunting glow. Francis had no idea how long he'd been there, he just knew he had to get out of the forest. Fast.

A howl ripped through the air, tearing through Francis' ears and into his consciousness. He turned around, running from the sound. It couldn't be a werewolf, could it? No, they're not real. What was he doing in the woods alone at night? Why had he come here? It didn't matter; he had to get out.

His slender body trembled under his pajamas. The werewolf leapt onto the path twenty feet in front of Francis. Its ears were forward as it listened to every move the small boy made. It stood like a man, walking on two legs as it licked its lips.

Tears poured from Francis' eyes and down his round cheeks. Every muscle in his body tensed with fear. The boy turned to flee, but his legs wouldn't work. He couldn't move. The beast had some kind of spell over him. Francis was forced to watch as the beast strode towards him, claws outstretched. It frothed at the mouth, drool escaping its long snout, oozing to the ground. With each step the beast took, Francis' terror grew. It was so close he could see its eyes, bloodshot and yellow as they stared at him, tasting him.

Try as he did, Francis could not break the trance and run. His clenched muscles were completely unresponsive. The werewolf stopped in front of the boy. Hot breath, reeking of rotten meat, billowed down on the tearful child. Francis called out, but even his vocal chords wouldn't respond. He wished for his Dad, but the man was nowhere in sight.

The wolf dropped onto all fours, snarling, hungry for child's tender flesh. The beast's mouth opened, revealing bloodstained fangs. Snot bubbled out of Francis' nose, oozing down his face, mixing with his tears, and clinging to his chin where it dangled, blown about in the wind. He stood submerged in dread, drowning in the horror of the imminent pain. Why couldn't he move? The wolf bit into his leg, tearing through the flesh to the bone. The wound burned violently, consuming the boy in an ocean of physical misery. His small body convulsed and dropped to the ground, writhing.

~

"MMMOOOOOOOOOOMMMMM!" Francis called out in agony as he rolled off his racecar bed, landing on the floor, leg muscles knotted in a fierce cramp. Sweat-soaked pajamas clung to his shivering body as he tried to straighten his leg.

His mom burst through the door, scooping him up. "Shhhhh, it's ok, sweet boy. You're ok."

Francis wrapped his arms around her neck. "M... my leg." Even as he said it, the muscles started to relax and he was able to straighten his knee.

She stroked the front of his hair with her palm. "What happened?"

"The w... w... werewolf bit me. I... I couldn't move." Francis said, his shaky hand rubbing a tear from his eye.

"Oh, honey, it was just a bad dream. There's no werewolf."

Austin stood in the door, sleep crusting his eyes, hair a wild mesh. "Ha, a nightmare. You shrieked like a banshee. I thought you were dying. Let me guess, you're gonna sleep with mommy now."

"Shut up, Austin." Francis wailed.

"Go back to bed. Leave your brother alone. This is your fault for showing him that stupid movie and filling his mind with that junk." Their mom turned to Francis. "You can sleep in my room if you want. There's lots of room since Dad's in New York."

Francis' limbs trembled. He didn't want to be alone, but he was scared that the smirk on Austin's face would turn into another month of ridicule. "No, it's OK. I can sleep here."

"Oh, Mr. Brave is growing up." Austin chided.

"Give him a break." Their Mom cut in. "Or do you forget crying and coming into my room to sleep when you were ten."

"Ha ha, you slept with Mom when you were ten."

"MOM."

"Go to bed Austin. You've got school in the morning."

Austin disappeared into the hall. Francis climbed into bed. "Mom, what do I do if the werewolf tries to get me in my dream again?"

"Your dreams are in your mind; you can control them. If the wolfman comes back, tell yourself that you're dreaming and make him go away."

"OK," Francis said, but he was doubtful.

"You OK now?"

"Ya, I'm fine," Francis sighed.

After kissing his forehead, his mom left Francis alone in the soft glow of his nightlight. He pulled the blanket up to his chin and looked around the room. His eyes flickered about the dark objects. A tree outside scratched the window, its branch looking eerily similar to the arm of a werewolf. Francis stared at it, telling himself it was just a branch. The wind moaned, exciting the limb. Francis shivered, then pulled the blankets over his head. He laid in the private protection of his quilt dome, calming himself. Then, after much contemplation, he slowly drifted back to sleep.

~

Francis stood alone in the woods. There was no trail, just trees and bushes as far as he could see. Darkness engulfed the forest, filling it with the unknown, chilling Francis with the feeling that his worst fears lurked behind every tree, waiting to tear his flesh from his bones. He walked with his hands outstretched to protect his face from unseen branches, or whatever horror might be lurking in savage anticipation of its innocent prey.

Coming to the edge of a swamp, the boy rested against a tree, lost and bewildered. Moss hung from a branch above his head like a giant green cobweb. The full moon reflected off the still water, casting a disturbing aura onto the surrounding trees. Francis let his head fall into his trembling hands. He wanted to be home, to see his mom, even his brother. But he had no idea how to get out of the woods.

The soul-shaking scream of a woman ripped through the still air. The boy froze. Another scream, closer this time, pulled him from his daze. Looking around, he anxiously searched for an escape route, but was blocked by the swamp.

Then came a howl.

Francis stared in the direction of the wolf's piercing cry. Through the bushes he could see the dark shape of a woman running towards him. Behind her, the werewolf ran on four legs, bared teeth gleaming in the moonlight as it snarled. The screams grew louder as the woman approached the swamp. Long blonde hair flowed over her torn nightgown.

Ducking behind a tree, Francis frantically attempted to form a plan. He peered out at the woman. The moonlight lit her face and he could clearly see Maria's graceful features. The wolfman was approaching fast, hunched and growling.

Francis frantically looked around. A path led away from the swamp. He could see his house at the end of the path. A light was on. His mom was in the window. He could sneak away while the beast attacked Maria. He looked back at the angelic woman. Horror wrinkled her face. She screamed for help. The werewolf was less than twenty feet behind her and gaining fast.

The boy began to flee towards his house, but the pleading screams of the woman stopped him. He couldn't let her die. But what could he do? He turned towards her. The werewolf would be on top of her in seconds. Francis turned instinctively and ran toward her.

The cold metal of a heavy object weighed down his arm. Glancing down, he saw he was holding a silver samurai sword. Had he been holding it the whole time? Lifting it above his head, he leapt between Maria and the beast. The wolf's head snapped at him, drool stretching from its fangs.

Swinging the blade in a wide arc, the boy severed the beast's head from its massive body. The body landed hard and began shrinking instantly, reverting into its human form. Francis stood triumphantly, sword shimmering in the moonlight.

Maria cried out in relief. She picked up the boy, smothering him with kisses and hugs. Her firm breasts pressed into his small body. Putting him down, she looked him in the eyes. "You saved my life, and because of your bravery I will show you my secret."

Francis watched in excitement as the woman knelt down. They were eye to eye. The wind blew her hair from her perfectly sculpted face. The moonlight accentuated the curve of her neck. She was the most beautiful woman the boy had ever seen.

She looked him in the eyes. "Are you ready?" She grabbed the front of her blouse.

"Yes."

Before Francis had a second to realize what was happening, Maria tore out of her clothes, instantly turning into a Unicorn. "Get on my back. We will fly to Heroland, where rainbows disappear into water-falls and monkeys surf on the backs of dolphins. There is candy and ice-cream and lots of other children to play with."

Francis hooked his sword in his belt and climbed onto the Unicorn. The two took flight and the boy looked out over the forest. As they flew towards the moon, Francis glanced back towards his house.

The werewolf was crawling into his brother's open window.

"Quick. Take me home. The werewolf is going for my brother."

The Unicorn swooped down to the house, her white feath-ered wings stirring up a mighty breeze. She hovered in front of Austin's window. Francis thanked her, then climbed into his broth-er's bedroom.

He was too late. The werewolf hunched over the sleeping boy and bit into his neck. It looked up at Francis knowingly, an evil smirk on its face. Blood oozed from its mouth.

~

"AAAAAHHHHHHH! The wolfman." Austin shot up in his bed, eyes in a blaze of terror. Beads of sweat clung to his forehead.

Francis stood next to him. "It's OK Austin. I'm here. It was just a nightmare. There's no such thing as the wolfman."

"Get outta my room, twerp. What are you doing with that broom?"

Francis looked down, surprised to see the broom in his hand instead of a sword. "I was just making sure you're all right."

"I'm fine. Just go away."

"You don't have to be scared, Austin."

"I'm not scared. GET OUT!"

"OK. Jeez."

Francis walked down the hall to his room. The moon shone in through the window, but it didn't scare him anymore. He unplugged his nightlight and got into bed. Looking around the room, he smiled, feeling peaceful. Then, drifting in and out of thoughts of unicorns, rainbows, and candy, he fell asleep.

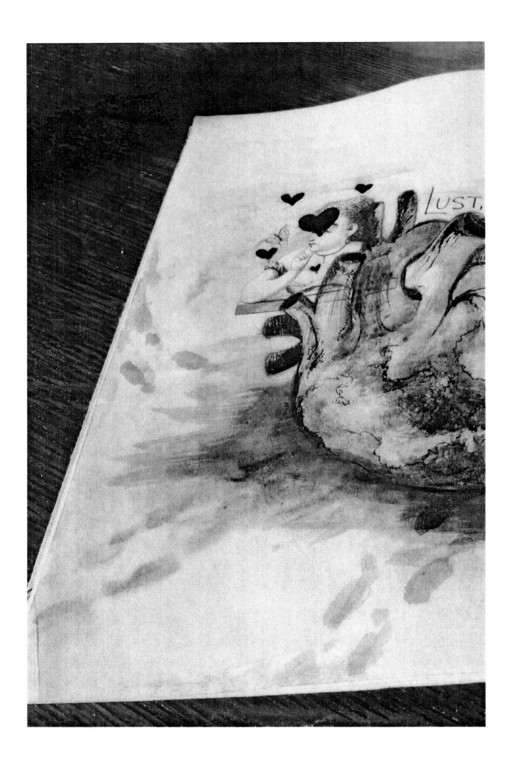

FERTILE MYRTLE was a shady lady
... always ... a party and
long ... know it. While
win... at ... ution to the
being pro... ... elieved in
take ... The Pill as her major protection
against any little ... hazards.
... time ... it ... or ... de
... was ... ly was no exception.
sh... began to forget to take her Pill
regularly. Weeks would ... Th... w...
... the vice squad ... needed. Th... w... a
midnight raid on her ... lace. ... he
tried a... ntended to two years. The
charge? You mig... well ask. She had
practiced license without a medicine!

Tom Falls in LOVE

TRY AGAIN...

9

TOM FALLS IN LOVE

She appeared so suddenly that Tom almost keeled over from shock. It was as if the clouds had parted and God had sent his most beautiful angel to the realm of humans so she could teach the world of true beauty. The raw vibrancy of the woman hit Tom with the force of a six-hundred pound sumo wrestler, slapping his mind into a feverish spiral, causing him to momentarily lose his balance. He steadied himself on the handrail. His heart fluttered in his bony chest. A thick haze of rapture swallowed his mind. He became aware of the tender plucking of a lute nearby. A rainbow appeared, even though it wasn't raining; leprechauns laughed and danced in a magical far-off land; and Tom choked on his own spittle.

It was love at first sight.

He recognized her instantly. She had been visiting his dreams for years. Tom watched her curly black hair bounce around her dark features as she walked toward the university library carrying a small mountain of textbooks in her arms. She kicked her foot up to the door handle and twisted her body, opening the door with ninja-like finesse. Tom admired her agility, stubbed out his cigarette, slid a peppermint Tic Tac through his thin dry lips, and then walked across the courtyard to the library. He wondered if his vision had played some sort of trick on him. Such overpowering allure seemed impossible, as if this goddess of love had come directly from Venus. He quickly opened the door and scanned the library. His heart beat so hard that he could feel the blood pound in his temples. He hurried past the computers, toward the stairs. When Tom finally spotted her sitting in one of the large chairs looking out over Nanaimo towards the ocean, he knew this was it.

He walked gingerly toward her. His hand shook as he cupped it to his mouth to check his breath. His palms were sweaty. He cut into an aisle to take cover behind the books, needing to calm his mind and think up an ice-breaker. Nervously tearing the pile of old receipts in his pocket into shreds, he thought; *I'll ask her for the time. No. That's lame. I'll tell her she looks familiar and ask her if we've ever had any classes together. No. That's stupid too. Come on. Yes, I'll walk over and tell her that she's beautiful. No, she probably gets that all the time. I guess I could just go and introduce myself. No. I know, I'll comment on the mountains; she's been looking at them long enough. She must like mountains.*

Tom ran his fingers through his hair to make sure that it had fallen right and was covering his hairline where he (falsely) believed his hair had started to recede. He approached her from the side, ten meters away. The sunlight poured in through the window, illuminating her gentle features. Her dark eyes shone. Her small nose sat above full red lips. Her olive skin was so smooth it appeared she'd been airbrushed. Suddenly paranoid, Tom looked down to see if he had sweat rings in his arm pits. Nope, he was all good.

Only five meters now. An irresistible magnetism drew him towards her, filling him with a voracious desire. His breathing quickened and he felt the sweat building between his toes.

Four meters, he could almost smell her.

Three meters, his mouth felt like a desert. His hands tightened nervously into fists.

Two meters, his tongue was sandpaper on the roof of his mouth. His nose twitched and he panicked, thinking he might have a stray booger.

One meter. Oh, she was so close. He could feel electricity building in the air. Tom breathed in, preparing himself to pour forth a torrent of smooth, flirtatious energy.

She pulled her phone from her pocket. "Hello?"

Shit, he thought. *Abort.* He walked past her and sat in a chair two over. He pulled a book from his backpack and pretended to read it. He flinched and thrusted it back into his bag when he noticed the large pink title: *How to Give a Woman Absolute Pleasure*.

The curly-haired goddess put her phone away, got up and walked upstairs. Tom followed just far enough behind that she wouldn't notice. She walked toward the large study area in the far corner, paused for a second, then turned and started back toward the study area in the other corner. She walked directly toward Tom. He panicked, not ready, no wit on the tip of his tongue. He took cover in an aisle and held his finger out at the call numbers, pretending to be searching for some all encompassing book of wisdom as she walked by. *Damn, she's turned me into a stalker,* he thought, looking around the corner. Her hips swung and her dark curls bounced with the rhythm of her step. His knees buckled and he grew faint. He grabbed the bookshelf to steady himself, watching her walk down the aisle. *This is it.* He thought *this is my defining moment. One day we'll be an elderly couple sitting in wooden rocking chairs on a rickety old porch looking back at this. The kind of moment in which dreams become reality and love conquers the world. I'm going to walk up to her, poetically express my love of nature, and especially mountains. I'll look her right in the eye and she'll be like, "Oh wow, this guy gets it". Then I'll whisper in her ear and she'll swoon. She'll know it's love at first sight, so I'll lean in for a juicy kiss. Then after we break apart, she'll look deep into my eyes and say that she's been waiting for me for her whole life. Then she'll pull out a couple tickets to Jamaica and say, "These babies are for us. I just won them from the radio station. You wanna go for a trip?" And I'll be like, 'Hells yeah,' then, I'll reach out and give her a high five and we'll go skipping out of the library hand-in-hand, mooning everyone and laughing as we go. It'll be awesome.*

Tom took a deep breath and started walking toward her. Excitement crawled up his spine. He was almost arm's length from his goddess. He cleared his throat to ensure his voice came out smooth.

Then, to his horror, a tall man with thick brown hair jumped out from behind a bookshelf, grabbed the girl's butt, and then jumped back into hiding. The girl flinched in surprise, shrieking as she turned around to look Tom in the eyes.

"What the hell do you think you're doing?" she said, her eyes blazing.

Tom stood mute. He opened his mouth to talk but nothing came out.

She approached, ready for a fight. "You think you're funny? Pervert."

Tom tried to swallow, but his mouth was so dry his tongue jammed in his throat. He lifted his hand, finger wagging in the air as if he had something to say, but still nothing came out. He considered turning and running. Then the handsome stranger sprang out from behind the bookshelf, picking the girl up in his muscular arms. They laughed, lips meeting in a passionate, make-out extravaganza. Just at that moment a flock of doves took off from outside the window. They soared above the mountains in the shape of a heart, the light bouncing off their wings and shining onto the lovers, causing them to glow in their fiery embrace.

"Shit," Tom muttered, as he stood stunned, feeling as if he'd just had his magic carpet yanked out from under him and he was now plummeting into an abyss. He turned around and headed back down the stairs, his every step heavy with heartache. "She wasn't that hot, anyway," he grumbled, his shoulders slumped in defeat. He walked out past the computers towards the door.

Then he saw her.

Cupid's arrow pierced his heart. She glowed, a lighthouse on an abandoned coast, summoning Tom to safety, her beauty radiating outward and into Tom's heart, warming it in a protective blanket. She smiled the-world's-cutest-smile as she sat at the computer typing away, deep in concentration. Blonde hair framed her golden skin and blue eyes, just like he'd always dreamed. He felt an invisible lasso come from her heart to his, reining him in. He was defenseless.

It was love at first sight.

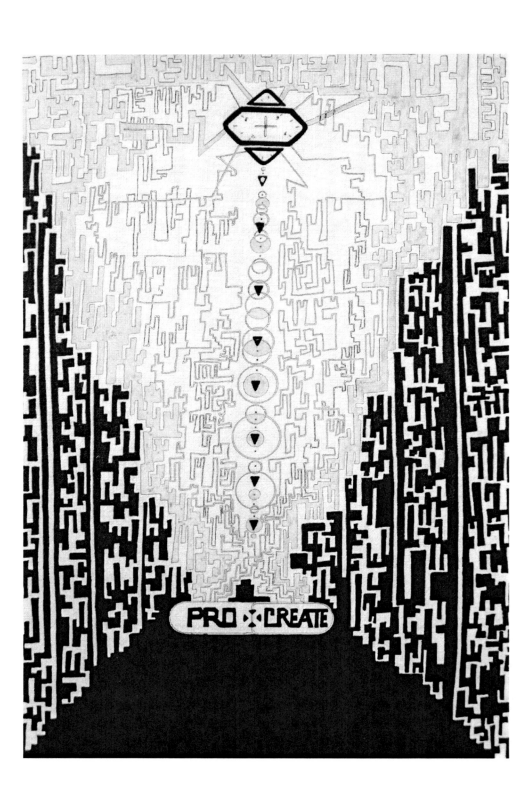

10

PRO CREATE

With nothing but a pink bathrobe covering her nakedness, Katrina sipped her coffee then took a bite of her pancake. She swiped the paper-thin tablet, opening the advice column. She rested her feet on Joe's as she read, giggling at the article and questioning its authenticity.

"Ha, Joe, check this out," she chuckled across the table. "Is this even real? Talk about why men shouldn't give advice." Katrina held up the tablet, pointing to the advice column. Sunlight poured though the window, illuminating her gentle features as she read. "Dear John." She upped the pitch of her voice to sound like someone else. "Last week I was on my way to work. I walked to the top of my building, got on my hover-bike, and hit the power button, but it wouldn't start. It sputtered and spat dark smoke, then nothing. The lights wouldn't even come on. After fiddling with it for a few minutes, I walked downstairs to my apartment to ask for my husband's help. I opened the door to find him on the couch having sex with our neighbor's daughter. I'm thirty five and my husband is thirty nine. We've been married over twelve years. Our neighbor's daughter is nineteen. My husband broke down and admitted that they've been seeing each other for over four months. I don't know what to do. I feel like I'm losing my mind, and my entire sense of trust is gone. Is my life over? Angela."

As Katrina read, the light shimmered lagoon blue in her eyes, making them appear as pools—deep and rich, gateways to playful treasure. She lowered her vocal timbre to imitate a man's. "Dear Angela. Don't fret too much over this. The hover-bike is repairable. It sounds like an electrical surge shorted the fuel injection system. The fuel injection system is located on the left side under the second panel, just above the engine. It is orange in color. Simply unscrew it and replace it. Make sure you tighten all four nuts well when you install it. Then check your fuel line for debris to avoid future clogs. If you want to test the electronics, your local mechanic can do it for around $30,000. I hope this helps, John."

Joe didn't respond. His chocolate eyes stared into nothing, his bushy brows wrinkling together as he sat, inattentively pushing his uneaten pancakes through a puddle of artificial syrup.

"Some men, eh?" Katrina prodded, searching for some kind of reaction.

Still no response.

"What's up, Hun? Where's that deep belly laugh I love waking up to?" Katrina reached across the table, taking Joe's hand.

"Oh, uh, sorry. I wasn't listening."

"I noticed."

"It's the annual Parenthood competition." Joe said, looking up nervously. "I want to try out."

"Oh." Katrina pondered. She fiddled with a strand of hair—a tell that she was giving her response considerable thought. "Do you think we'd really stand a chance? You know only the top two-percent win the right to have children. Besides, I'm moving up at the law firm. A baby'd really stall my career." Sipping her coffee she slipped a stack of highlighted papers into her briefcase.

"Kitten, what's a job compared to bringing life into the world?"

Katrina got up and walked to the window. "I know we've looked forward to this, but I'm scared. What if we're not chosen? I'd be heartbroken."

"We're running out of time. The cut off's thirty-five."

Twirling a golden lock around a slender finger, Katrina looked out the window across the top of the clouds. Closely built skyscrapers dotted the horizon as far as she could see. A sky-train rumbled past on one of the many tracks weaving through the city. Faces peered out from the windows as the sky-train cut its way through the white fluff. She silently weighed the pros and cons of having a child, her eyes absently watching people zip about in the hover-bike lane. A kid would mean a great deal of extra work, but it would make Joe so happy. And it would bring them even closer together. Plus, being granted the right to conceive was the greatest honor one could receive.

Below the clouds, glass-encased bridges connected the buildings. People filed through from building to building like worker ants; but not exactly like ants—ants work together for the colony, people work for themselves. Megatropolis was truly a multi-layered city in which people could go months without ever stepping foot on the ground.

Katrina looked down at the rooftop garden of another building. Three young children played joyously in the garden's playground. The sight made this conversation with Joe suddenly real, feeding her innate need to become a mother. She hadn't realized how much she wanted it, or more accurately, she hadn't let herself realize it. But now that Joe brought it up, it was a real possibility. The alarm on her biological clock was ringing.

Letting out a sigh, she turned to Joe. "Do you really think we stand a chance? There are twenty-seven-billion people in the world. Why would they choose us?"

"Babe, you're too hard on yourself. You're a government lawyer, you were a star runner in college, and you're beautiful. Trust me they'll choose you."

"What if we're not both chosen? You're just a gardener."

"Just a gardener! Babe, I'm insulted. I love my job. I love working outside. Besides, tilling the rooftop gardens keeps me fit. I'll have an advantage over all the office workers in the fitness tests."

"Yeah, and God knows you'll pass the looks test." Katrina laughed. "But people get hurt in the races."

"Oh, that's rare. We'll be fine."

"OK, it's worth a try. Nothing will ever happen if we don't at least try."

"YES!" Joe jumped over the couch and picked Katrina up in a playful embrace, twirling her in a circle. "I love you."

"I love you too."

~

Joe and Katrina sat on the sky-train, heading towards Gustafson Arena. Katrina gazed out the window as she mentally prepared for the competition. She'd been training tirelessly for the last two weeks, running all one-hundred-and-fifteen flights of stairs in her building every day, along with reviewing math, logic, and problem solving equations. Being a lawyer had kept her English and language skills sharp, so she hadn't needed to practice writing.

For almost an hour she looked out the window as the sky-train wove through the dense forest of skyscrapers. Every once in a while she would catch a glimpse through open blinds into someone's life—a man, virtual-reality goggles over his eyes, lost in the trance of a digital world, a family sitting down to lunch, an elderly woman huddled on a chair by the window reading, surrounded by robocats.

Joe squeezed her thigh, "You're gonna do great, Kitten."

"Thanks, Babe."

"We're gonna crush this competition."

"I hope you're right. There'll be twenty or thirty-thousand people competing. Maybe five-hundred to a thousand will win the pill."

"We'll get it for sure. Don't worry your cute little bum about it."

"OK," Katrina sighed. She tried to relax into her seat, but the thought of the impending eight hour evaluation of her physical, mental, and emotional stature was nerve rattling. She hated being judged, yet it never seemed to end. As a child, she'd been judged to determine what elementary school she belonged in, then again before high school, and again for university. The pressure never ceased. Exams followed by races, followed by exams, followed by races, followed by the bar exams and job interviews. Now the pressure mounted daily in the courtroom. There seemed to be no escape. It seemed life was one big competition.

She looked at Joe. How was he so calm and confident? She loved his halcyon nature. He didn't care what others thought, and breezed through life without ever being rattled by their judgments. So what if he went to a frightful college and works as a gardener. He's healthy and wakes up in the morning looking forward to his job. That's more than she can say for most of her friends working in offices. He'd even been offered a job on one of the lunar mines. It would have paid five times his current salary and he would have gotten every second month off, but he turned it down. Said he wouldn't be responsible for the chemical trails in our atmosphere. He'd rather grow food, thought it was more noble.

She placed her hand on his. A smile parted his lips, just enough to expose his sparkling teeth as he looked eagerly out of the window.

He was going to float through this competition on the same easy cloud that he floated on through the rest of his life.

~

After signing in, men and women were sent to opposite ends of the stadium. Joe wrapped his strong arms around Katrina. She nuzzled her face into his neck, inhaling the mango scent of his skin before kissing him and wishing him good luck. She watched him walk away. Sinewy muscles bulged from his lean calves with each step. She wasn't worried about him in the fitness tests, but she wished he'd studied more in school. He was wise in many ways, but they didn't test wisdom—only concrete knowledge—and in that he lacked. And, to make it worse, he refused to be implanted with a memory chip.

Katrina breezed through the language exams, finishing the questions and crafting a well written essay on cultural symbolism in less than two hours. She passed the problem solving tests easily enough. It was natural for her to follow the logic in the language and to decipher what the problems were really asking. The basic math didn't trouble her either, although she struggled with a few of the calculus questions.

After five hours of sitting through exams and an hour being photographed to have her beauty assessed, she lined up for the physical tests. The fitness tests were the second last—before the blood work, so that the contestants wouldn't be drowsy from giving blood.

A tall man, black hair slicked back, called her over to the track. Katrina lined up with seven other women at the starting line. Cameras mounted high above them broadcast the races live across the globe. She looked around while stretching. The competition looked fierce, momentarily filling her with doubt. Had she trained hard enough? Being a track star in college, she had thought that her physical conditioning was superior to others. Suddenly, she wasn't so sure. Two weeks' notice hadn't been enough to fully get back in shape.

A young brunette readied herself in the lane next to Katrina, dusting off the loose gravel from her starting point so she wouldn't lose traction. The girl appeared to be in her early twenties. Muscles bulged from her thighs with a tautness that comes from years of training. She wore a sports bra, sun glistening off her body, muscles twisting upward like knotted rope. Katrina looked away, nervous and suddenly feeling old for the first time.

She studied the course. It was a four part race. Run, hover-bike, climb, underwater wrestle. She tied her hair in a tight bun; this race was about to get unruly. She inhaled deeply through her nose, trying to calm her heart, which fluttered in her chest like a phonebook in a dryer. It had been almost a decade since she'd competed, but there was still the spirit of a champion in her. Closing her eyes, she steadied her mind.

Bending low, she opened her eyes, knuckles turning white as her fingers and toes dug into the ground. She eyed the hover-bikes four hundred meters away. Four bikes, eight women.

The gun sounded and she sprinted toward the bikes, each long smooth stride propelling her forward. She breathed deep, in through the nose and out through the mouth. Even breaths, just as she'd been trained.

The women ran in a vicious pack, elbows flying, trying to yank each other down by the hair. Katrina's breath heaved. A spot of fire erupted in her lungs as she sprinted, trying to pull ahead of the pack. Ducking an elbow, she drove her shoulder into the robust woman on her right. The woman tripped, taking out another.

Katrina reached the hover-bike first, starting the engine as she swung her leg over the seat. Two ropes dangled from a platform high above the far end of a six hundred meter pool. She took off at full speed, angling upward toward the closest rope. Half-way there, a hover-bike rammed her from behind, sending her into a speed wobble and almost tossing her off her bike. The cracking force of the jolt was like a whip at her back, spurring her forward in a possessed fury. She wasn't a girl racing to make her parents proud, or a teenager racing to win a scholarship. She wasn't competing for a medal. She was racing for the existence of her unborn child.

Climbing a few feet in elevation, she hit the brake. The woman behind her slammed face first into the back of Katrina's bike. That'll teach you, Katrina thought, all empathy lost as the competitive spirit over took her. No bitch was going to steal her right to conceive.

Another woman approached from the right. She swung a fist, but Katrina veered left. The two approached the bottom of the rope, side by side. They collided, battling mid-air. The woman grabbed hold of Katrina's arm, trying to pull her from the bike. Katrina braked and turned hard into the back of her competitor's bike, sending her spinning. Both women leapt from their bikes. Katrina grabbed the rope. Her competitor missed the rope, but managed to grab Katrina's leg. Once abandoned, the hover-bikes flew back to the starting position via autopilot. Katrina held tight with both hands, the woman dangling from her leg. She felt the woman's weight through her entire body, stressing her joints. The rope bit into her palms. Her shoulder ached under the strain. She couldn't shake the woman loose, but couldn't climb with the added weight. Another competitor reached the second rope and scrambled up it, gaining the lead. Katrina looked down at the woman on her leg and kicked. There was no other choice, it was kick, or lose. Her foot caught the woman in the shoulder, sending her falling to the water below. Now only one woman stood in her way.

Katrina ascended the rope with the intuitive agility of a monkey, then ran the length of the platform. The other woman had already leapt into the water. Katrina dove, arcing into the water in a polished swan dive, torpedoing strait to the bottom. Her hands and eyes searched the bottom for the H20 to O2 conversion mask. Her competitor approached from the side, increasing the pressure. Katrina turned from her competitor in a desperate search for the mask. Her pulse raced, stealing her oxygen. Her lungs burned as she fought the impulse to inhale. Claws of panic formed a strangle-hold on her mind. If she surfaced before finding the mask, she would automatically forfeit. She feared that she'd been stalled too long on the rope and her competitor had already found Katrina's mask.

The woman loomed threateningly close. Then, just as the need to swim for the surface overwhelmed her, Katrina's hand closed around the mask. She pulled it on.

Before she had time to turn, the woman was on her, hands at her throat, trying to grab Katrina's mask—the match was won by forcing your competitor to surface. usually by removing their mask so they needed air. Katrina kicked backward, catching the woman in the stomach. Turning, she managed to grab the woman's arm. She held tight as they wrestled at the bottom of the pool. Nails dug into Katrina's forearm, drawing blood. The woman was strong, too strong. A thumb painfully dug into Katrina's ribs. She grabbed it and twisted it back, feeling it dislocate, causing the woman to back off.

Wrestling was not an option; Katrina was out matched in terms of strength. She would have to rely on her speed and swimming skill. Crouching low, she pushed off the bottom, propelling herself toward the woman with a perfectly executed dolphin kick. The woman struck out for Katrina's face, but Katrina anticipated the move, dodging left and seizing the woman's mask, tearing it off as she swam by. The woman continued after Katrina, desperate to regain her mask. She grabbed at it, but Katrina held tight. They battled, new age gladiators in an underwater coliseum, fighting for their future children's existence. The woman twisted Katrina's arm, but couldn't pry the mask from her. Katrina used her legs to wrench herself free from the woman's grip. She kicked at her rival and swam away as fast as she could, the woman close behind. Then, beaten by the desperate need for oxygen, her rival turned and swam towards the surface.

Relaxing, Katrina let her body float to the top of the water. She had passed the physical test.

~

After the blood work, Katrina joined the crowd of women waiting for the final results. Only ten percent were left. She looked at their worn-out faces. Tension permeated the crowd. She thought about Joe, wondering if he'd finished his tests yet, hoping he'd passed. She couldn't help but fear what would happen if only one of them succeeded.

The women were united in hope, yet they were separate, aware of the others as competition. Katrina observed the women's eyes darting about, sizing each other up, judging. She thought about how competition can divide people, causing them to perceive each other as opposing forces. She wondered if there had ever been a time when people had been more connected, living with a greater sense of community—before overpopulation threatened Earth's natural balance, causing the World Government to set strict limits on reproduction.

But then again, there had always been competition of some sort. People had competed for jobs, money, land, and pride. War and greed were prevalent throughout history, reaching dirty fingers into all aspects of life, including government and religion. She wondered if it would ever be a predominant aspect of human nature to act for the whole, as well as the self.

A man stepped up to the podium, declaring that the results had been finalized. Katrina felt tightness in her chest. The crowd fell eerily silent as the women looked up at the scoreboard, desperate to find their names. Then, shrieks of both delight and agony filled the air.

Katrina searched anxiously for her name, her heart pounding, hands trembling. Her breath grew quick and shallow as her eyes scanned row after row of names. Then, to her great relief, she found it. She was going to be a mother. An image of herself, sitting by the window holding a baby, flashed in her mind's eye. She hadn't even allowed herself to believe it possible, but now it was going to happen. She had beaten the odds. The miracle of new life was going to be hers. What an honor! Her genes would carry on. With blurred vision, she wiped away her tears.

~

A river of bodies flowed steadily from the stadium gates as Katrina waited for Joe. Morose faces pushed passed her, twisted by the pain of shattered dreams. She felt for them, wanted to comfort them, but couldn't. What could she do? Katrina's hand fell to her stomach and she imagined a life growing inside her. The thought filled her with excitement, but she tried not to show it, not wanting to celebrate in front of the broken-hearted.

Joe was nowhere to be seen. Anxious for the results of his competition, she pulled her Eye Phone from a case in her purse and slipped the contact lens into her eye. Joe answered and her lens created an image of him as clearly as if he was standing on the sidewalk in front of her. He stood, overwhelmed, eyes down, face pale. She knew instantly that he hadn't been chosen.

"I'm waiting at the sky-train station." His voice limped out, broken.

On the sky-train home, Joe stared blankly out the window. His body seemed shrunken and deflated. He didn't speak until they were almost home. Looking directly into her eyes, he said, "I understand if you want a divorce. I won't blame you if you want to be with someone who can father your child."

Stunned, Katrina replied, "What? Never! You're my man. We'll figure something out. We'll buy a fertility pill on the black market."

"With what money?" He looked defeated. "I'm not worthy to be a father."

"Don't talk like that. We'll find a way."

~

Less than a month later, Katrina looked across the hotel room at the strange man undressing before her. The thought of fucking him made her sweat, covering her with a film of shame. He looked at her the way a hungry dog looks at a piece of meat, salivating with anticipation. She wanted to run away, but wouldn't. She would be a mother, even if this is what it took.

The man's hair was peppered with grey and balding on top. The muscles of his pale legs were underdeveloped and his body was soft in the middle. As he stepped out of his boxer-briefs, Katrina couldn't help wondering how this man had won the right to be a father. He must have bribed someone. He certainly wasn't half the man Joe was. She pushed the thought of Joe from her mind. She couldn't think of him, not now. She still loved him too much, wishing it was him here instead of this rich sleaze.

Wearing nothing but dress socks and a haughty grin, the man approached her, lamplight reflecting off his bluish-white chest. Shuddering, she looked away and unbuttoned her blouse. Two white pills sat on the bedside table next to a glass of water.

The man molested her with his eyes as she stepped out of her underwear. She could feel his gaze move up and down her body. He was ravenous, a wolf; she was a doe, scared and alone. He licked his lips.

She forced a smile as she handed him a pill. Taking it in his sweaty palm, he stepped so close he pressed into her hip. The warmth of his cock made her want to twist away, but she stood strong, determined to go through with this.

"Bottoms up," he said as he swallowed the pill. Then he leaned in so close his thick breath settled onto her neck.

She sat on the bed, closed her eyes, and wished for the experience to pass quickly.

~

At home, Katrina turned the shower off and reached for her towel. No matter how many times she lathered her body in soap, the feeling of filth clung to her, sullying her body and mind inside and out. She brushed her teeth again, spitting the white froth into the sink and letting it slither down the drain. Wrapping herself in her pink bathrobe, she sat on the living room couch and stared out the window. Time slipped by unmeasured as she tried not to think. She let her head rest on the back of the sofa and closed her eyes, but the image of that creep on top of her, panting, squishing her into the mattress, caused her to open them, to look out the window, desperately searching the outside world for a distraction.

Joe came in whistling, oblivious to the personal hell that Katrina had just lived through. He kissed her on the cheek, then grabbed the milk carton from the fridge and took a swig, not noticing the distress in her eyes until he had gulped down almost half a liter.

"What's wrong, Kitten?" he asked.

"I had a tough day."

"What happened?"

She pointed to the coffee table. Two white pills sat on the glass, reflecting the sun from the window.

Joe stared for a moment, confused. Then said, "Are those what I think they are?" his face lit up. "How'd you get em?"

"It doesn't matter. I have them now and you can be a father." Katrina shifted in her seat, avoiding Joe's gaze.

"Babe, I have to know how you got them. I'm your husband. Look at me."

Katrina looked him in the eye. How was he going to react to this news? Her skin felt clammy. Breathing deep, she blurted it out. "I met with one of the single men who passed the tests, and switched the pills with vitamins so he didn't know."

"What? Babe, that's so devilish of you. I didn't know you had it in you." He sat next to her on the couch, excited as the realization that he would be a father sank in. "How did you get away with it? Didn't you have to tell him your name in order to meet up?"

"I did it for you, Joe, so you could be a father." Her voice cracked with uncertainty.

Joe's jaw dropped, as if weighted by a sudden realization. "Oh my God! Did you kill him?" he joked, leaning back, eyes wide as he stared at her inquisitively.

How could he joke at a time like this? "Don't be ridiculous." She quipped, not in the mood.

"How then? How did you get away with the pills?"

Katrina looked out the window. She couldn't withstand Joe's probing eyes. They were drills burrowing into her, and any second she would burst. Her hands shook as she spoke, her voice small and scared, squeaking like a mouse cornered by a cat. There was no easy way to say it. "I switched the pills, then I f... f... fucked him so he wouldn't know. It was the only way."

Joe sat silent, face pale and twisted, too stunned to react. Silence hung in the air, thick and malevolent, blanketing the room with tension.

Katrina couldn't take it. "I... I did it for you. So you could be a father."

"YOU FUCKED HIM?" Joe stood, disgusted, as if the information had suddenly clicked in his mind. "Fucked him? No. I... what? Whore." He turned away from her. "I can't believe this shit." He kicked the couch, sending it sliding backward with her on it. "Why don't you go fuck the president so you can get a whole bag of fertility pills?"

Katrina flinched, shrinking. She stood up, reaching for Joe, but he pushed her hands away and stepped back, repulsion painted across his face.

"Joe, it's not like that," she blurted, "I didn't want to, but, but, it was the only way the government wouldn't find out."

He stared at the floor, hands trembling, saying nothing. The silence tore into Katrina, festering inside her like a hive of maggots.

Unable to bear it, she blurted, "We have the pills now. We can start a family."

"I can't start a family with you. I can't even look at you." Joe walked to the door and put on his shoes, looking back as he opened the door. Pain twisted his eyes. "We're done. I can't do this."

Before Katrina could speak, he left, slamming the door. She collapsed onto the tile floor, the last of her strength drained from her body. The dam that had been holding back her emotions crumbled, pouring forth a tsunami of anguish. She lay, crumpled, crying for what felt like an eternity. Why didn't he understand? He had wanted so badly to be a father. This was their chance.

The sun set as she lay on the floor sobbing, tears streaking down her face, puddling on the tile floor. She had never felt so alone. The only light now was from the lamp in the living room. The fertility pills sat on the coffee table, staring at her, two beady white eyes taunting her. They meant nothing without Joe. She had just wanted to make him happy, help him fulfill his dream of fatherhood, and now he was gone.

She wished they had never gone to the competition. Her life was ruined, and all because of those two stupid pills. She hated them, little demons that came between her and her love. How could she have been so foolish as to think that Joe would see past the act she had to endure in order to get the pills? She was the one who had to live with the memory of that creep on top of her, breathing, sweating, fucking her, his slime inside her. She shivered at the thought, wanting to vomit.

Standing, she took the pills in her hand—repulsive little things, filthy and evil. She had to get rid of them. Crushed under the burden of heartache, she tossed the pills out the window. Good riddance. The room felt lighter without their sinister presence.

Still crying, she pushed the couch back to its place in front of the coffee table, desperate to put some part of her life back in order. She slouched onto it and buried her face in her pillow, wanting to sleep, to disappear from this nightmare, but her mind was too tormented to find the stillness sleep requires. Instead she lay curled into a ball, muscles clenched as her mind was swept about in an ocean of confusion, haunted by grief.

After some time, the door slowly opened and Joe stepped into the room, shamefaced. Katrina stared at him with anxious silence. She wanted to run to him, to hug him and tell him it meant nothing, it had all been for him.

Joe spoke first. "I'm sorry I stormed out. I was in shock."

"No, I'm sorry. I shouldn't—"

"It's ok. I understand why you did it. I went to the ground to sit and think. I can't think clearly this far away from the ground. I should be thanking you, not yelling at you. After all, we're actually going to be parents. How sacred is that?"

A wave of relief broke over Katrina as Joe's words sunk in. She ran to him, wrapping her arms around him. "Thank you. I knew you'd understand."

He kissed her forehead. "Let's put the pills somewhere safe for now. After you have your period and we know there's no chance of that asshole getting you pregnant, we'll take them."

Suddenly weak-kneed, Katrina braced herself on the side of the couch. Her head spun. Her strength waned. Dizzy with nausea, she could barely find her voice. "Th...the pills are gone."

"What? What do you mean gone?"

"I was upset. I thought you were going to divorce me. I threw them out the window."

"But...what about the baby?" It was Joe's turn to be weak in the knees.

"I didn't want a baby without you. When you left, I was heartbroken."

Joe slumped onto the couch, emptily gazing at the floor. "So it was all for nothing."

Overwhelmed, Katrina walked to the window. "They could be down there. On the ground."

Joe sprang up. "Let's go." He ran to the door.

Once on the ground, they scoured the concrete below their window.

"It's no use" Katrina said. "They must have shattered into a thousand pieces. Our window is over a hundred stories up."

"It can't be," Joe said, slouching to his knees. He didn't want to believe it, but he knew the pills wouldn't have survived the fall.

Then Katrina noticed the crack in the concrete. A weed was growing up through it. The end of the weed blossomed into a cup-shaped flower. Inside it, something white gleamed in the streetlight. Katrina bent forward to look inside. Miraculously, both pills were safe inside the flower, looking up at her in their white purity, the glowing eyes of an angel.

11

MAOISTS, MOUNTAINS, AND MILK

Part 1

At twenty-three years old, and three years into a spiritual quest across Asia, I felt like the king of the universe. I was full of youthful passion—or arrogant stupidity, depending on your frame of reference. I felt unstoppable. The dengue fever that had stolen thirty pounds from my already slender frame and cursed me to ten days in a Singapore hospital didn't kill me. Neither did the crocodile that chased me out of a lake in India.

In my youthful delusions of invincibility, I believed myself to be guarded by an all-powerful, celestial benevolence. So much so, that I never clued in to the danger of riding a motorcycle across Thai islands while blitzed on ecstasy, mushrooms, alcohol, and ganja at the same time. Even after I'd watched friends hit the ground, some of whom would never walk again, others who would never see another sunrise, I still believed that I was invincible.

That was, until I found myself staring down the long, cold barrel of an AK-47. At least, that's what I thought it was—my mind was too busy trying to drag itself out of the frigid, black pool of trepidation it was drowning in to get a closer look. I liked to think that I was the most badass, audacious, ass-kickin' troubadour who had ever stepped onto the planet—until I was slapped into reality by the backhand of fear. Then, I quickly crumbled into a terrified child, afraid of pain, afraid of the unknown, afraid that my short life would be torn away from me before I had had the chance to fulfill my ever-expanding list of hopes and dreams.

So there I stood, during the height of the Nepalese revolution, in a small village five days hike into the Himalayas, surrounded by guerrillas, losing a staring contest with the hollow eye of an assault rifle, and on the verge of collapsing into a whimpering buffoon. The kid with the gun laughed when my shaky hands raised to the heavens.

His young voice puffed from his mouth, drifting upwards to become one with the ice blue sky. "We are the Maoists. We are the other government of Nepal. The government of the people."

Shit I thought, *Maoists*. I'd heard stories of these guys bombing schools and taking prisoners. But then again, I'd also heard that it was the government that bombed the schools so they could diminish the Maoists growing popularity. I didn't know who to believe. I was just a dumb kid caught in a tumultuous time.

I looked at the gun and had a flash-fantasy of myself busting into some deadly kung-fu and taking all seven guerillas out with my lightning-fast lethal-limbs. But I was far too chicken-shit to turn myself into Rambo. I was going to have to rely on my meager intellect to get me out of the situation.

"Do you guys want to sit down and have a beer? You can teach me about the Maoists," I suggested hopefully.

This threw the gunslinger right off. He eyed me, his head cocked to the side like a bewildered dog. The mountain people were poor, and beer was an extreme luxury reserved only for tourists.

"Come on. I wanna buy you guys a beer to show my appreciation for your liberation of the people."

The gun went down and the kid looked around at his posse. They looked thirsty.

"Yeah, OK."

So we walked to the only restaurant in the three-building town, and I ordered a round. Sandeesh, the leader of the guerilla pack, launched into a practiced monologue on the injustices of King Gyanendra. Not wanting to pick sides, my exhausted mind slipped away, swept up by the landscape. All around us, frozen titans thrust their jagged white heads above the clouds. With a daunting glory, the mountains overshadowed the insignificant wanderers sitting and talking politics on a rickety wooden deck. For how many tens of thousands of years, I wondered, have these mountains loomed skyward, housing people as they came and went, passing through the cycle of life. I imagined a yeti, older than time itself, roaming the slopes and guarding the path to Shangri-La. I noticed the Buddhist temple on the edge of a peak hundreds of meters above the village. I thought about the monk who lives there, alone, dedicated to a life that strives to understand that which lies beyond our immediate reality. As I looked out onto the untouched terrain, it seemed entirely possible that there exists a land beyond the reach of modern humanity, nestled in a forgotten valley in which magic thrives, kept alive by belief.

Sandeesh's laugh brought me back to the conversation as he explained that the Maoists maintained control of eastern Nepal and the majority of the countryside. "If the king not step down," he warned, "the Maoists will make him."

I ordered another round, and the vigilantes gratefully thanked me, slapping my shoulder and shaking my hand. Sandeesh's eyes glimmered as he spoke of liberating the people and installing democracy. He didn't seem the least bit dangerous now. His enthusiasm for the cause made me realize that these were good people, good in that they truly believed that they were doing the right thing. Sure, there might be some collateral damage, but ultimately they believed that they were fighting for the people. In their own minds, they were heroes, fighting a great evil that had befallen their land—much like those who fought the tyrannical rule of Hitler.

I wondered if the essence of what makes a man 'good' lies in his intentions rather than his actions. The ripple effects of one's actions are unknown, especially in the extreme conditions of war. I sipped my beer, trying to comprehend the complexity of the moral choices these young men navigate daily.

The thought came to me that the spectrum of human morality is not linear, with good and evil lying at opposing ends. Rather, it is many dimensional, with a multitude of lines reaching in an infinite number of directions, each representing different human dualities—honesty and deceitfulness, courage and cowardice, generosity and selfishness, etc. But what do I know? I'm just a kid trying to enjoy a beer with a gang of gun-slinging rebels.

Like the mountains, beers in Nepal are two and a half the size of the ones in Canada. Add to that the thinning of the blood that occurs at high altitude and the small size of my new drinking partners, and it's safe to say that after a few beers and countless anti-government cheers, we were practically kin. A couple hours into our intercultural exchange, Sandeesh noticed that the sun was about to disappear behind the peaks of the monstrous Annapurna range. "We go," he said, standing up. "There is not many daylights, and we go to next village for rally."

With that, the group staggered down the stone path, leaving me alone, buzzing from the beer and looking out from the roof of the world, once again the unstoppable, fearless globetrotter.

Part 2

The next morning, I continued my trek into the mountains, walking towards an ancient culture frozen in time—the assimilating effects of globalization not yet having penetrated this deeply into the Himalaya. After eight hours of navigating alpine forests, dragging myself up jagged rock-faces, and crossing glacier streams, I came across another small village. My legs ached, and the sun was about to drop behind the mountains, so I decided to bunker down for the night. Haggard and breathless, I wandered into the stone courtyard of a guesthouse and looked around for someone in charge. Lush foliage, richly green and dotted with an assortment of flowers, lined the edge of the courtyard. There wasn't a soul in sight, so I walked around to the back of the building. Behind it, a field of marijuana plants stretched as far as I could see. I dropped to my knees and bent forward until my head disappeared into the greenery, and I inhaled the sweet, skunky aroma.

A wooden shed housing two shaggy yaks sat on the hill next to a greenhouse. A round woman, short grey hair tied up over a face weathered by many hard years of mountain living, stepped out of the greenhouse. She walked toward me, beaming a grin that was heartfelt, welcoming, and unabashedly toothless. Radiating happiness, she welcomed me to her home and offered me lodging and dinner. After dropping my backpack in a musty wooden room, I sat at the table in the courtyard, happy to rest my weary legs. The woman disappeared for a moment, and then came back with a glass of milk in her hand. She handed me the glass. "I have very special treat for you."

I took the glass. It was still warm. "Thank you."

"Yak milk. Fresh," she said, nodding her head to the long-haired creatures in the shed.

I looked down at the glass. It came complete with rubbery white chunks floating in it, tints of yellow throughout, and mini pools of oil shimmering on the surface. I looked back at the grey-haired woman. She looked so proud of the milk. I smiled back, "Thank you," then put the glass on the table, planning to pour it out when she went inside.

"Drink, drink. Bring energy after long walk. Make you strong." She pushed the glass towards me and nodded her head, looking at me expectantly.

I picked up the glass and brought it to my nose for a smell test. The warmth rose to meet my lips. It smelled fine, but I nonetheless imagined the ghost of Louis Pasteur standing behind the woman, gesturing wildly while yelling at me not to drink. The woman's almond eyes observed me so tenderly that I couldn't refuse her. I touched the glass to my lips and let the thick liquid pour in. A lump of the rubbery curd slid passed my lips and into my mouth, touching my tongue. It half melted in my mouth, leaving behind chunks stuck in my teeth. I gagged and almost spat it across the courtyard. Milk seeped from the corner of my mouth as I tried to choke it down. A lump slithered down my throat, almost alive. The old woman smiled amiably. And I tried my best to mask my look of total disgust behind a smile.

The woman nodded her head to the glass. "Drink up. Long walk tomorrow."

I smiled and looked at the glass. It was still nine-tenths full, but I tried my best to see it as one-tenth empty.

Part 3

The next morning, I woke early, ate breakfast with my gracious host, hugged her goodbye, and then set out on the trail. I followed the river as it twisted up the mountains. My excitement grew as each step brought me deeper into the mountains, carrying me upward into new climates.

A few children passed me on their way to school.

"Where are you going this early?" I asked the older boy.

"Our school is in Chamje." Apparently the English classes were working.

"Isn't that five hours away?"

"Haha, for you five hours. We Nepali. For us two hours."

And with that, the children laughed and ran ahead. I watched them go—little legs carrying them up the jagged slope. I tried to keep up for a few minutes, but couldn't match their pace.

That night I came to another small village and checked into a quaint guesthouse. A British man sat on a balcony looking up at the mountains, smoking a joint, and drinking a beer. I was happy to see another foreigner and sat next to him, introducing myself. As we sat talking, a woman appeared with her young son. A Harry Potter gash on the boy's forehead dripped blood down the side of his face. Danny, the British man, pulled out some bandages from his backpack, cleaned the wound, and patched up the kid's head. The woman thanked us profusely and then told us to stay there while she got us a gift. A few minutes later, she appeared with two glasses in her hand. *Oh great*, I thought, *here we go again*. She handed us the steaming glasses and I was relieved to find tea inside.

That's when things got weird.

A fawn ambled up to the woman and tugged at her skirt. The woman sat on the ground and lifted up her shirt, exposing two huge, milk-filled breasts. Danny and I exchanged a quick smile, barely able to take our eyes off the 'mountains.' Then the deer latched on to the woman's nipple, entering into a feeding fury, shaking its head and bucking its legs as it suckled the woman's milk. The deer sucked so hard that I thought it would tear the woman's nipple from her breast. I winced, wanting to look away, but was completely entranced by the visually magnetic episode. The woman laughed, seemingly enjoying herself. Danny and I watched for a few minutes, too stunned to speak.

When the deer finished, the woman looked up at us and smiled nonchalantly.

"No momma. If I no feed, then die." She explained before disappearing into her house, leaving Danny and I alone.

I sat, quietly contemplating my journey, appreciating how the originality of each day nourishes a childlike awe, encouraging me to open to the diversity of both nature and humanity, and to the untapped wonders of my senses.

I thought about my experiences on the road, how my perceptions of reality are constantly stretched as my mind is challenged to expand to include ideas and ways of being that I previously thought impossible. The open road leads to unchartered territory. It breaks us out of old patterns of behavior, forcing our minds into new areas of perception. In one day a person may encounter love, anger, joy, boredom, depression, humiliation, peace, solitude, amazement, exhilaration, confusion, fear, and relief. By necessity, one learns to slow down and take it as it comes. The beauty present everywhere becomes more apparent. One begins to see, feel, and experience the ultimate mystery and power of the journey that is life.

As I sat, mind lost in thought, Danny turned to me, a mischievous smile twisting his youthful face. Sparking another joint, he winked, "I love this place."

12

PERILOUS KISS

I find her in the deepest recesses of my subconscious. I'm on a routine search, digging, probing, banging my head against the desk, hoping my skull will crack open and brilliance will pour out. I hunger to create art, but I dig too deep. She appears suddenly, vague at first, then jumping into focus, an old unwanted dream. My mistress hunches behind a cabinet of memories I'd hoped forgotten. Naked and feral, she peers into me, eyes haunting, beautiful, darkly exotic. Tattoos twist up her taut flesh, wrapping her body in their inked dance.

She sees my face. My real face, not the mask I show others. I want to run, to scream, but my eyes are locked to her in fascination. Her smile twists, grotesquely magnetic, mesmerizing like the scene of an accident. I stare, knowing that what I'll find will haunt me forever. She lusts after me, not just my flesh, but also my soul. She longs to grab me, fuck me, devour me, drag me to hell. I crave her more than I crave air. Seductively threatening, she promises to give me everything. But she'll leave me with nothing—exposed and alone, ashamed.

Her sex-toys lay spread out on the coffee table, taunting me—a spoon, a rubber tube, and a needle. Cinnamon lips kiss my skin, inviting one more dance with the devil. Wrapping the tube around my arm, I vow yet again, that this will be the last time.

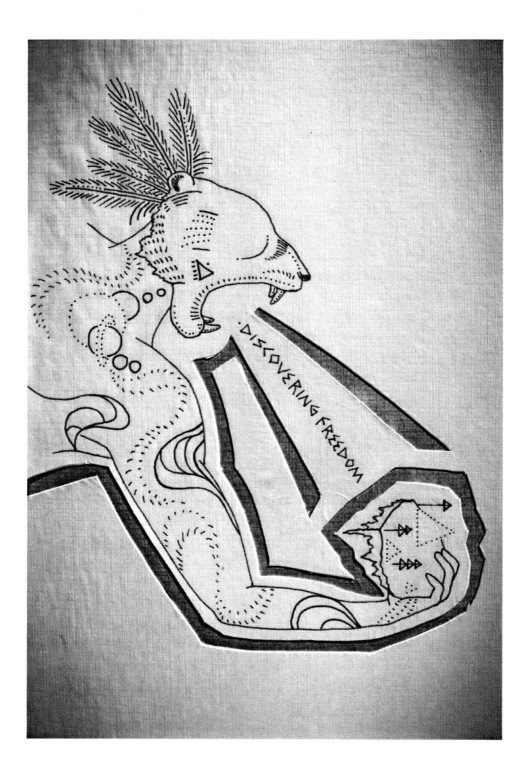

13

DISCOVERING FREEDOM

It was the summer of 2012. The war on terror raged on. The stock market was in a state of uncertainty. CERN announced the discovery of a new particle with properties that matched the Higgs Boson. *Curiosity*, the Mars Science Laboratory Mission's rover, landed on Mars. Hippies danced in psychedelic trances on the beaches of Goa. Republicans and Democrats battled for apparent control over the USA political system. The Mayan Long Count Calendar approached the end of the thirteenth B'ak'tun. Dolphins played joyously in the waves of every ocean. And a series of explosions killed over two-hundred-and-fifty people in the Republic of Congo.

Leo, however, had no knowledge of any specific events taking place anywhere on earth other than the seven-and-a-half-square-kilometer island he lived on. Why? Unbeknownst to himself, he was an illegal experiment—the world's first genetically enhanced human—hidden from authorities on an island in the northern Pacific.

He sat at his desk, brow furrowed, holding his pencil like a spear, attacking an equation with every ounce of mental strength he could muster. Shaggy brown hair, thick and lustrous, hung with unkempt gusto over his sharp features. Scratching out the equation, Leo flipped the paper over to try again. *I must be missing some crucial factor*, he thought. *I've accounted for energy, mass, light... what is the final element?* He stood abruptly and strode over to his bookshelf. His shirt stretched around his powerful frame as he ran his finger along the spines of the books.

He'd spent the majority of his twenty-year existence searching for the meaning of life, examining every inch of the island on which he was confined. But something was missing. He'd turned over every rock, literally, including the ones at the bottom of the island's river, climbed every tree, and read all six-hundred-and-fifty-seven books in the library countless times. He'd stood on every corner of the island, staring into the surrounding watery void, wondering if there was more to the world than the doctors or books let on.

Having exhausted the library and the minds of all others on the island (five biomedical engineers), Leo turned to math, hoping he could discover some insight that would give meaning to his isolated existence.

Down the hall, in the kitchen, Dr. Gustoff turned to Dr. Hiener. "He's been in his room for weeks pouring over those math and physics books. It's not healthy."

"I know, I know. He's getting too old to keep here, but what can we do?"

"Unveil our research to the scientific community. Leo needs to be at a lab on the mainland so we can begin integrating him into society."

"The punishment for experimenting with human genetic modification is too severe. We'll lose everything."

"When the world sees Leo, they'll understand. Just look at him. He's got an IQ of over two hundred he's stronger and faster than any man on earth, he can play ten instruments, his body has effectively fought off every cold and virus ever given to him."

"But he's still not happy."

Dr. Gustoff looked directly into the eyes of his colleague. "Neither intelligence nor physical prowess are precursors to happiness. Happiness is a state of being that comes with knowing yourself and your place in the world. Happiness in its truest form only comes when one has found peace within oneself. How can we expect this of a man confined to this island, whose entire upbringing has been a controlled experiment? His spirit isn't free to explore the world."

Dr. Hiener shifted his weight from one foot to the other, letting out a sigh. "We must act cautiously. There's no doubt he's a miracle of science and technology, the future of mankind even, but if the world finds out about him before they're ready to accept what we've accomplished, they'll imprison him and shut us down.'

Leo thumped down the hall and stepped into the kitchen. At six foot five, he towered over the scientists. "I'm going for a walk. I've got to clear my mind."

The two scientists watched him go, knowing that nature had a soothing effect on him. Leo walked past the garden to the edge of the front lawn and looked across the cedar and fir forest to where the river poured out of the small lake, carving its way across the island to the ocean. He sat down, hulking body thudding onto the grass, and let out a sigh. He yearned for someone to talk to. Really talk to. Not like the doctors. They were different from him, guarded about so many topics. He longed to share from the heart, completely and openly, without judgment.

If only there was a way off this island. Nobody ever came or went. A couple years back, while standing on the beach and gazing into the horizon, Leo had glimpsed a boat in the distance. It had spawned notions of being able to leave, to sail away. The more he had thought about it, the more his curiosity had amplified, spinning into an obsession that had lasted months, consuming him, driving him mad. Finally, he had attempted to make a raft and escape. He had constructed the raft hurriedly and in the secrecy of night. His haste, coupled with the fact that the doctors had consciously withheld any nautical information, led to an unseaworthy vessel. He didn't know which direction the mainland was, and knew nothing of the strength of ocean currents, but, regardless, set sail in the darkest hour of night. His raft had sunk a few miles away and he had almost drowned fighting the cold ocean currents while navigating his return by light from the lab.

Leo loved the doctors, but couldn't shake the nagging suspicion that they were lying about their being banished to this island by the government, and that leaving would be courting severe punishment or maybe even death. How could they not know who his father was? Would his mother not have told them before she died in childbirth? He craved change, to see the world, to go out into the unknown and experience life in its rawest and truest form. This yearning boiled in him, burning him from within, driving him into his own mind. It seemed a cruel trap to know that a vast but unreachable world existed beyond the horizon. He longed to fully embrace life, to dive in and surrender to its mercy and flow. He hungered for understanding, for knowledge beyond book learning, wanting to really feel the world, to experience each moment as deeply as possible.

He stood up, restless, and walked to a tall cedar. Grabbing the lowest branch, he pulled himself onto the tree and climbed. He sat in the tree and looked into the forest, noticing a new tree growing out of a rotting log. "From death comes life, and from life comes death," he whispered to no one in particular, pondering how molecules and atomic particles are continually recycled into new organisms. He thought about his own body, how the molecules he was composed of could have once been part of a fish, a rock, a dinosaur, anything.

Going back in time far enough, Leo reasoned, the very elements and subatomic particles that now make up his body had once been elements of the cosmos. Leo smiled, his body could have once been part of a shooting star and might be a shooting star in the future.

The thought led him to consider time. Is time infinite? If so, then the elements that form his body at this very moment could potentially have been almost anything, including creatures that have yet to be created. If the dimension of time is taken out of the equation altogether, and we imagine that all of time is happening at once (it is only experienced as unfolding linearly from a state of individual consciousness), then one single element is potentially everything at once. And our bodies share their molecular make-up with an infinity of other things. Everything is connected. All life is one.

As he sat in the tree, a faint roar above roused him from his musings. His curious blue eyes searched the sky for the source of the unusual sound. Suddenly, as if in a dream, a massive beast appeared, bursting through clouds, slanting towards Leo as it flew. He lowered himself to the ground, mind reeling as he stared up at the flying creature, circular wings rotating above its head. His muscles twitched, readying themselves for action. It approached at incredible speed, slowing as it neared the front lawn, stirring up a great wind. As it hovered, Leo saw through its front windshield that a man controlled it from inside. The beast was actually a machine, a helicopter. Leo was shocked into motionlessness as he tried to sort out the meaning of this strange appearance.

The scientists came running out of the house as the helicopter landed on the lawn.

Bill McGruff, CEO of Biotech, stepped out of the helicopter, the sun reflecting off the silk fibers of his Armani suit. Leo stepped out from behind the tree, his mind racing. This was the first visitor to the island since he'd been born. The man stood before him, dressed in bizarre clothing with a striped piece of fabric dangling from his neck.

Dr. Gustoff ran up to McGruff, panting, "What are you doing? You're going to jeopardize everything!"

"There's no time. We've got bigger issues at hand. The Monkergle has escaped from the interior lab and is roaming free in the Kootenay Mountains. Our trackers can't keep up to it in the thick forests. Leonardo is the only one fast enough to catch it. We need him."

"What?!"

McGruff turned to Leo. "I'm Bill McGruff, the owner of this island and the employer of these scientists. You need to come with me immediately."

Leo's mind spun. Was he about to get off the island? Had he been lied to by the doctors? Where did this man come from? He felt the urge to be alone with his thoughts, to run into the woods. But this helicopter was his chance to get off the island and find out the truth about why he was trapped here. It was his ticket to the world. He looked at the man. "I don't understand. What's an employer?"

"I'll explain in the helicopter."

Dr. Gustoff interrupted, "No, he can't go. He doesn't know enough about the world. It's too dangerous."

"He has to, Doc. If the public finds out that Biotech has been genetically crossing animals, and has created a creature that's part monkey, part tiger, and part eagle, we'll be finished. Game over for everyone. No more island. No more Leo. Got it?" McGruff turned to Leo, "Get in the helicopter."

Frightened, but overcome by curiosity, Leo looked at Dr. Gustoff, then at the helicopter. Unlike the others, Dr. Gustoff had always treated Leo with tender compassion. Leo didn't want to say goodbye, but the lure of the helicopter was too great. A shiver slithered up his back—the serpent tempting him to eat from the tree of knowledge. The sun glistened on the machine's smooth red surface, tantalizingly beautiful. He'd dreamt about what the world was like, now he was being given the chance to see it. Maybe he'd even find the missing key that would unlock the mystery of life.

He got in.

~

Leo stared out the window of the helicopter. The approaching mainland spread out as far as he could see. He marveled at the lush mountains rising from the sea in jagged arches. Patches of mist clung to their edges, held in place by the mossy branches of cedar trees. Synapses fired rapidly in the folds of Leo's grey matter as he pondered the possibilities of the world, wondering how big it actually was. He clenched his hands unconsciously as he thought about the island. A tightening sensation spread throughout his chest. How much of what he'd been taught was a lie?

McGruff's voice pulled Leo away from his contemplation, "Pay attention. This is extremely important. Do you understand that the men on that island were not banished there? They are biomedical engineers, and you're the world's first genetically enhanced human. You are the fastest, strongest, smartest human on earth. It is up to you to catch the Monkergle. If the public finds out about it, the government will check all our labs and find out about you too. Biotech will be shut down and you'll never see the doctors again. You'll become the subject of extreme experiments."

Leo cradled his head in his thick hands as he processed this new information. He was going to have to sort through almost everything he knew about the world in order to discern the truth. If only there was some sort of device that held information about everything. He looked up, uncertainty in his eyes. "Am I not already the subject of extreme experiments?"

"No, you are our child. Biotech is your family. We're preparing to teach you about the world and release you, but first we need you to do this for us. There's a team waiting for you in the Kootenay Mountains. Do you understand your mission?"

"Sure. Catch the Monkergle and bring it back to the lab."

"Good. Follow the trackers. They'll lead you to the beast. Sneak up on it. You're the only one fast enough to get within shooting range. Once you've tranquilized the Monkergle, the trackers will radio the lab. We'll have the helicopter pick you up. It's imperative that no civilians spot the Monkergle."

~

The helicopter landed twenty kilometers north of Biotech's Kootenay Mountain Laboratory, hidden deep in the overgrown forests. Two rustic-looking men, one tall and bearded, the other short and bald, waited in a clearing in the woods. As Leo stepped out of the chopper, the bearded man walked up to him and shook his hand. "Leo, good to meet you. I've heard all about you, and I'm looking forward to seeing you in action."

"Just try and keep up." Leo smiled.

"Here's your tranquilizer gun. D'ya know how to shoot?"

"Yeah. McGruff showed me in the helicopter."

"All right, let's get a move on. The Monkergle's got a head start. Plus it can fly, so it's tricky to track. We've followed it this far, but it gets away every time we get close. It's too fast. That's where you come in. Get within range and take the shot. Do not hesitate. This animal is dangerous. It'll rip you limb from limb before you have time to blink."

The trackers entered the forest, signaling Leo to follow. He stopped at the edge just long enough to watch the pilot and McGruff take off in the helicopter. Cedar and fir trees covered the steep hills of the mountains. Ferns grew up from the forest floor. The earth here was springier than on the island, mossier. The sun beat down from high in the sky, softly penetrating the forest's thick canopy to where the three men followed the Monkergle's tracks. Leo jogged easily beside the others.

The bearded man led the way up the mountainside, stopping briefly to examine a clump of orange hair on the side of a boulder.

"It stopped here to scratch itself." Examining the needles of a nearby branch, he turned to the others. "This way."

The group continued up the mountain until the tracks suddenly disappeared. The bearded man looked around. "It must have flown from here. Look for marks in the trees."

Leo pointed, "There."

"Where?"

"Scratches. Halfway up that big cedar."

"Well, you got vision. That's for sure. That cedar's gotta be a hundred meters away," the smaller tracker said, impressed.

The bearded man put his finger to his lips. "He's close."

The air filled with a distant, whooping growl. The raw power of the sound sent a chill up Leo's back. He turned to the others. The smaller man's eyes bulged out of his ghostly face. His hands shook. Following the tracker's gaze, Leo spotted a shaking treetop a few hundred meters away. What strength, he thought, to bend such a thick tree. Leo grew eager to see this extraordinary creature. He sprinted alongside the men, guns held tight.

Leo's shoes dug into the forest's floor as he propelled himself forward with superhuman speed. It was impossible for the trackers to match his pace, and with each stride of his powerful legs, Leo ran further ahead of them. They were more than fifty yards behind by the time he neared the beast. An orange blur overhead caught his attention. Leo aimed the gun, but couldn't get a clear shot.

Leo sprinted after the beast, adrenaline coursing through his veins as his muscles clenched. Never in his twenty years on Earth had he felt so alive.

A new sensation arose within Leo—a connected bliss felt when the focus is so sharp, it cuts away all distractions and allows the mind to concentrate only on what is present—a hyper state of awareness that comes with a complete forgetfulness of self. It comes to lovers in the throes of passion, comes to artists as they are consumed by creative force, comes to the lion as he pounces on his prey, and it came to Leo as he sprinted through the forest, free from the restraints of the life he'd known, and in search of an understanding that would lead him towards liberation.

Leo continued his pursuit, weaving through the trees and jumping logs, his legs pumping like pistons. He crashed through bushes. His thick hands protected his face as he ran swiftly over the top of the mountain and down the other side. He ran for over an hour, lost in the excitement of the chase, unable to stop long enough to get a shot off.

When he finally halted in a small clearing, the trackers were miles behind. For the moment, signs of the Monkergle escaped Leo's senses. He listened intently. The forest whispered a language forgotten by man, a language of subtly and instinct, where dire meanings hang on the slightest of sounds. A breeze rustled the braches above him, carrying with it the melody of a small bird. A woodpecker struck a rhythm nearby. A squirrel above cracked a nut. Leo rested against the soft bark of a cedar tree and scanned the air. The forest was denser here than on his island, and the trees bigger. Sunlight shone through the treetops, illuminating the large ferns sprouting in clusters from the springy matt of twigs and cones that lined the forest floor. Dust in the air caught and held the light. Moss clung to the northern sides of the trees, drooping from their branches. The gentle trickle of a river aroused his thirst, drawing him towards the source of the sound. He walked downhill to the river's edge, and dropped to his knees, thrusting his face into the cool water and filling his stomach.

Drinking from the stream brought a sense of calm. Through this simple action, he felt connected to this forest and these mountains. The rivers were the veins of this land, and he drank the lifeblood, inviting it to become one with his body. The thought came to him that he could get away from the trackers, escape his old life, and begin anew. He longed to be free to discover the world on his own terms. But he shrugged the thought away. He had a job to do and wanted to do it well. He could make his escape after capturing the beast.

Wiping the water from his chin with the back of his hand, he glanced down the river. Fifty or so yards downstream, the Monkergle hunched, face to the river, quenching its thirst. Leo crouched, stealthily approaching the creature. As he got closer, he had his first good view of the beast. Its fur was striped orange and black, and large wings folded across its back. A long tail curled toward the sky, flicking back and forth. It looked to weigh around two hundred pounds.

Leo ducked behind a log twenty yards from his prey. Steadying his breath, he aimed the gun at the beast. Before he could bring himself to fire, the Monkergle began walking downstream. Leo followed. He crouched again, taking aim, but as he held the beast within his scope, it sniffed at the air and turned in Leo's direction. The creature's blue eyes shone dramatically, framed by the furry orange face of a primate. Leo shuddered upon seeing the alarmingly human-like features. It seemed to be smiling, enjoying the sun. Then it turned fully towards Leo and made eye contact, a look of inquiry appearing in its intelligent eyes. It seemed to be wondering how to react to this newcomer. It walked toward him.

Leo's finger rested on the trigger of the tranquilizer gun, the barrel pointed at the beast's chest. It was fifteen yards away, staring Leo in the eyes. The creature approached on all fours. The sun glistened off its white fangs. Leo stepped back, awed by the beast's powerful beauty. The Monkergle stood on its hind legs and scratched at its side with a large furry hand. Leo watched cautiously as it took a few steps forward on its hind legs.

The pounding of Leo's heart made his aim unsteady. The beast was now ten yards away. It breathed through its cat-like nose. Whiskers stuck out from the sides of its face below its curious eyes. Suddenly letting out a breathy whoop, it lowered onto all fours, eyeing Leo suspiciously. Its back feet resembled hands more than feet. Muscles rippled under its fur as it took a few more steps toward Leo.

Stretching downward like a sleepy cat, it nodded its head, watching Leo cautiously before proceeding.

Leo felt a surge of compassion as he looked the animal in the eyes. Was he imagining a wave of camaraderie passing between them, an awareness of a kinship that only those who have been subject to the same evil can know—a bond forged by similar hardships?

No wonder this creature had escaped. It was far too magnificent to be locked in a cage. This creature had accomplished what Leo had dreamed of countless times. He watched it. Every hair on its sleek body glistened. A potent intellect burned behind its eyes. The Monkergle wasn't that different from him. Memories of the island flashed through Leo's mind. It had been his cage. He let his gun fall to his side. This animal was his brother; he couldn't shoot it.

Once the gun was down, the Monkergle relaxed. It smiled and nodded to Leo. Leo laughed and the animal let out another whoop whoop, then turned playfully on the spot in a quick circle and looked back up. Leo imitated it, turning in a circle, then began laughing. The Monkergle stood on its hind legs and spread its wings—a collage of orange and black feathers. Its wingspan was nearly fifteen feet across. Leo spread his arms.

The beast took another few steps toward Leo. It was so close that he could feel the warm air from its nostrils. He tried to calm his own breathing. Swallowing hard, Leo took a step towards it. The possibility of danger intensified the experience, making it seem surreal. Slowly reaching out a hand, he touched the beast's forehead. It closed its eyes and rubbed its head into Leo's palm, purring. Exhaling deeply, Leo scratched under its chin. He was surprised by its tameness, but then realized that it must have gotten used to being around people in the lab.

Remembering the trackers, Leo glanced back. They were still miles behind. He could return the beast to the trackers, but what good would come from that? They would cage it, and possibly him too. Life, Leo suddenly realized, doesn't flow in a linear chain with each day an equal segment on the calendar of existence. Rather it courses from defining moment to defining moment, forged by the choices that shape the soul. He was standing at the edge of one of these precious moments, at a fork in the path of life. He could be the tracker's puppet, doing what he's told, or he could think for himself, being true to the virtue in his own heart.

He walked away from the trackers.

The Monkergle looked at him inquisitively. Leo smiled and motioned with his hand, "Come on." The animal ran to his side, lifted an orange hand to the tranquilizer gun, and let out a gentle whoop.

"What? You don't like this gun?"

The Monkergle stopped walking, staring up at Leo intently. Its eyes flicked from Leo to the gun. Leo looked at him. "You really don't like it." He dropped the gun on the ground. "Ok, have it your way."

The Monkergle walked at Leo's side.

~

Slowing his pace, Leo folded his arms across his powerful chest to shield himself from the brisk night air. He and the beast had been running for hours and he felt comfortable enough with their head start to ease up. It would be tough for the trackers to follow in the dark. Squinting, Leo examined his surroundings. The Monkergle seemed to have better night vision than he did. Leo rubbed behind its ears.

Not really understanding the proper usage of the term doctor (everyone he'd known on the island was a doctor), Leo decided to name the Monkergle Dr. Monk. "Yeah, that's what I'll call you, Dr. Monk. What do you think?" Leo asked, still rubbing the soft fur behind its ears.

Dr. Monk smiled.

Leo sat on a log to rest his legs. He massaged his strained thighs, not used to such mountainous terrain. Dr. Monk flopped onto his side next to Leo, letting his massive head fall onto Leo's feet. The extra body heat comforted him. Leo reached down and began rubbing Dr. Monk's velvety belly. A breeze rustled the leaves and Leo closed his eyes to listen to the night sounds. He could hear a bird in the distance, and a small animal scurrying about, preparing for the night in a nearby tree. A faint, far-away rhythm was slightly audible. Hunger amplified his curiosity. He stood to investigate the source of the noise. Dr. Monk followed, happily running zigzag patterns through the bushes.

As they drew closer to the sound, a deep beat-driven music became perceptible. Glowing lights flashed in the distance, lighting the sky, and Leo could hear the happy shouts of many voices. Dr. Monk grew uneasy, hesitant to go too near the noise. He whimpered, refusing to walk any further.

"Fine then, if you don't want to find out what all the fun is, you can stay here." Leo said.

The creature looked pleadingly into Leo's eyes.

Leo pointed to a large rock that overhung the side of a small cliff. "Stay here, OK. I'll be back with some food. Stay!"

Dr. Monk nodded, sadly but obediently.

Leo turned and began walking toward the noise. Dr. Monk watched him vanish into the darkness, and then lay under the rock with a sigh.

~

Leo stood at the edge of the forest and gazed across a clearing. On the far side of it, an array of laser beams lit the night sky. Primal rhythms echoed toward him and, even from this distance, Leo could feel the vibration from the bass throbbing rhythmically in his chest. He wondered what sort of event was taking place, some sort of celebration. People walked and danced throughout the clearing, more people than he imagined would have ever been in one place. A city of tents, so close they touched one another, filled the field. A man dressed in a turtle costume exited a tent near Leo and stretched, yawning. Leo wondered if the small fabric dome was the man's home. Did these people live here in this neon-electric city? Entranced by the laser beams and wanting to discover the source of the music, Leo strode across the field of tents.

At the far side of the clearing, various paths led into the woods. Leo wandered down the middle path, staring at a few brightly dressed people. A man dressed as an octopus danced down the path, shaking all eight limbs to the beat. A samurai walked up to the octopus and drew his plastic sword. The two broke into an energetic dance frenzy that lasted less than a minute and ended in a mock battle in which the octopus strangled the samurai. Laughing, they slapped their hands together and danced off in different directions. As Leo observed the lively exchange, a plethora of costumed people danced down a path through the woods.

Leo followed. The music intensified as he neared the speakers. At the far end of the path an area opened to a white pyramid. Neon lights flashed above. The music swelled with heaving rhythms, at once fierce and playful. Leo felt the vibration penetrate his core, massaging his innards. How was the sound so powerful?—so physical?—so consuming?

Rounding the pyramid, Leo stumbled upon a crowd of nearly a thousand jumping in time to the thunderous music. Lasers lit the trees, bass shook the earth, and people flung themselves about. A skinny, shirtless man, eyes bigger than any Leo had ever seen, stood in front of a stack of speakers, pumping his fist in the air in time with the beat. The man contorted his jaw in circus-quality facial-aerobics.

Leo stared in disbelief at the throng of wild people. In all his years of fantasizing about the world, he had never imagined this. Two men worked electronic gear from a platform in the center of the crowd. Lasers shone onto a group of dancers suspended on bridges and platforms in the trees. A fuzzy yeti shook its furry limbs in a state of wild abandon. People held glowing jellyfish on poles above the crowd. A man with an afro and neon tights held a sign, *GET GROOVY.* Another man, naked, held a sign on a pole, *FUCK CLOTHES.* A shirtless gypsy held another sign, *IF YOU'RE LOOKING FOR A SIGN, THIS IS IT.*

Leo began moving his hips, swinging his arms to the music. His head bobbed and he let out a loud whoop in the fashion of Dr. Monk. He leapt in the air. His feet carried him around the periphery of the crowd. He imitated the movements of the others and danced in joyous circles. Bouncing with the drums, he threw his body about. The sound was so thick he felt as if he could swim through it.

A young man tapped Leo on the shoulder. "Here, dude." He passed Leo a joint.

Leo took it in his fingers and looked at it, confused. Smoke drifted up from its glowing tip. The man modeled what to do by putting his fingers to his mouth and breathing in. Leo copied. The smoke burnt his throat. He coughed out a cloud, passing the joint back to the man. His skin tingled as he swayed to the music, opening and closing his hands as if he had just discovered them. He breathed deep as this new sensation spread through his body. His eyes explored the crowd, absorbing the scene.

Large screens in the trees flashed cartoon images in time to the music. Lights reflected off a disco ball suspended in the trees. Balloons floated above the crowd. Consumed by the mob-like energy, Leo danced with unrestrained joy, jumping up and down and flinging himself about, surrendering to the music. It washed over him, wave after wave of pleasure filling him with glee, tantalizing him, sending his mind on wondrous journeys of imagination. He became the music—the physical manifestation of the sound. It bubbled within him, brewing delicious emotions, screaming joy, and filling him with awe. Twirling in bolder and bolder circles, he felt the energy flow out from him. He imagined a web of energy connecting each person in the crowd, flowing freely, alive with love. His face stretched in a blissful smile and he began noticing the smiles of others in the crowd.

Some people were dressed as animals, some had their faces painted, and others wore nothing at all, letting their body parts bounce and swing freely to the rhythms.

Then he saw her—the first woman he'd ever seen outside of a book.

The sheer force of her beauty hit Leo in the chest, knocking him backward. His knees almost buckled. His mind began to whirl as a new, profound emotion overtook him, drilling a series of cavernous realizations into his psyche that would forever change the way he experienced the world.

Her skin glistened with dance-party sweat as she flung her dark hair in circles. Her hips gyrated in time to the music, exuding a raw sexuality so powerful it could turn men into animals. Glancing up between fervent moves, she noticed the man watching her with ferociously luminous eyes, muscles straining the seams of his shirt. Her pulse quickened and her cheeks flushed at the sight of this Adonis incarnate—never had she seen such untamed masculine beauty.

She danced in front of Leo, her perfumed hair inches from his face. His gaze followed the curve of her body. He felt a powerful urge to grab her and pull her to him. She twirled, letting her fingers brush his. His loins pulsed. His heart fluttered. And he nearly lost control of his inner animal.

She looked up through tangled hair, flirting with her eyes. Leo smiled and extended his hand. She took it. He wanted to pick her up and tell her how happy he was. He wanted to scream to the world that he was finally free, but instead he just smiled, trying to fit in. She smiled too, keeping enough distance to feel safe, but close enough that Leo almost exploded with sensual enthusiasm.

After half an hour of painfully flirtatious dancing, she let Leo pull her close. His hand ran down her side to her hip, gently squeezing her supple flesh. She shivered with excitement.

She leaned in until her chin touched his shoulder, "wenna gtues so wa."

"What?"

"I'M THIRS YLETSOMWA."

Her words were drowning in dub step. She took Leo's hand and led him away from the speakers. "You wanna get a drink?"

"Yeah."

"Come on." Holding Leo's hand, she led the way toward a central area. Paths led in different directions to various stages where parties raged. Hundreds of people danced in a rock pit in front of a ten piece funk band. Across an open area, three large temples rose from the grass. Lasers shot out of the top of the tallest one, filling the sky. People danced on various platforms on the temples as well as in a large crowd surrounding them.

"You look a little overwhelmed. First time at Shambhala?"

"Yeah. I never knew."

"I know, eh? This party's wild. It's my third time."

They passed some food vendors. The smell brought Leo's hunger to the forefront of his mind. His stomach gurgled and he thought about Dr. Monk. He had to get back soon, before Dr. Monk got restless.

The woman filled a bottle of water from a tap then turned to Leo. "My name's Celina, by the way."

"I'm Leonardo. But call me Leo."

"Do you want to walk to the beach to watch the fire dancers and smoke a joint?"

"Yeah, but...I have to get back to my friend. I told him I'd bring him some food."

"Oh."

"You can come. He's not far. I just can't leave him too long. He might run away."

"Run away? What stage is he at?"

"He's waiting for me in the woods."

"In the woods? Is he sick?"

"No. He's scared of the noise and all the people."

"Sounds like a bit of a weird guy."

"Oh no. He's not human. He's a Monkergle."

"A what?"

"It's a new breed of animal. Part monkey, part tiger, and part eagle."

She lightly slapped his chest, letting her hand linger. "Get outta here. There's no such thing."

"No, seriously. I befriended him after he broke out of the lab."

"Stop pulling my leg. Let's go smoke this joint. I wanna watch the fire dancers." She pulled him toward the beach.

"I can't. I need to get some food and get back to my friend."

"If this is your way of trying to get me into the bushes, it's not working. I'm not that easy."

"No. Wait. What?"

A clown on stilts walked by, juggling some glow-in-the-dark balls. He bent down, "You guys want some mushrooms?"

"Yeah, I'm starving. I haven't eaten since breakfast." Leo answered.

Celina looked at Leo incredulously. "I don't think he was talking about those kind of mushrooms."

"These mushrooms will take you to the moon." The clown cut in.

Leo looked at the moon perched high above the forest. "That's impossible. The moon is 384,400 kilometres away. Even if you converted all the mushrooms in the world into biodiesel, the energy needed would…"

The clown touched his fanny pack, "I've got uppers, downers, lefters, righters, and little blue pills that'll make you spiral into yourself." He winked at Leo, "What you two beauties need is a couple of these Foxies. Pop these then cross the bridge, find a spot under the stars, and lose yourselves in the ancient art of fuck."

Celina looked up at the clown. "We're all good here."

"Alrighty. Party on." The clown walked away, talking over his shoulder, "Look for the clown if you wanna get high."

Celina squeezed Leo's hand. "You're different. I like it."

"Yeah, I guess you could say I haven't gotten out much. What was that guy talking about?"

"He's selling drugs."

"Why would we take drugs if we're not sick?"

"Get outta here. We're at Shambhala."

Leo looked down, laughing nervously, feeling left behind by the conversation. "Please come meet my friend."

"Friend better not be code word for penis!"

"What? No, I—"

"I will mace you." She laughed. "Ok, I guess we'd better get some food."

~

Leo and Celina walked through the bushes, stomachs full of veggie burritos and frozen yogurt. He called out, but Dr. Monk wasn't under the rock. He looked around, holding a veggie burrito in the air, enticing Dr. Monk with the scent. "He's around here somewhere. He wouldn't leave me. He's my best friend."

"What does he look like?"

"Part monkey, part tiger, part eagle."

"Come on. You mean Labrador?"

A loud whoop came from the trees above, and Celina jumped behind Leo. Dr. Monk sailed down on spread wings and landed with a thud in front of their feet. Celina grabbed Leo's waist from behind, her arms shaking. "No Fuck'n way. No Fuck'n way. What the fuck is that?"

"I told you. A Monkergle. Don't be scared. He's friendly." Leo rubbed the top of Dr. Monk's head and handed him the burrito. Dr. Monk ate it in one bite.

Leo looked at Celina. "What was that word you said?"

It took her a moment to answer. "What word?" Her eyes were glued to Dr. Monk like ugly to a mullet.

"Fuck."

"What do you mean, 'what is it?'" Her voice trembled.

"I mean, what does it mean?"

"Are you kidding?"

"No." Leo suddenly felt ashamed of being unaware of something that was obviously common knowledge. "I've never heard it before."

"Fuck that, Mr. Proper. Are you given me a hard time? I'm a grown woman; I can say fuck if I want. Fuckety fuck fuck." Celina slapped Leo's arm, keeping him between her and the beast.

"But what does it mean?"

Celina eyed Leo, her head cocked to the side like a puzzled dog. "You're serious? It means have sex, but it's just a word people tag into sentences when they're not clever enough to think of a better word."

"Oh. What's sex?"

"Fuck off!" She slapped his arm again. "I'm not falling for your bizarre sense of humor."

Leo dropped it, embarrassed by his ignorance. "Men from the lab are tracking us. They'll be here soon. We need a safe place to hide."

"Can I pet it?"

"Go ahead."

Biting her lip, Celina reached out a shaky hand, flinching but holding steady when Dr. Monk rubbed his face into it, purring. "I have five acres in the mountains an hour from here. We can take my van."

Dr. Monk rolled onto his back, wanting his belly rubbed.

"Where's your van?" Leo asked.

"In the clearing on the way to Fractal Forest."

Leo bent over and began enthusiastically rubbing Dr. Monk's belly with both hands. "He won't go near the people. He's scared."

Celina stepped out from behind him and joined in the belly rubbing. She looked at Dr. Monk's monkey-like hands and noticed the retractable claws. "He's amazing. And so soft."

Dr. Monk smiled.

Celina continued, "I'll drive the van to the edge of the clearing and pick you up."

~

Celina's house was nestled between two clusters of cedar trees. A large garden full of herbs and veggies took up most of the backyard. The van rumbled to a stop in the gravel driveway and three dogs came running to meet it. Leo and Celina stepped out and Leo opened the side door for Dr. Monk. The dogs went berserk when they saw the Monkergle. They ran in circles around the van, barking and growling. Celina tried to settle them down, but failed. Dr. Monk stepped out of the van and stood on his hind legs, spreading his wings to their full glory. One look and the dogs cowered, knowing they were no match. They whimpered behind Celina. Laughing, she took them and put them in their kennel.

Dr. Monk waited outside as the humans went into the house. Prayer flags hung above the door. A rich maroon-colored hall led to a living room full of large leafy plants. Celina pressed play and a stereo emitted chill beats layered with ethnic instruments and deep bass-lines. The house smelled of incense. Leo looked around the room, thrilled to see the home of someone from off the island. He examined the fish tank closely, looking the fish in the eye, laughing at the miniature castle. Then he sat on a worn couch with a patchwork blanket draped over its back. He wondered what the rectangular plastic and glass box mounted on the wall in front of the couch did. He had never come across the word on it, Samsung.

Celina brewed some chai, and then sat on the couch with Leo. He had pulled a large pile of books from the shelf and was flipping through them.

"You have so many books. I had no idea there were this many books in the world."

"What do you mean? There are millions of books in the world."

"Millions! I've got a lot of reading to do. Have you read them all?"

"All the books in the world?"

"Yeah."

"Don't be ridiculous. Nobody's read all the books in the world."

"Oh." Leo looked Celina in the eyes, craving to understand more about the world. "What is life like for you?"

"What do you mean? Like what am I all about?"

"Yeah, sure."

"Well, I live here with my two friends. They're still at Shambhala. I teach yoga and waitress at the Outer Clove in Nelson to pay the bills."

Leo wondered what bills were, but didn't ask because he didn't want to appear ignorant. "What makes you happy?"

"Sitting here with you makes me happy. I love working in the garden, being in nature, walking my dogs, snowboarding in the winter. I moved out here to Nelson from Calgary because I was tired of the big city. I was beginning to feel like everyone I knew was a lemming. Like they were just all cookie-cutter versions of each other. Sometimes I feel like all the rules of society just make people lose their individuality. So many people just believe what they're told about the world—act the way they're told to. They don't challenge their beliefs by expanding their world view and breaking out of the mental box that society has locked them in through a lifetime of social conditioning."

"I know what you mean."

"There's lots of ways to live. It's the people who keep their imagination and see the world with childlike awe who find happiness. Sorry if I'm getting too deep."

"No, I love it. I'm really interested."

"I guess what I'm saying is that you've got to choose a way-of-life that resonates with you and helps you to express your unique spirit. That's why I love it here. I'm free to be me. No judgment. How about you? What do you do?"

"Oh, I like reading, playing music, swimming in the river."

"Music, eh? What's your weapon of choice?" Celina asked, turned on by creativity.

"Oh, no. I don't believe in violence."

"Get outta here, you goof. What instrument?"

"Oh. Guitar, piano, saxophone, drums, violin. I like to play all the instruments on the island I live on. It's one of my favorite things to do."

"I have a guitar. Will you play for me?"

"Sure."

Celina pulled an acoustic guitar from a case in the closet and handed it to Leo. It looked like a child's guitar in his hands. She turned off the stereo.

Leo began gently, pressing the strings, bending them as he plucked melodies between chords. The music poured out of the guitar, gypsy-like, rolling over itself in haunting layers, swelling with rhapsodic fire. Leo's fingers climbed and climbed, pushing the tone higher and higher, until, no further left to climb, the music suddenly disintegrated into a rhythmic fury, full of guttural bass. Leo stomped his foot, flung his head about, and cried out as he bent the sound to his will.

The music growled like a feral animal as Leo's fingers dug into the lower strings. He pounded the guitar, bestial and passionate, full of delicious wrath. Then his hand was high up the guitar's neck, tapping harmonics, savoring the succulent silence between notes before building to a blistering climax—a fierce melody, dangerously erotic, brutally sweet like the kiss of death.

Celina sat in wondrous silence. The music burned with richness and flavor, containing inner longing and complete surrender. It burst with emotion and teetered on the edge of sanity, reaching to the deepest recesses of her soul, seeming to touch the gates of Heaven and Hell, uniting them, shaking the world with its vibration. It was completely of the world, yet somehow wildly separate from it. It spoke to her of a way-of-being that transcended anything she'd ever known, activating an inner-wakefulness deep within the young woman's core.

True art, she realized, has a way of making the outer world melt away, consuming the audience in the eternity of the moment—to the point where nothing exists but the art, as it brings the gifts of enlightenment. Art pushes the human race forward by taking the imagination to places never before charted. It comes from a world beyond our own, beyond the confines of logic or language, a world that cannot be seen or touched, only felt. It is a state of being that every one of history's great artists have known well, a state only achieved by those with the courage to delve into themselves, a state that, once achieved, will forever change the way the world is perceived. Leo was tapped in.

By the time the song ended, every inch of Celina's skin tingled. The sound had ceased but the energy continued to resonate throughout the room, like ripples in a pond. A hunger awoke in her that she could no longer ignore. She slid over until she was inches from Leo. She took the guitar from his hands, setting it on the edge of the couch. She looked up at him with eyes impossibly blue—luminescent pools full of life and love and tenderness and passion and everything beautiful about the world. Their hands met. Fingers interlaced. Leo leaned in, reveling in her scent. Their faces were inches apart, drifting closer—her breath warm. Leo's lips were alive with blood.

Standing, she pulled his shirt over his head. He stood with her, his heart pounding, mind racing.

Lamplight shone on his skin. Celina's eyes traced Leo's body; muscles rippled under tight skin with his every small movement— muscles that she hadn't even known existed. How was this man possible?—so beautiful, and so passionate.

Letting her fingers trace his abs, she pressed herself into his chest and felt herself melt. His hands ran down her shirt to her hips. She leaned back, seductively peering up. Then she slowly removed her shirt and tossed it to the floor.

Leo's inner lover awoke like a fiery dragon, dangerous and powerful and blisteringly hot.

Celina's fingers traced Leo's skin from waist to back, summoning a trail of goose-bumps. He pulled her close, arms around her waist. Their lips met—gently at first, tenderly exploring, building into passion, savoring the experience with all senses. She moaned. The sound penetrated Leo's core. The dragon took flight. Arms encircled flesh. Hips ground together. Organs swelled. Celina gently bit Leo's lower lip, throwing him into a roaring ocean of sensation. His heart fluttered in his chest like a sparrow in a glass box. He held Celina close. Their bodies moved as one, hearts in sync, drunk with passion, arms exploring skin, squeezing, rubbing, lips and tongues entangled fervently.

A small hand found its way to the top button of Leo's pants and undid it, relieving some of the pressure his raging erection exerted on his jeans. The brushing of her hand against his penis unleashed the primal desire inherent in men, and he realized that the sexual acts he performed on himself in the bathroom were not meant to have been solitary activities. He wanted to cry out, but breathed deeply through his nose to calm himself. A world of possibilities was opening.

Celina slid Leo's pants down past his hips. She cried out in both fear and excitement when she saw it. It curved upward; long, thick, and muscular. She'd never seen anything like it, so powerfully animalistic. She lost herself in impulse at the sight, reaching out and wrapping her fingers around its vascular shaft. It pulsed in her hand. "Oh my God," she gasped, "you have a... a... a TAIL!"

With a shattering sound, the front door flew open, sending splinters flying. Two tranquilizer darts flew into the room, hitting both Leo and Celina. Their strength quickly waned. He dropped her. The room spun. And they fell to the ground, unconscious.

The trackers ran into the room. The bearded one turned to the little one, "Oh shit. Our man moves fast. Good thing for that tracking device. Imagine the shit-storm if he impregnated her."

The little tracker stared at the bodies. Leo lay on his back. "Ha," the little tracker guffawed, "Look at that!" He pointed to Leo's penis. The organ lay on its side, put to sleep by the dart.

"Stop acting gay and get some rope."

While the smaller man got some rope, the bearded tracker ran his hand up Celina's stomach and squeezed her breasts.

~

Leo woke in a small cell meant for an animal. He looked around, eyes still heavy from the effects of the dart. His cage was just big enough to lie down in, and contained only himself, a wool blanket and a pillow. He shook his head to clear the grogginess.

The cage was in a large, sterile, concrete room. Florescent lights hung from the ceiling. There were three other cages like his, but all were empty. He felt a desperate need to know if Celina was ok. A wooden table across the room had various open files on it. Leo sat on the blanket in the back of his cage, his head between his knees.

The bearded tracker walked into the room, a crooked smile taunting Leo. "Thought you could out smart us, eh?"

Leo stared, grinding his teeth in impotent fury.

"You might have the body of an Olympian and a genius IQ, but ya ain't street smart. You're missing the building block to success. Ya know what that is?"

Leo stared unresponsive, fists clenched.

"Experience. You're like a lost puppy. You're lucky we caught you. You couldn't handle the big bad world." The tracker picked up one of the file folders and waved it about. "You think you could figure out the equation for life? I'll tell you what life's about. Power. That's it. Power makes the world turn. Our whole society is based around it. Everyone wants it. Money represents it. And right now I've got it and you don't."

A pain-filled whoop echoed into the room from down the hall. Leo looked up. "Dr. Monk."

The tracker stood close to the cage, mocking Leo. "Don't worry; your friend's gonna get his. Tonight they're gonna clip his wings. That glorified housecat ain't ever gonna fly again."

Before the tracker had time to flinch, Leo shot across the cage. Banana like fingers wrapped around the tracker's neck and Leo lifted him from the ground. "Open the door or I'll crush your windpipe."

Leo's grip was so tight the tracker couldn't even cough. The tracker's beard scrunched up around his face like a dead chipmunk. Leo pulled him in, clanking the rodent against the bars. "How do you like this experience?" he growled into tracker's panicked face.

A tazer met Leo's arm just above the elbow, shock causing his hand to tighten around the tracker's neck. Leo groaned as his body convulsed. He didn't let go.

The tracker's feet pressed the bars of the cage with all his might. He broke free from Leo's grip, flew backwards, and landed with a thud, his head bouncing off the cement floor.

Leo stood tall, muscles shivering from the jolt. The tracker rolled over and slowly stood, checking the back of his head for blood. Coughing and breathing heavily, he looked up at Leo, making sure he was out of reach. "Fucking gorilla."

"You wanna see power?" Leo grabbed the bars of the cage, the sinewy muscles of his forearms twitching as he pulled. The metal groaned under the strain.

The tracker backed away in horror, but the bars didn't budge. "Good luck. These cages can hold any animal in the world. Including you." With that, the tracker walked out of the room, rubbing the back of his head.

~

Leo huddled in the corner of the cage, wrapped in a blanket as he sat. The bars pressed uncomfortably into his back, but he didn't care. His head hung limp. Dr. Monk cried out from another room. Leo thought about captivity, about the doctors and trackers, and how the mind can be held captive by social conditioning and misguided ambition, just as the body can be held by physical bars.

Dr. Gustoff stepped into the room. "Pssst, Leo. Over here."

"Dr. Gustoff, what are you doing here?"

"Getting you outta here. I can't stand to think of you being trapped in here. You're like a son to me, Leo. I've watched you grow your whole life. My loyalty is not with Biotech, it's with you." Dr. Gustoff took a key from a ring attached to his belt and opened the door to the cage. "Biotech will never let you go. You need to get out of here. There's a whole world out there. It's time for you to go become the man I know you will become."

"Thank you." Leo stepped out of the cage and embraced the doctor. "Come with me."

"I can't. I'll slow you down. Do you remember when you were working on the equation for life?"

"Yeah. I was wrong. Life is too big to summarize in one equation."

"I've been thinking, Leo, and I believe that life exists to evolve. To continually grow in increasing complexity. Mankind is at the forefront of evolution on earth. We have the largest scope of consciousness, and are increasing our knowledge of the universe daily. That's why I dedicated my life to helping man take the next step of evolution through science. That's what you are. The next step."

"So, I'm the first of my kind?"

"There's no time for this conversation. We'll meet again."

"Where's Celina?"

"I don't know."

"I've got to find her."

"OK, but first there's something that must be taken care of if you are to stay free. There's a tracking device implanted behind your left ear. You have to cut it out, or they'll find you."

"Ok." Leo's fingers traced a small, almost undetectable, bump behind his ear.

"Go."

~

The small tracker slept on a chair in front of Dr. Monk's cage. Leo grabbed him by the neck and lifted him up. The tracker awoke instantly, his legs and arms flailing uselessly against Leo's strength. He tried to scream, but Leo's grip was too tight. The tracker reached for his tazer, but Leo crushed the device in his hand, tossing it to the floor.

Dr. Monk paced back and forth. Leo slammed the tracker into the side of the cage, pulled the key from the tracker's belt, opened the door, and threw the tracker inside with the beast. "Where's Celina?"

"I don't know." The tracker backed into the corner of the cage. Dr. Monk stepped close, licking his lips. The tracker looked pleadingly at Leo. "Please!" He pulled a small knife from a case attached to his belt.

Dr. Monk swatted it from his hand. The knife slid to a stop at Leo's feet. Leo picked it up. The beast pounced on the small man, pinning him to the ground. Its lips pealed back, allowing the light to glisten off its fangs.

"OK, OK. We drugged her so she would forget meeting you and dropped her back off at the festival."

Leo opened the cage, let Dr. Monk out, then locked the tracker in. "That wasn't so hard was it?"

~

Leo and Dr. Monk crept stealthily down the hallway towards the exit. A beam of sun shone through a small window on the door.

Leo picked up his pace. He could see outside. A grassy field stretched towards a forest. Mountains rose in the background.

A loud barking echoed from one of the rooms which lined the hallway.

Leo turned slowly.

The noise had come from the second door on his left. He peeked through a Plexiglas window on the room's door. Two scientists sat at a table, lost in conversation. The room was full of cages. Each cage held a different animal. Leo quickly surveyed the room for weapons, saw none, then opened the door and stepped in.

The scientists looked up. "What the—"

"One word and you're dead. Give me the keys."

Dr. Monk stepped into the room behind Leo. The scientists stood wide-eyed, backing slowly into a corner. One of them pressed the silent alarm button next to the computer station.

Leo stepped forward. "Cooperate and nobody'll get hurt. Understand?"

The scientists nodded in unison. Grabbing the keys from the belt of the smaller man, Leo turned towards the cages. There were ten total. He walked to the first one and tried a key. It didn't work. Inside the cage a small Chihuahua-like animal with bat ears and wings ran excited loops. It stopped when Leo removed the key. A floppy tongue hung from the side of its mouth as it sat panting, looking up curiously at Leo. The next key Leo tried opened the door and the small creature ambled out.

One of the scientists protested. "Stop. You don't know what you're doing. These animals represent decades of research. They're going to change lives, not just as pets, but as biological test subjects, working animals, seeing-eye guides—"

Leo shot him a glance that shut him up. Dr. Monk stepped closer to the men to make sure that they didn't try anything.

Flipping through the keys, Leo searched for the match to the next cage. Inside was a zebra-like animal with wings.

As Leo tried to find a key to the cage, the door to the room flew open, hitting the wall with an angry smack. The bearded tracker shot a tranquilizer dart. Leo turned. The dart grazed the fabric of his shirt, then ricocheted off a cage bar and hit the wall.

Leo charged.

The tracker shot another dart, but Leo ducked. The dart flew past his ear. Before the tracker had time to squeeze the trigger a third time, Leo snatched the gun from his hand and threw it into the corner of the room. One of the scientists made a move for the gun, but Dr. Monk put his foot on it and bared his teeth.

The tracker threw a punch at Leo, who ducked, picked the tracker up, and threw him across the room. The tracker slammed into the wall, snapping his collar bone. He fell limply to the ground, rolled over, and moaned. Lines of agony twisted his face, and his eyes scrunched shut. Leo grabbed him by the arm, dragging the screaming man into the open cage.

He looked at the scientists. "Get in." They did.

Leo locked the men in the cage, then looked the tracker in the eyes. "You dare to talk to me of power? Your feeble mind knows nothing of true power. Power is not an aggressive quality. It doesn't come from your muscles or guns. It's not a way of controlling one's surroundings, or a command gained over others. No, that's simply willfulness. The only real power is power over the self. Power over the outside world is an illusion, a temporary trick. It will always leave you wanting more. Those who strive for power over the external have no real power. They are simply too oblivious to see that they are slaves to a force they cannot see or understand."

The scientists nodded thoughtfully, but the tracker only groaned, rendered deaf by his pain. One by one, Leo proceeded to unlock the remaining cages and let the animals out. A muscular mule-gorilla-cross, obviously created to toil on a farm or industrial complex, ambled out the door. When all the animals were free, Leo looked at the scientists, bluffing, "If anyone from Biotech follows me, I will go straight to the government. I have a list of names connected to illegal experiments."

He ran out the door, down the hallway and outside, Dr. Monk at his side. The sun shone in full glory—a yellow orb hanging in the blue sky above the mountains. The forest stretched in all directions. An eagle soared above the trees. The flying zebra joined it in flight. A breeze rustled Leo's hair and he breathed in deeply. A wolf-goat stood tall on its hoofs, leaned its sleek head back, and howled at the sun. Leo howled too, tears streaking his smiling cheeks as he ran, leading the stampede to freedom.

14

NAKED

By now you must have seen the picture on Facebook. I know you'll wanna hear all about it, so I'll tell you the story. I'm getting a little fed up with everybody asking, but I suppose all the telling helps me tell it better. I'll tell it right for you, though. I won't spare the juicy details like I did when I explained it to Kyle's mom last night, or to my parents this morning.

I tried to get out of the house without seeing my mom, but I swear she's got an inbuilt tracking device. Like last summer, when you were visiting and she busted us getting high in the tree house. This is worse, though. Smoking pot's normal teenage curiosity, but her parenting books don't cover this. I bet she's home right now, Googling it. Anyway, my Dad came downstairs and they questioned me for, like, twenty minutes. It was soooooooo awkward. My Mom had this concerned look on her face that depressed the shit outta me. She tried to hide it, but that made it even worse. My Dad kept saying, "Don't worry. We're here for you." They were so morbid about it, treating me as if I have a terminal illness. I'm perfectly healthy. There's nothing wrong with me. This is who I am. Deal with it.

I barely managed to get out of there before I was late for class. And school this morning's been nuts, everyone stopping me in the halls, congratulating me. I can't walk ten feet down the hall without someone stopping me. I guess this is what it's like to be popular. I'm not going to complain, but I doubt it'll last. I'm just the flavor of the week. Truth is, I just want people to stop. I want to forget about it. I'm all twisted up. If life had a face, I'd punch it. That's why I'm spending my lunch hour hiding in the library and writing you. You've always been like my personal shrink.

It happened last night at Kyle Greenwood's party. I was hanging out with Tom, like usual, sitting on the couch, shooting Captain Morgan's from the bottle, and trying to get the courage to go over and talk to Lara. She looked gorgeous. Long brown hair. Eyes like beacons. A smile ten feet wide. A tight Billabong shirt. But of course, being popular, she was surrounded by people. People who didn't even know I existed until last night. I wanted to go talk to Lara, but how could I? As soon as I look at her my heart starts clawing at my chest like a cat in a wet paper bag.

She's the nicest of the popular girls, the only one to smile at me in the hall. I have no idea why she's dating Allan. He's a shaved gorilla—walking proof that evolution can go backwards. All muscle, no brain, and with the compassion of a hand grenade. I don't believe in hate, but if he was on fire and I had a bucket of water, I'd drink the water. He's a year older than me, and the captain of the Clippers. He was standing amid a group of jocks, shot-gunning beer and talking jock-talk. Rating girls on a scale of one to ten, or making fun of all the guys that don't play sports—something that doesn't require much brain activity. He wasn't paying Lara any attention. Not that he usually did.

It's obvious to everyone but Lara that he only wants her because she has that stripper-fit body that makes idiot men drool like dogs. He doesn't care that the poems she writes in English class touch real emotion, which is hard to do. Mine keep ending up cheesy. He doesn't care that she sang in the school play, or that when a bird flew into the window and broke its wing during social studies, she took the time to nurse it back to health. All Allan sees in her is tits and ass. His brain is so underdeveloped he's barely human. Lara is a queen, a goddess with a mind like an ever-blossoming flower. She could never be satisfied with a chiseled Neanderthal. Allan could fit his entire vocabulary into a single sentence. Lara needs someone who can bend their awareness and look at life from a multitude of angles. Someone who contemplates. Someone who'll talk to her. Me! Or so I thought.

Anyway, there I was on the couch, bottle in hand, Tom jabbering about the new GTA, when Lara looked up from the depths of her circle and made eye contact with me. My stomach leapt out of my body. Her eyes were tractor-beams, drawing my gaze, exerting an alien force that rendered me immobile. I stared at her, expecting her to look away. But then she smiled. We gazed into each other's eyes from across the room, seeing each other from opposite corners of a social universe. A moment of mutual recognition passed between us. Her head even nodded, I swear. I felt it like lightning. Then, Kaylee grabbed Lara's arm and her attention was taken away. The moment was lost, but its excited energy continued to pulse through me.

Gradually, my attention reverted back to Tom. He was onto his talk of how we're going to get the band its first gig—his favorite subject these days. I didn't feel like a brainstorming session, so I told him I sing for fun, not to show off. Honestly though, the thought of a gig is nerve-racking, even though people keep telling me to get out there. I can't stand the idea of that many eyes on me. I just want to keep it in the garage for now.

I wanted a drink to calm my nerves, but I couldn't stomach the thought of another shot, so I said to Tom, "Let's find some mix" and nodded toward the kitchen. He grunted something about a "piss break" and wandered toward the bathroom. So I walked to the kitchen by myself and tried to blend in. I felt kinda awkward standing alone. Allan and his gang of primates were still in the corner, pointing and laughing at people. Tom and I refer to their 'crew' as the cactus club, because they're all pricks. Luckily, I went unnoticed: passing under the social radar is a skill I've been developing my entire high school career.

My mind wandered. You know how active my imagination is. Sometimes my mind just conjures these images at the most inopportune times and I just burst out laughing. Like when we went to that yoga class and everyone was meditating, and I imagined smashing two cymbals together and startling everyone. I could picture everyone's faces—so serene while meditating, then smash go the cymbals and everyone's freaking out, leaping in the air and screaming. I couldn't stop laughing. The teacher gave me the evil eye. It was so awkward I had to leave the class. And then it still took me like ten minutes before I stopped laughing.

Anyway, I stood alone in the kitchen, imagining that the reason I feel like an outsider is because I'm actually a three hundred year old vampire, frozen eternally in this sixteen year old body—I've been watching *The Vampire Diaries* on Netflix lately. I likened my feelings to that of the vampire, ever on the outside of society, attempting to blend in as I hunt my prey. I scanned the crowd from the shadowy periphery. The need for blood pulsed within me—the craving burning with feverish, consuming flames, peeling away the last of my humanity, leaving only a hungry fiend. I imagined the warmth of fresh blood running down my throat, heating my cold body. Who was I going to drink tonight? Would I kill them? Or simply drink the 'little drink,' and let them walk away?

The party was full of life. Sweet life, waiting to be feasted upon. My hungry eyes rested on Allan and the jocks. They were laughing at one of the freshmen who was so drunk he couldn't stand. They were trying to get him into the bathroom. Lord knows what they would do to him in there. I swear Allan thinks arrogance and stupidity are virtues. I could feel the evil resonating off him. I decided I would drink from him tonight. I might be a cold-hearted killer, but I prefer to feed on the wicked. It soothes my conscience to envision myself as a cleanser of evil, rather than a random killer of the innocent. Like it somehow justifies the evil in me if I use it to wipe out other evil.

I licked my lips. Allan was not innocent. He thought he wielded some power that gave him reign over others. I would show him true power. And then I would drink the delicious life from his body, finishing him. Today would be his last on Earth.

I found a glass and poured the rest of my rum into it. I filled it with Coke from a random bottle from the counter. It wasn't blood, but it would have to do while I awaited my opportunity to feed upon Allan.

A voice behind me pulled me from my fantasy. "Hey, wuddya doin'. That's my Coke." I turned, meeting Lara eye to eye. I was so stunned I just stammered. Then she smiled and slapped my arm. "I'm just giv'n ya a hard time. I don't know whose it is. I'll take a top up though." She held her empty glass out, ice tinking against the side.

I was so shocked she was speaking to me that all I could do was pass her the bottle. She pulled a bottle of vodka from the freezer.

"Cool party," I said, instantly beating myself up for it. So unclever. Mr. Mathews writes on all my papers how witty I am, but I don't know where that wit goes when I need it. I guess it's easy to be witty on an English paper; you can sit there and think about it, preconceive it. Thinking on the fly is different.

I can't even describe how blue Lara's eyes were. How enchanting. How their iridescent shine ignited a passion in me that caused every cell in my body to suddenly wake up. She leaned closer, keeping eye-contact, and said, "I heard you singing in the shower after everyone left gym." The words bit into me, leaving me dying in anticipation. *And?* I wondered. The seconds of silence stretched toward infinity, time seeming to bend in upon itself endlessly…

…

…

"It was sexy."

I nearly dropped dead when she said it. Sexy! My pulse pretty much doubled. My mouth turned into the Gobi Desert, tongue stuck to the roof.

"I admire you, you know," she said.

I couldn't believe what I was hearing. I watched her lips—the soft pink tissue delicately pronouncing each syllable. I wanted so bad to press my lips to hers, to feel her, taste her.

"You do what you want," she continued, "I wish I could be more like you. I feel this controlling need to fit in, to be liked. It's stifling. You have a social freedom of expression."

I was floored. Was this a joke? But she continued, stepping closer as she spoke. "You never try to impress anyone. You don't give in to social conventions. You could be so hot if you didn't always wear baggy jeans and a hoodie. Look at your body, it's hot. If you wore something tight, showed off your ass, maybe let your hair out of that ponytail, so many guys would want you. Maybe people would stop thinking that you're a lesbian."

I nearly spat my rum and coke all over the kitchen when she said that last part. How did they know? Zoe, you're the only person I've ever told. Is it that obvious? My heart jammed in my throat, causing me to choke on my words. "People… ahem… mmhg… think I'm… gay?"

"Well, aren't you? You've been staring at me all night."

"I… Um… Well…"

"Cuz, I've always wondered what it would be like to kiss a girl."

The blood rushed to my face, hot and awkward. Did I hear her right? Her eyes were on me, her gaze drawing mine. She smiled softly, encouragingly. How could she be so confident in this situation? My heart felt like it was going to burst. I was sweating. The kitchen felt like it was shrinking. I looked around self-consciously. It felt like the whole party was listening. Lara put her hand on mine. Her skin was so soft.

I realized it was now or never. If I didn't respond, others would wander into the kitchen and the moment would be lost forever. She squeezed my hand.

"You're beautiful." I blurted, wishing it had been something more suave. "I couldn't help staring." I fumbled for something sexy to say.

She got right to the point. "What's it like? You know, kissing a girl." Her directness was enticing, her gaze hypnotic.

"I don't know," my voice limped out, a fraction of itself." I've never kissed a girl."

"Really. Well, we should try. Bedroom?" Her eyebrows arched play-fully. She turned, still holding my hand, pulling me toward the back of the house.

The next thing I knew, my back was up against the wall of Kyle's parent's bedroom. My hoodie was coming off. Lara's lips were on mine, tasting of raspberry. I kissed back. Her hair smelled of mango and coconut. Her shirt like lemon. She nibbled my ear, whispering.

She grabbed my belt, pulling our hips together. I pulled her shirt over her head. The light caressed her perfect body. I could feel her sweet breath on my neck as she undid my belt, letting my pants drop to the floor. My heart raced. I could feel the passion in my chest, radiating outward, consuming me. How was this happening? Was I dreaming?

She was pulling me toward the bed. Her small shorts were flung to the corner. I stared at her little waist, circled by a thin G-string. Her mouth was on my breast, sucking my nipple, gently biting. The sensation coursed through me. We fell to the bed, me on top. She wrapped her legs around my waist, moaning in my ear. I could feel her warmth through her panties. The next thing I knew, my panties were being flung off. Our bodies writhed against one another. Her thighs squeezed my hips as I pushed into her. Our lips and hands roamed the valleys and mountains of each other's silky flesh. Her hands were on my breasts, massaging. Then I felt her finger between my thighs, exploring.

But how? I was holding both her hands.

I turned. Allan was there. Naked. Hand to my crotch. He had this look on his face, tongue hanging out like a hungry dog.

I jumped about six feet off the bed. "WHAT THE FUCK?"

"Shhhh, it's OK," Lara said. "Just go with it."

"I'm not touching that jerk." I was practically shouting. My whole body shook. I felt dizzy with nausea.

"Shhh. It'll be sexy."

"Gross." I practically spat.

"Don't tell me you're not into guys." Allan grunted.

"Guys are fine. It's you that disgusts me."

This really pissed him off. Hit him where it hurts, the ego. His face contorted into a mask of anger. "Big words from a lesbo-whore."

I wanted to smash his idiot face right there. I looked to the dresser, but there was nothing that could inflict enough damage. "You moron," my voice cracked hysterically. "Your insults don't even make sense. How can I be a virgin *and* a whore?" I was collecting my clothes, pulling them over my body. I turned to Lara. "Was this all a fuck'n set up? Huh? HUH?"

"No. Shhhh. I'm sorry." Lara looked ashamed. "It wasn't supposed to happen like this. He wasn't supposed to sneak up on you. He said he'd knock first. I thought you'd be into it."

Allan had a smug grin on his face.

"Fuck you" were the only words I could find.

"Tried to," he barked.

I slammed the door, pulling on my hoodie, feeling the filth cling to me as I left the room. I heard Lara yelling at Allan as I walked away. "This isn't a fucking porno. You can't just sneak up on somebody."

I just wanted to go home, to forget myself in sleep. I pushed through the crowded hall, looking for Tom. I knocked into a table, spilling drinks, but didn't stop to clean it. I checked the living-room and porch, but couldn't find Tom. I was so desperate to get out of there that I was about to give up and walk. Then Tom came racing up to me, out of breath. "Jen, your phone. Facebook." He was anxious, but too out of breath to express himself.

I pulled out my phone. There on Facebook, the very first news feed, was a picture of me in my underwear, pressed against another girl whose face was conveniently hidden. The picture was titled, *Jen the lesbo whore.*

I turned on the spot, walking straight back into the thick of the party. Allan stood in a circle of assholes, his back to me, showing his phone to some jerks, laughing like a crazed hyena.

He didn't see me coming.

I wound up and kicked him between the legs from behind, focusing all my hate of him into his testicles. He whimpered and dropped to his knees. I stepped in front of him. The whole party went silent, everyone's eyes on me. Allan's face was pale. I kneed him in the face. It hurt my knee, so I knew it musta really hurt his face. He spat blood and fell forward onto his hands. He looked dazed. He put up a hand to protect himself. Blood ran from his mouth, but I didn't stop there. I was so mad. All the emotion of the night had turned to anger. He moaned something about me being a 'clam eater'.

I wanted to kill him. "Does your ass get jealous of all the shit that comes outta your mouth?" I spat. A few people roared with laughter. Then I kicked Allan in the ribs, feeling the force up my leg and into my hip. He fell, clutching himself. I took out my phone, stood over him and took a picture. Then I uploaded it to Facebook, titled, *Allan getting his ass kicked by a lesbian.*

.The owl scans the darkest nights
.The hawkeye delivers death from distance
.The heron spans ecosystems
.And then there was...

Blind Date
Bob

15

BLIND DATE BOB

Pouting, Marsha examines her reflection through heavily mascaraed lashes. Her hand—festively decorated with crimson nail polish, three rings, and a silver bangle—holds her thick brown hair in a temporary bun as she slowly pivots 360 degrees, admiring her full glory. She looks good. Not quite as ferociously sexy as she did ten years ago, but still good—at least a seven and a half out of ten. Bob is in for a treat.

Brown eyes beam back at her in the mirror. Her black dress hugs her curves like a formula 1 race car, screaming sexy in a stylish Italian accent. She loves the contours of her voluptuous body, an ivory cello waiting for the vibration of a taut bow. Hopefully Bob's one of those guys who likes a little junk in the trunk, a little cushion for the push'n, a real woman, big and beautiful, not one of those salad eating stick women—if not, she'll just leave his superficial, media-manipulated ass in the restaurant. It wouldn't be the first time she'd walked out on a date. Why waste time?

She spritzes another cloud of vanilla perfume onto her neck, just in case the first two weren't enough. Winking at herself, she walks out of the bathroom; her work is done—two hours to transform herself into a real Aphrodite—time well spent. It's a lot to ask for, but she hopes Bob looks as good as she does. Blind dates are nerve racking. It was her overbearing mother's idea. The old bag is always meddling in Marsha's personal affairs.

"You're thirty-four now," her mom had badgered. "You're no spring chicken. Better hurry up the man hunt if you wanna husband."

"Jeez mom, I'm not eighty. I don't have cobwebs between my legs. I'm waiting for the right guy."

"Well, you know, lionesses hunt, pigs wait around to be fed."

"Mom!"

"Cool down. I'm just giv'n ya a hard time cuz I want grandbabies."

Marsha hates that conversation even more than she hates being single. And to make it worse, her mother can't let it go, bringing it up at least every few weeks, as if Marsha has forgotten that time is slipping away. She wants a steady man in her life. She'd almost been married once, had a ring and everything. But then she'd found the asshole in bed with her best friend and she cut them both out of her life.

Bob's late. Not a good sign of character. Hopefully he's a better date than the last guy, who'd trumpeted his arrival by blowing a melody of colors into his handkerchief. What kind of man carries a rag full of snot in their pocket? It's disgusting. And snotty pants hadn't even paid for dinner. She'd never get serious about a guy that didn't treat his woman like a queen. At least he wasn't Steve, who'd leaned over at the end of their only date and whispered, "Does Marsha want her marsh plowed?" Perverted jerk! She'd slapped that smug grin off his face in a hurry. A man has to earn her rosy jewel; he can't just buy it with a steak dinner and a slice of New York cheese cake. Scumbag.

He sure was cute though. Too bad he'd had to go and open his dirty mouth; she would have enjoyed a jolly rogering. It feels like forever since she's had a man. A dry spell? – more like a drought. Maybe Bob will be the rain maker.

The doorbell rings and she sizes Bob up through the peeking-glass. He's tall, which is good. Broad shouldered too, so he probably has a big dick. His hair's thinning, but she could handle that—he'd get a few good years out of it before his hairline retreated too high and he'd have to shave it all off and grow a goatee to compensate. She'd be in her late thirties by then. Women in their thirties date bald men. It's totally normal. Bald guys can still be cute, unless they're too skinny. Then they look like aliens. At least Bob's a solid hunk of man, even if he is soft in a few places. He brought flowers too, which means that he's not cheap and will pay for dinner, so that's a relief. There's no worse way to end a bad date than by coughing up forty bucks.

It's his sweater-vest that bothers her. Who wears a plaid sweater-vest in the twenty-first century? He probably has some boring job like a salesman. All in all, she decides he's a six—which is good enough, considering her eggs are drying up.

~ Meanwhile ~

Bob wonders why 'what's her name' is taking so long to answer the door. He must have caught her in the bathroom. The wooden porch groans as he shifts his weight nervously from foot to foot, cupping his hand in front of his mouth to check his breath. Minty fresh, his gum performs its job marvellously. He wonders what the world must have been like before gum—horrible, that's what—people every-where walking around with bad breath. One thing he can't stand is a close talker with bad breath. Bob's sight is poor at best, but his olfac-tory abilities are almost canine.

His mom set up this date. Bless her heart; she cares so much about Bob and his brother. He trusts her. Apparently 'what's her name' is the daughter of one of his mom's cribbage friends. Something like that, anyway. He can't quite remember. He's too nervous. He hasn't been on a date in over a year—a fact that makes him feel like he's inside a pressure cooker. Looking around to make sure he's alone, he takes advantage of his last moment of privacy and picks out the polyester underwear that's wedged between his buns like sandwich meat.

He wishes he could remember his date's name. His mom had told him, but it slipped his mind, vanished like a forgotten dream. Not knowing her name had annoyed him to great length the night before, when he'd wanted to masturbate and couldn't check out her picture on Facebook. Masturbating without an image is like going down a waterslide without the water. Sure it's possible, but it takes longer to finish and usually leaves you with friction-burn.

The best tactic for learning her name, he decides, is to introduce himself right away so that she introduces herself in response. The longer he waits, the more awkward it'll become to ask.

Wondering if he should ring the doorbell again, he leans forward to see if he can see through the peeking-hole in reverse. A dark shape behind the glass moves suddenly and the door opens.

A waft of perfume billows out from the open door. It envelops him, sinking in—a sharp chemical concoction with the undercurrent of vanilla. It attacks his nostrils so ferociously his eyes water. He can barely breathe; she has the fragrant pungency of a burning brothel.

Before he has time to react, the big eyed, curvaceous beauty smiles and says, "Bob, I presume." She hugs him, pressing her firm, round breasts against his chest—the excitement of which almost makes up for the fact that his nose is inches from her perfume drenched neck.

"Bob's my name, don't wear it out," he replies, stepping back, mentally cursing himself for the cheesy opening line. Why couldn't he be more suave? He'd watched hundreds of romantic comedies, read books on dating, and watched dating tips on YouTube, but just couldn't seem to hone the skill. At least he looks sharp in the new sweater-vest his mom helped him pick out.

"Ready for a night to remember?" He asks, wishing he had asked her name, but impaired by a sudden attack of shyness.

She giggles, "You bet. Let's get going."

He extends his arm to lead her towards his Prius parked across the street.

~

Marsha bats her eye-lashes at Bob. He's a little nerdy, but in a cute way. His opening line was corny, but she's willing to pass it off as nervousness. He has a great smile—earnest in the way it creases his cheeks. And she likes the way he's holding out his arm like a gentleman. Maybe chivalry isn't dead, after all. Maybe the nerds have kept it alive—hooked to life support and barely breathing, but alive none the less.

She notices him holding his breath and thinks he must be in shock. She can't blame him though—she is rather breath-taking. His eyes even look a little watery; he must be overwhelmed by her exquisite feminine stature. Her goddess-like powers never cease to amaze.

As they walk arm in arm, she gives Bob's bicep a subtle squeeze, slightly disappointed by its doughy consistency. If they start dating, he'll have to begin an exercise program. She's good for men like that, influences them to better themselves. Men need a good woman behind them, pushing them in the right direction. At least Bob drives a new car. Toyota's are a practical choice; they run forever—he must be the kind of guy that thinks about the future.

Once inside, he starts the car. To Marsha's disappointment, distorted rock guitar blares through his speakers. It sounds like a bunch of guys using instruments to jerk off their egos by showing off how fast they can play. Outwardly, she smiles, but inside she thinks it's time for his musical tastes to mature.

Grabbing his iPhone from the docking station, she slides the screen to unlock it and brings up Soundcloud. "Time for some Soul Docta to get us in the mood. Don't you think?"

"Oh, ya. Play whatever you want."

Female vocals, oozing Auto-Tune, fill the car, backed by the tech-pop groove of electronica. "So, what do you do for a living?" she asks—partly because she wants to make conversation, and partly because of the role it plays in the direction the date is headed.

"I'm a salesman." He replies, flashing his smile, which suddenly looks fake—like a personified sales pitch. "It keeps me busy. I'm getting a little tired of flying to Asia every second month though."

"Oh, what do you sell?" She asks, really wanting to know how much money he makes, but knowing it's rude to ask.

"I'm a sales rep for Toyota. Sell to car lots all over the West Coast."

Impressed, Marsha smiles, importing cars sounds lucrative. Maybe Bob's a seven after all. "Sounds like a good job. I'd love to travel one day."

"Yeah, it pays the bills. All my travelling so far has been work related. I'm getting to know Tokyo pretty well. One day I'd like to stay in Asia, maybe get a tan on the beach in Thailand. I just need someone to come with me. How 'bout you?"

"Oh, I'd love to come to Asia."

"Ahhh. No. I mean what do you do?"

"Oh, of course. Haha, silly me. I make women beautiful. I work at Heavenly Springs Spa. Hair, nails, facials, I do it all. A Jill of all trades, haha."

Marsha stares at the road ahead, nervous about how fast Bob's driving, but not wanting to risk saying anything and sounding bossy on the first date. And what's the deal with having the window all the way down? It's February for God's sake. They pull up to Earls, and she's disappointed with the unoriginality of his restaurant choice—with all that car importing money, you'd think he'd really want to wow her.

~

Bob gets out of the car as fast as his chubby body can, and inhales the fresh air, finally free from the perfume's death grip. It's the aromatic equivalent of Genghis Khan, raping and pillaging his nostrils with the force of a ruthless army. He'd practically had the pedal to the floor, trying to shorten the agony of the drive.

Taking 'what's her name's arm, he leads her to the door. Their reflection stuns him. They look natural together, elegantly radiant. Her beauty leaps from her voluptuous body and her dark, attentive eyes. It envelops him in its glow, making him look like a stud worthy of such a prize. He wants to linger in front of the reflective glass, but doesn't dare. He can't risk seeming weird, or worse, desperate.

Once seated at a table, he attempts a conversation. "So, what do you do for fun?"

'What's her name' smiles, "Shopping. I could spend hours in the mall. I love the new mall on Fitzwilliams St. The one with the glass elevators. They've got a great new Cineplex in there, too."

"I love it in there. Sometimes I get lost just window shopping." Bob lies. The mall is his personal hell. In and out, that's his motto. The only good area is the food court. It's his favorite place to eat because you can mix and match. Where else can you have New York fries with a slice of pizza and an A & W root-beer?

"I've been going to a lot of dinner parties lately," she says. "My friend Sam started dating an artist. He's been taking us to art shows. I never knew how fun it was—the wine and snacks and conversation."

An artist. That's intimidating. Now he's going to have to try twice as hard to seem cultured. He fears 'what's her name' is probably already bored. Under the cover of the table, Bob nervously twists his napkin as the pressure mounts. He worries that the conversation's going nowhere. He's drowning, wondering why he can sell cars so well, but can't sell himself. If only his dick was a car, he'd sell it to her all night long. *Holy cheese wiz. Get your mind out of the gutter*, he warns himself. *Focus. Be witty. Close this deal.*

He wants to change the subject, but his mind is blank. Why is it so damn hot in this building? He worries he'll start to sweat, which would be mortifying. The thought seems to increase the temperature. He can't blow this date; it's the best opportunity he's had to meet a woman in over a year. If only she'd give him a chance, she'd see how much love he has inside. He would walk the length of the earth to make her happy, if she would just free him of the torment of being alone.

The silence grows, surrounding the table, enveloping them in an awkward calm that hangs thick with self doubt. Bob feels a bead of sweat trickle out of his armpit, gathering momentum as it snakes a horrifying trail down his lumpy side to his polyester boxers, where it's absorbed, mingling with his ass sweat. The room seems to be shrinking. The air is so thick he can barely breathe. For a brief moment, Bob thinks that his best bet is to get up and run. But then the waiter arrives, saving Bob from the manic chidings of his self-conscious mind.

"How are you two tonight?" the waiter asks.

"Great! We're on a date," She replies, eyes shining.

Soothed by her enthusiasm, wanting to loosen up, Bob orders two glasses of Chardonnay. The waiter quickly disappears, leaving the love seekers to themselves.

~

The waiter retrieves the wine. It's a slow night so he watches the couple by the window, eavesdropping on their conversation each time he checks up on their table. The man looks nervous; his eyes shift as he drinks his wine a little too fast. To pass the time, the waiter creates make-believe lives about the people he serves. He decides that the man is an accountant from out of town, here on business, foreclosing properties of families hit hard by the economic crash. His date is a hooker. She'd be quite beautiful if she toned down her make-up and lost twenty pounds. But, by the way she put back a steak dinner, slice of chocolate cake, and a bottle of wine, he doubts she'll lose the weight. She's quite animated, but in a high-pitched annoying kind of way. The man hardly talks, just nods and smiles thoughtfully, peppering the conversation with just enough verbiage to keep it alive. The waiter imagines himself on a date with the woman. He'd probably sleep with her, but wouldn't call her after.

~

Bob picks up the check, happy to treat such a beautiful woman to dinner. When the waiter shows up, 'what's her name' is in the middle of a story, so Bob sends him away with his Visa. She's talking about work, some customer's little dog. The lady had wanted her hair cut to match her poodle's, or some such stupid shit. Bob's mind keeps wandering, but his date doesn't seem to notice. Her beauty is distracting. She laughs at her own story and Bob picks up the cue to laugh along. He imagines what she looks like naked. He'd love to see her lying in the sun by a river.

He drives home even though he knows he's had a little too much wine. It's not characteristic behavior, but he doesn't want to take a cab—can't come across as unmanly. He's only had a few glasses; he's not drunk by any stretch of the mind. They arrive, tipsy and enthusiastic, and he smiles, "Thank you for such a lovely evening."

"Oh, you are very welcome, Bobby boy. It was my pleasure."

Her lips glisten in the soft streetlight. He wants to kiss her, to grab her sexy black dress and pull her close. He longs to rub his face in her big breasts, sucking on her nipples, kissing her flesh all over. He wants to run naked with her through a field and fall into her embrace. He yearns to dive into her, feel what it's like inside her, the slippery warmth of her womanhood.

Instead, he rests his hand at his side so she doesn't see it tremble. They look each other in the eyes. Deep in his loins, the gods-of-love dance their fiery tango. Longing rises up, consuming him, burning from within. But he can't bring himself to action.

Then she leans in, pressing her cherry-red lips against his, simultaneously thrusting him into Heaven and Hell. The sensation of her lips, her smooth tongue as it explores the contours of his mouth, is brilliant, but it comes with a catch. The onion and garlic mashed into her potatoes remains ripe on her breath. The flavor makes him want to gag, to turn away in disgust, but he can't. It feels marvelous to finally be kissing a beautiful woman. Her lips are so soft, and her hand is on his chest, rubbing, exploring—God, it feels good. It makes him feel like a man. A sexy, desirable man. He holds his breath as he kisses back, eyes closed as his pink, flubbery tongue fumbles around the inside of her mouth, touching her teeth as much as her tongue.

She breaks away, opening the car door and getting out. Her eyes are like stars in the night air. Her radiance shocks him as she lingers by the car door, angelically illuminated in the glow of the streetlight. For a second he thinks she's going to invite him in. His heart batters about in his chest like a panicked cat in a sack. His mind suddenly jumps to the prehistoric condom he's been optimistically carrying around in his wallet for years. It's so old, he wonders if it will hold. It's probably fine though, he's no superhero in bed.

"What's her name' speaks first. "I had a beautiful time with you tonight, Bob." She kisses him again, this time lightly on the cheek. "Call me," she whispers, handing him her business card.

He glances at the card to learn her name. Marsha. Marvelous Marsha. Magnificent Marsha.

"Me too, Marsha," he replies. "You are exquisite. Thank you."

"Goodnight, Bob."

"Goodnight."

She turns and walks towards her house. He watches her all the way to her door, admiring the gentle swing of her hips, the bounce of her delicious ass. Then, once she's safely inside, he starts the engine and drives to the end of the block. Once out of view, he parks the car and calls a cab, not wanting to drive home drunk.

While waiting, he coughs, then pulls one of Marsha's hairs from his mouth. *Gross*, he thinks, and then laughs at himself. At what point do body parts become no longer beautiful? All night he had been in awe of Marsha's hair, yearning to touch it, to kiss it, to run his fingers through it. And now here it was, on his lips, and it repulsed him. Why?—because it is no longer part of her. Once plucked from her head, it transforms from beautiful to disgusting. So what is it then that we are attracted to, he asks himself. It's not solely the body. He longs to kiss her leg, but sever her leg from her body and he couldn't get away from it fast enough. Would her leg still be part of her if it was detached? No. So, at what point would we no longer be ourselves if we slowly removed our body parts?

The cab pulls up and Bob gets in, laughing at himself for his drunken musings. He's had too much wine.

~

Marsha leans against the inside of her front door. She can still feel Bob on her lips. He'll call. He'd be crazy not to. He'd been stunned by her beauty and charm all night. And that kiss in the car had definitely sealed the deal. He's not stylish or handsome, but she'll give him another shot. She imagines them together, lying on a beach in Thailand. Then she walks upstairs, lights three vanilla scented candles, and runs a bubble bath.

~

Once at home, Bob sits in front of his computer and turns it on. There's a box of Kleenex next to the screen. He pulls out Marsha's business card and kisses it. It smells like Vanilla. Her perfume lingers on him. The scent gently arouses recollections of her adorability. In a gentle voice, he repeats her name a few times, enjoying the musical lilt of it. Then he signs into Facebook and types the name Marsha Lane into the search bar.

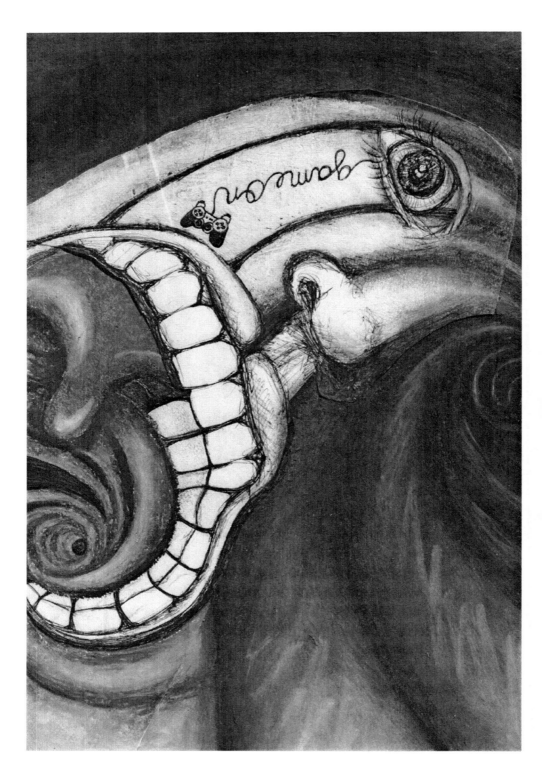

16

GAME ON

The school bell sent the class into an ecstatic rush. Binders slapped closed, backpacks zipped shut, and children bolted for the door amid a symphony of laughter.

"Don't forget that your science projects are due next Wednesday. The science fair is a week Friday, and I want you all to be ready," Mrs. Jacobs called out.

Jackson sat at his desk until the rest of the children had left the room. He made himself seem busy so as not to draw attention from Mrs. Jacobs, who was marking the math quizzes. He doodled in his binder, adding a sword to the hand of a warrior elf. For added effect, he outlined flames coming from the sword, licking upward toward the top of the page. When he figured that the coast was clear, he got up and walked to the door and looked out.

Mrs. Jacobs called him over to her desk. "Is everything all right, Jackson? You seemed a little distracted today."

"Oh, I was just thinking about the science project."

"OK. I'm counting on you, Jackson. Our class could really use that new computer, and you're our best hope for winning. How are the ants?"

"They built lots of tunnels, and I already drew a map. They build slower in the cold. I haven't mixed the red ones and blacks together yet though."

"Ok, well don't wait too long; you need a full report on how they interact under the various stimuli."

"I won't."

"See you tomorrow," Mrs. Jacobs said. She looked old and tired.

Jackson thought it must be hard to be a teacher. He smiled and touched her hand. "Thanks for your help."

The hall was almost empty. Jackson strode towards the door, looking over his shoulder to make sure no one was following him. Once outside, he crossed the playground to the bike parking lot and quickly unlocked his bike, letting out a sigh of relief.

Billy stepped out from behind a dumpster and started walking towards Jackson, pounding his palm with his fat fist, his face twisted with a sadistic grin. Jackson mounted his bike. His hands shook so violently that he could barely hold the handlebars as he began to pedal. Before Jackson could get his momentum up, Billy ran in front of the smaller boy and kicked the bike's front tire, sending Jackson over the handlebars. He landed on the gravel face first, scraping his chin and biting his lip. Picking himself up, he tried to hold back his tears while he looked at Billy.

"Please, just let me go. I didn't do anything."

Billy scoffed, "You're dead meat, Jackson. You think you're special because you won the math game today? Huh?"

"No, I—"

"You're just a weak nerd. You know what happens to weak nerds?"

"They get good jobs when they grow up," Jackson said. He winced, wishing he had kept his mouth shut. The older boy's fist slammed into Jackson's eye, sending a flash of light behind his eyelids and snapping his head back. A sob escaped, and a tear rolled down his cheek. He wiped it away.

Billy laughed, "You little pussy. Why don't you go cry to mommy?" He grabbed Jackson by the collar of his shirt and pulled him close. "What's the matter, wimp? Scared?" The bully's foul breath engulfed the undersized boy.

"Leave me alone."

Billy threw Jackson on the ground and then kicked him in the ribs. Jackson rolled into a ball, unable to hold back his tears. His body heaved as the salty drops streaked down his cheeks. Billy kicked Jackson again then snickered and walked away. "See you tomorrow, Jackie."

* * * # * * *

Jackson parked his bike in his back yard. He paused on the rotting wooden steps leading up to his back door and took a deep breath. The handle on the sliding door was broken off, so he pressed his palms flat on the glass to open it. It rumbled on its track.

"How many times have I told you not to smudge the glass?" his mom said, giving Jackson 'the look'.

"Sorry, Mom."

"It's OK. Just try to remember."

Roger sat on the living room couch, a beer in his hand. A large, empty bag of Zesty Taco Doritos sat on the floor next to him, the remains of which lay sprinkled in his beard and on the cushions. A plump, hairy hand explored his belly button for lint. His eyes didn't leave the Raiders game.

Jackson's mom sat at the kitchen table reading a romance novel. Her thick red hair was tied up in a bun, and her reading glasses rested on her freckled nose. Jackson walked into the kitchen to grab a cookie from the jar. His mom looked up at him. "Oh my God. What happened to your face?"

"It's nothing. I just wiped out on my bike."

Roger looked up from the game. "Is that kid pick'n on ya again? It's time to man up, boy. You're ten years old. I'm tell'n ya, if you don't toughen up, people are gonna walk all over ya your whole life. Come 'ere, lemme see your face. And bring a beer."

Jackson took a Pilsner from the case in the fridge and walked over to the couch, handing it to Roger. The greasy man took it and looked at the boy's face, grabbing it around the chin, squishing the boy's lips into fish lips. Jackson flinched.

"Stop being a baby. It's a scratch." Roger tapped Jackson's cheek with his palm.

Jackson's mom said, "Go clean yourself up. Barb might come over later, and I don't want her to see you like that."

Jackson washed his face then went to his room. He peered into the ant farm on his dresser, looking at the new tunnels. Dropping in a small lizard, Jackson wondered how the ants would react to the threat. Then he sat on his bed, opened up his science notebook, pulled out a pen, and began to write. *Roger's a penis head.* He quickly scribbled over it, looking over his shoulder. He knew Roger would never come into his room, but he didn't want to risk it; one beating was enough for today. He closed his book, deciding to work on his homework later. He turned on his Playstation.

Game On

Jackson the Mighty Warrior Elf rode his stallion towards the village. His long blond hair flapped gallantly in the wind. A dragon circled above, threatening the village and, more importantly, threatening Princess Athea. Jackson took aim with his bow and shot an arrow at the dragon's heart. It missed. The dragon looked down and saw the elf. It dove towards Jackson, setting the roofs of the huts on fire as it drew closer. Jackson fired another arrow, which bounced off the dragon's thick scales.

The dragon landed heavily in the middle of the village. The villagers fled in all directions, screaming for their lives. The beast caught a villager in its jaws. With one solid crunch, it swallowed the man. It turned to look at Jackson, the yellow of its eyes glowing with malice. Smoke seeped out of its nostrils, hovering around its blood-stained teeth before dispersing into the air. Its snake-like, smoke-tarnished tongue jutted from its ugly mouth, licking its lips.

Jackson dismounted from his horse and let it run to safety. Drawing his sword and shield, he looked the dragon in the eyes, preparing himself for battle. The dragon let out a blast of fire. The elf crouched behind his shield. The metal turned red, burning him. His health dropped to 90%.

The dragon stopped the flame to inhale. Seizing the opportunity, Jackson rushed towards the dragon. It turned and struck out with its tail. Jackson slid on his back as the spikes of the tail passed over him, grazing his armor. The elf stood and raised his sword, slashing the dragon's back leg. It kicked out and caught the elf in the chest, sending him skidding across the dirt road. Jackson's health fell to 78%.

He sprinted in for another attack, leaping onto the dragon's back, and grabbing hold of its scales. The beast twisted its neck around, trying to bite the elf. Jackson held on, just out of reach of the dragon's teeth. Huge leathery wings beat the air, raising a thick cloud of dust. Jackson coughed and closed his eyes as the dragon took to the air. It flew, twisting and turning, trying to throw the elf off. Holding on with one hand, Jackson raised his sword. His arm rippled with strength as it came down, driving the point of the sword into the dragon's back. The beast shrieked with agony, writhing as it fell from the sky. Jackson grabbed the sword with both hands and thrust it deeper into the monstrous creature as they fell. They crashed into the ground, spewing debris in all directions. Jackson tumbled across the dusty road, his sword still stuck in the dragon's back. 44%.

In one quick movement, the dragon leapt on top of Jackson and pinned him to the earth with its talon. Jackson's health plummeted to 26% as he was crushed under the weight of the beast. Its sharp heel pressed so hard into Jackson's chest that he thought it might pulverize his insides. The dragon bent so low its face was inches from Jackson's, its thick breath engulfing him. Smoke billowed from the dragon's mouth, making Jackson cough violently. 18%. Jackson could see the blood vessels in the dragon's eye as it twitched with wickedness. A drop of blood-tinged saliva slithered out from the dragon's mouth and landed on Jackson's cheek. Claws dug into Jackson's shoulder. 9%. A red alert flashed in the sky, warning Jackson that he was at critical health.

The elf frantically reached into his pouch. The dragon's mouth opened wide, revealing rows of large fangs. Its head came down fiercely, snapping at the elf. As the beast's head came down full force, Jackson thrust a dagger into its mouth, piercing the roof and driving the blade into the dragon's brain. The beast fell dead with a thud. Jackson wriggled out from under its mass, his health now at 2%. His body blinked yellow, meaning one more hit and he would die. He pulled the last remaining magic potion from his pouch and drank it, restoring his health to 100%.

Looking up, he saw the Red Army storming the castle. Drat, he thought, I've got to save the Princess. He whistled for his horse.

Pause

Jackson saved the game and rushed to the bathroom, unleashing a torrent of yellow bubbles into the stained toilet bowl. He dribbled a little onto the floor, but didn't stop to wipe it up. As he hurried back to his bedroom, his mom called out, "Jackson, dinner."

They ate in front of the TV, Jackson shoving bite after bite of his pizza pocket into his mouth. His mom turned to him, "What's the rush, little man? That game's still gonna be there in twenty minutes." Jackson smiled, his mouth bursting with processed cheese. His mom rubbed his head. "Tell me about school. Do you have any homework?"

Roger turned his head from the episode of *Family Guy*, "I'm try'n to watch this."

Jackson's mom looked at him. "Let it rest Roger. I'm trying to talk to my son."

Roger's eyes narrowed and he clenched his jaw. "Don't take that tone with me, girl. Don't forget whose house this is."

Jackson squirmed in his seat, wishing he could eat in his room. His mom spoke up again. "Don't you forget who pays the bills around here."

The ogre staggered to his feet. Realizing how drunk he was, Jackson's mom quickly apologized, but it was too late.

"You fuck'n skank. After all I've done for you. Letting you and your little shit son live in my house."

A sudden urge to stab Roger with his knife overcame Jackson. In his mind's eye, he pictured himself standing over a cowering Roger, scaring the meanness right out of the thug. But he knew it was no use. Roger was too big and emotionally ugly for Jackson to fight. How could a boy battle a man who is bitter to the core? Overwhelmed by his own inadequacy, knowing he couldn't protect his mother, Jackson started to cry.

The brute turned to him and grabbed hold of his shirt, "Time to man up, you little pussy." He slapped Jackson's plate out of his hand.

It smashed on the coffee table, sending shards of porcelain tumbling across the shag carpet. "Crying's for babies."

Jackson's mom began picking up the pieces, trying to hold back her tears. Roger dropped Jackson then turned to her, yelling.

Jackson snuck away, tears streaking his pale cheeks. He shut the door to his room and turned up the volume on his Playstation, but could still hear Roger's voice thundering up the stairs.

✳✳✳Game on✳✳✳

Jackson the Warrior Elf rode fearlessly into battle against the Red Army. With his sword drawn, he rode straight into the thick of the crowd, chopping off the heads of his enemies. A shrill scream pierced the air, echoing out of the princess' tower. He fought his way to the gate, cutting through the crowd with his sword. A large ugly troll stood guarding the gate. Jackson shot it in the chest with an arrow. Enraged, the troll charged. Jackson shot the troll again, but it kept coming. Jackson's horse reared up and Jackson swung his sword. The troll smashed the horse in the face, sending both the horse and Jackson tumbling to the ground. His health fell to 96%. Towering over the elf, the troll grabbed hold of Jackson with both hands, picking him up and holding him face to face. Jackson head-butted the creature in the bridge of the nose. Blood poured down its chin, but it didn't let go. It growled, deep and guttural, then started to crush Jackson in a bear hug. Jackson's sword fell to the ground and his health began to drop. 94%, 92%, 90%. Jackson kicked the troll in the balls. The troll squeezed harder. 86%, 82%, 78%. Pulling his dagger from his belt, Jackson drove the blade into the side of the troll. It let go. Jackson picked up his sword and sliced it upwards in one quick swoosh, severing the troll's head from its body.

The elf ran through the gate into the castle, quickly slamming the door to shut out the Red Army. Another scream echoed out of the princess' tower. Jackson sprinted up the castle stairs and kicked down the door. The Red Prince stood over the princess. She was backed up in the corner screaming, her night gown torn up the side.

The Red Prince turned to face Jackson. A scar ran from his forehead, across his right eye, and down his cheek. His skin was blood-red and his mouth was full of sharp metal teeth. Drawing his sword, he smiled at Jackson. "Welcome to the party."

Jackson rushed at him, swinging his sword at the Prince's head. The villain blocked it and kicked Jackson in the ribs, sending him stumbling back into the wall. Jackson's health fell to 70%. The Red Prince swung his sword, but Jackson somersaulted to the side to escape the blow. The fiend swung again. Jackson blocked the blow with his blade, sending sparks flickering down. He slashed out and their swords clanked together. The Prince's sword grazed Jackson's hand, knocking his sword to the ground. 55%. The Prince rushed in. Jackson dodged the attack and kicked the Prince in the ribs, then grabbed him around the neck, putting him in a head lock with one arm, and holding the Prince's sword-bearing arm with the other. He stepped onto the Prince's foot and twisted his arm until the sword fell to the ground with a clank.

Wriggling free, the Prince turned, catching Jackson in the face with a left hook. The elf stumbled backward, his health falling to 30%. The Prince leapt on him, tackling him to the ground. Straddling the elf, the Prince began raining down a fury of punches. Jackson's health swiftly plunged. He drew his dagger from his belt but the Prince immediately struck it from his hand. The red warning flashed a critical health alert. Jackson bucked his hips trying to throw off the prince, but the prince was too strong. The Prince struck the fatal blow.

Game Over.

#

Jackson got up and kicked the Playstation in frustration. He hated *Legends of Old* anyway. It was a stupid game. He flopped onto his bed and started to cry, eventually falling asleep with his face pressed into a wet pillow.

The ant farm rested by the window, forgotten.

The next day after school, Jackson stepped onto the playground and stealthily walked to his bike. Billy was nowhere in sight. Jackson mounted his bike and began hurriedly riding home, stopping when he saw Billy across the playground sitting on a young boy's chest and slapping a younger boy in the face. Jackson could see the crying boy's eyes, his torn shirt, and his bloody elbows. Jackson gripped his handle bars so tight that his knuckles turned white and muscles rippled up his thin forearm. He had a vision of himself smashing Billy in the head with a rock and saving the boy. He fantasized for a few seconds about confronting Billy. Then he began peddling home, shoulders drooped as he stared at the ground in front of his bike. What could he do to stop the bully anyway?

The guilt of failing to act hung heavily on his shoulders, slowing his pace to a crawl. Was he really someone who walked away in a world where evil flourishes when left un-confronted? On the surface, Jackson felt the pain of being a victim, but there was a deeper pain, a pain that struck to his core. It existed within a layer of himself too deep for his child's consciousness to access, but it was there none-theless. It was the deeply rooted knowledge that one creates themselves through their thoughts and actions, and that by riding away, he was creating himself as a coward instead of a hero.

Once home, Jackson slid the glass door open and stepped inside his house. His mom sat on the couch watching TV. As she looked up at him, Jackson could see the fresh bruise forming under her sunglasses.

"Where's Roger?" he asked. He had noticed Roger's car parked out front.

"Gone for a walk in the woods. He had to burn off some steam." She winced, holding her ribs as she spoke.

Hatred for Roger flowed through Jackson's veins. How could the world be so cruel? His mom never did anything to deserve this. Somebody had to do something. If only he could turn himself into a warrior elf, he'd make Roger pay.

Jackson walked upstairs to his bedroom and sank into his bed. Tears blurred his vision. He drove his small fist into his pillow, clenching his jaw so hard that his face vibrated. Sitting up on his bed, Jackson looked out his bedroom window. He thought about the boy that Billy had been tormenting. He thought about Billy walking home, unpunished. Was there no fairness in the world?

He looked at his ant farm, remembering the lizard. Panicked, he picked up the glass cage, fearing for the lives of his ant friends. How could he have released a bully on them? The dirt crawled with their movement. Relieved, he looked for the lizard. Its dead body was covered with ants. They had dealt with the threat, turning it into ant food. They had protected their queen. But how was that possible?— the lizard was so much bigger? A paradigm shift in the boy's reasoning occurred, as he realized it is possible for the small to defeat the big. The gears in his mind spun.

He walked downstairs. His mom stared blankly at the TV, not registering Jackson's presence. Her wounds were more than just physical. Her spirit was broken. If he didn't do something, her suffering would get worse. He had to protect her, like the ants protected their queen. Taking Roger's key from the hook next to the front door, he stepped outside. Roger's Plymouth sat in the driveway, the sun reflecting off its red paint.

Jackson got in and slid the key into the ignition, turning it just like he had seen his mom do thousands of times. The engine rumbled to a start. He could barely see over the steering wheel. He put the lever to the R like his mom did when she backed out of the driveway. The car lurched backward onto the street and then came to a sudden stop as Jackson's foot found the brake. He pushed the lever to the D, and the car leapt forward. Jackson smiled; driving in real life wasn't that much harder than in video games.

He drove down the quiet street a few blocks, then made a left onto Billy's street. His lips curled with a smile as he saw Billy riding his skateboard home. Pushing the pedal down, Jackson sped up as he approached Billy from behind. He looked at the speedometer, 30 Km/h. Jackson turned the wheel and the front bumper of the car caught Billy in the hip. The boy slammed onto the hood and then rolled off to the side, landing on the pavement with a thud and sliding to a stop. Jackson slowed the car just enough for Billy to look up at the license-plate, then Jackson hit the gas and the car peeled away.

That night, as Jackson sat in front of the TV eating dinner with his mom and Roger, there was a knock at the door. Roger opened it, and was startled to see two police officers standing in the doorway.

The tall, thin officer asked, "Are you Roger Lane?"

"Yeah. What's this all about, officer?" The scent of rum spilled from Roger's mouth with every word.

"Put your hands behind your back; you're under arrest."

"What are you talking about?"

"This afternoon at approximately quarter after three, you hit a young boy down the street with that red Plymouth in the driveway."

"What?"

"The boy suffered a bruised hip and broken elbow and you just drove away."

"What are you talking about?"

The officer handcuffed Roger and began walking him towards the car. "People like you make me sick. Hit and run is a serious offence." He turned to Jackson's mom, "If you'd like to see Roger, you can come by the station. You might want to think about getting him a lawyer."

Roger tried to wrestle free. The officer slammed him onto the hood of the cop car before shoving him into the backseat. Once in the front seat, the officer turned to Roger, "You're going away for a long time, buddy."

The car pulled out of the driveway and drove down the street, leaving Jackson and his mom standing in the driveway. Jackson's mom looked down at Jackson, confusion wrinkling her freckled forehead. Jackson grabbed her hand and looked up at her. He felt light and free, as if he could fly. "Don't worry, Mom. Everything's going to be OK."

17

SOMETHING ABOUT LOVE

Vladislav picked up the broom and used it to knock on the ceiling, warning Tom that he was late for their daily walk. Tom answered with three knocks of his own, signaling that he'd be right down. Vladislav unlocked the front door of his bachelor suite, then shuffled past the stack of books cluttering the hall and stepped into the bathroom to relieve himself once more, so he wouldn't be inconvenienced in public.

The pee was slow to come so he rested his hand on the wall and leaned his weight into it. His legs felt tired. He observed his reflection in the mirror, noticing how the dark skin sagged under his eyes. Time had morphed his cheeks into jowls and caused his neck to resemble that of a turkey. He'd been losing weight ever since

Inga's death, shrinking until one day he would disappear from this world altogether.

His apartment still felt foreign to him. It had been kind of Dmitri, his son, to agree to pay the rent until the house sold. Dmitri had even found an apartment in Vlad's best-friend's building. But what Vlad really wanted was to see his children and grandchildren more often. He secretly wanted to move in with Dmitri, but would never ask. It's unfortunate how life works, he thought. You have children. You love them, make sacrifices for them, dedicate yourself to them, and move to the other side of the world to secure their future. Then they grow up, get caught up in a culture that values image and material progress over family, and they move away, visiting just enough so they don't feel guilty for being an absent child. He wasn't bitter though. He loved his kids and wanted them to be happy. He just wished he was more a part of their lives.

For forty years, Vladislav had lived in the same house with Inga. He'd imagined them dying together in that house. He hadn't imagined this. Her gone, and him left—eighty-two years old and with a body healthy enough to make it to a hundred, the last years of his life drawn out and lonely. But still he was glad that he'd outlived her. He wouldn't wish this loneliness on her.

The small apartment was tangled with trinkets from his life with Inga, a life vanished from his present existence, a life that could now only exist in memories. A collection of porcelain dolls took up residence in every corner, sitting on any and every available space, be it refrigerator, windowsill, or countertop. He'd always thought the dolls trite, with their little dresses, rosy cheeks, and glass eyes. But after Inga's death, the dolls had become precious reminders of the life they'd shared. Pictures spanning the spectrum of their life covered the walls: photos of their wedding, photos of them together with the kids, photos of them as teenagers in Russia before the war had ended and they'd come to Canada to start over.

Tom knocked on the door and Vlad shuffled past the worn couch. His knee creaked. The couch was far too large for the small living room, not to mention that the seams were torn and it sagged in the middle. He could never get rid of it though. How could he give up the couch he and Inga had conceived their second child on?

Tom let himself in before Vlad reached the door. Tom was all smiles—always was at this time of day, when the sun was high and the day fresh and full of possibilities. It wasn't until the sun was down that his mood would falter—when he would go home to his apartment alone, sit in front of the TV or stereo, and continue whatever vintage bottle of scotch he was currently 'testing'. A boyish charm glistened in Tom's crescent eyes, which were just slightly marked by the seventy nine years that had taken his hair and fattened his belly. He'd stop people wherever he was—on the bus, in the line at the supermarket. He'd break the ice with a joke, then talk and talk as if he'd known them for years. He'd tell them about his life, his travels, his wives, keeping on until they grew impatient and politely excused themselves. It was a game to him, really.

He made sure to leave his apartment everyday and talk to someone. His biggest fear was that nobody would notice when he died. To die alone, the world continuing on as normal for days or even weeks, unaware of the rotting corpse in the apartment until the smell grew so pungent it seeped into the hallway with enough clout to alarm the neighbors; that's the worst possible end to life that Tom could imagine. It would be like his life meant nothing to anyone. The fear drove him to talk to every clerk or public service worker within five blocks from his house. So that when he was gone people would say, "I wonder whatever happened to that nice old man who would come in here every week. He sure was friendly."

In spite of his fear of dying alone, Tom was full of the satisfaction of having really lived. He'd been a successful surgeon, travelled the world, and always sought adventure. "The body," he'd once told Vlad, "is not a temple to be meticulously kept pure. It is a vehicle to be used—ridden and driven. And when I die, it'll be unexpectedly, scotch in one hand, cigar in the other, in a body thoroughly used up and worn out."

The two men embraced before leaving the apartment. Vlad draped a leather coat around his thinning shoulders. Once outside, they began walking the three blocks toward the harbor. The sky was blue and the sun high, but the air skin-tighteningly brisk. It nipped at their noses and ears, causing them to check that their jacket zippers were zipped tight.

"I'm in love." Tom blurted.

"Again?" Vlad's head tilted with the question. He secretly thought Tom didn't respect the word love—that he threw it around, using it to mean he fancies someone. "Who is she this time?"

"Maggy. She was a nurse. Retired now though. Widowed." Tom had had seven wives, two families, and countless mistresses. He claimed that while Vlad had loved one woman, he had loved women, all of them, the entire gender. He thought them all beautiful and had no preference for hair-color or body-size. All he wanted was to shower them with affection—and for the affection to be returned. He called them 'God's perfect creation'. "We met last Sunday at the Opera."

Vlad rolled his eyes. "You can't love somebody you've known for a week."

"Of course you can. If you have the courage."

"You don't know them well enough. What you're feeling, comrade, is lust."

"Give me a little credit. I'm seventy nine years old. I think I'm past the age of lust. Think about when you first met Inga. Was it not love at first sight?"

"That was different. She's my soul mate. Love is not something that just happens. It's built over a lifetime." Vlad remembered seeing Inga for the first time—her lanky pubescent body and straight brown hair. He'd been fourteen when her family moved to his neighborhood. He'd first seen her through her front window, laughing, lit by the fire's glow. She'd been a year behind him at school and it had taken him weeks of watching her in the halls before he'd conjured the courage to talk to her.

The two men slowly shuffled along the busy sidewalk, the ocean's briny scent beginning to overpower the city's myriad aromas. Tom inhaled deeply, feeling refreshed by the salt in the air. "I see it differently, my friend. Love is something grown within oneself and given without expectation to anyone deemed worthy. You can't limit love. It's fear that keeps us from loving."

Seagulls flew overhead. A man on the corner sold hotdogs. Two teens walked hand in hand, giddy and gay, passing the slow-moving old-timers. Vlad smiled, feeling the sun on his face as he spoke. "I'm talking about true love. True love comes only once. It shakes you to the core and turns your world around. It allows you to remove all masks. You tell that person everything you've never been able to say to anyone else and they absorb it all, wanting more. You laugh together and cry together. You grow together. And there's no pressure or competition or jealousy. You are free and encouraged to be yourself and loved for who you are. Insignificant things like a wink or a caress transform into invaluable treasures that will stay with you your whole life, held and cherished in the heart. And, as our lives pass, we realize that life is not about things or accomplishments. There is only love. And to love with all of ourselves, to surrender, to give everything that we are, is why we're on earth."

The brisk autumn air had transformed the street into a feast for the eyes—the trees a cornucopia of fall colors. From where the men walked on the hill, the ocean was visible. The tide was out and children played along the shore. A kite joined the birds in flight. Tom pulled out a handkerchief and trumpeted a melody into the fabric before returning it to his pocket and answering.

"I agree, my friend. But why is true love limited to just one person? What is a soul mate?" The question was rhetorical. "A soul mate is a mirror. Someone who reflects you to yourself, exposing not only your triumphs, but also your shortcomings. They don't take your shit. They expose your weaknesses, tear down your barriers, and slap you awake. They come into your life as teachers. They reveal new layers of yourself to you. They love you and help you build yourself. But in the end, in one way or another, whether they stay with you for six months or sixty years, they leave you. They must leave, because ultimately we are alone. They break your heart wide open. But you know what happens when your heart is broken open, new light gets in. And we have the opportunity to take all the lessons our soul mate has given us and to recreate ourselves, stronger and even more full of love."

"Thomas, how many years have I known you? How many women have I seen pass through your life? You only say this because you've never met your Inga."

"No. There are many ways to love. It doesn't have to be limited to one person. You love your children."

"But that's different. We're talking about romantic love."

"No, we're talking about love. Love is bigger than romance. It's the beginning of everything that matters in this world. To truly love is to love all. This is what we must learn. To love everyone. And not only people. Love the trees, the sky, the ocean, ourselves."

"I see what you're saying, but we're still talking about different things. You're talking about loving all. I'm talking about loving one with all that you are."

"Everything, love included, has its season. Love is like those maple leaves. It grows, blooms, turns a brilliant color, but ultimately falls from the trees, gets blown by the wind and then disappears into the very earth it came from, returning to its source. It's not that love ends. Love is an eternal energy. But it changes form. This is life. You and I will do the same one day. Like those leaves, our bodies will soon return to the earth. But this isn't negative. It is the natural order. After the leaves have served their purpose, they fall from the tree in order to make room for new leaves to come in the spring. In the same fashion, love falls from our lives to make room for new love. Life departs from this realm in order to make room for new life. Every end is a beginning. The danger is not that love ends. The danger is in not allowing it to begin again."

"Are you saying that I should love another? I would have no idea how. I have loved Inga my entire life."

"I'm not saying for you to take another lover. If and when the time is right, only you will know. I'm defending my newfound love. But you have space in your life now that Inga has passed. I'm not saying to fill it with a woman, but I am saying fill it with love."

The men arrived at the beach, the harbor on one side, rocks stretching away from them on the other. They sat on a bench overlooking the water. A sailboat sliced across the horizon, swollen sails bathed in sunlight. The men sat in comfortable silence for a few minutes. Then Thomas spoke again. "Maybe no one truly knows what love is. Maybe it's too big. Or maybe we all know what love is, but it's so big we can only understand a piece of it. See it from one angle."

Vlad nodded in thought. Behind them the city bustled with the lives of millions going about their day. Above them, the sun shone, seagulls flew, and a cloud hung in the distance. Below them, the earth turned and worms tunneled. In front of them, a woman walked hand in hand with a small boy. The boy held a stuffed dinosaur. The ocean gently lapped at the shore. The tide, pulled by the moon, turned and began its slow journey in. And inside their slowly failing bodies, two old men felt the warmth of friendship.

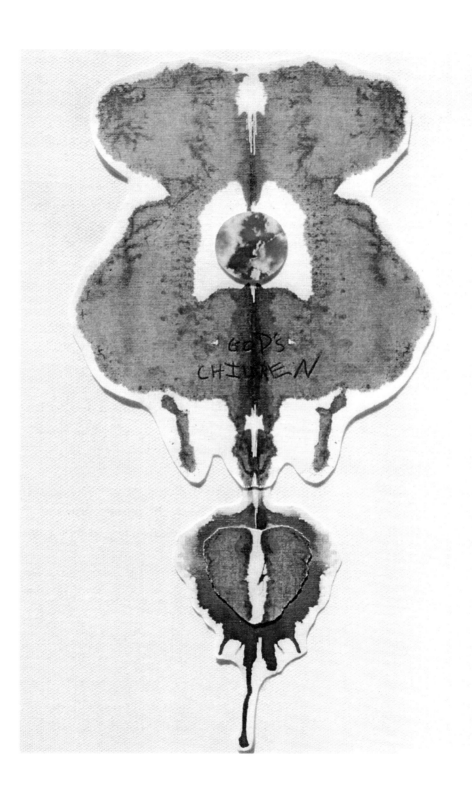

18

GOD'S CHILDREN

The boy is up to his elbows in blood. This is my fault, he thinks, as he stares at the pile of guts trailing to the ground. The deer hangs from its hind legs, dangling from the lowest branch of a tree. Its eyes are set with the horror of death. The boy can't look. The disappearance of life behind the eyes is still too fresh. He hates himself.

The boy pulls at the guts, slopping them into a pile on the dusty grass. The doe sways, tongue flopped out the side of its mouth. The smell of shit and death hangs thick in the humid air, clawing up the boy's nostrils and deep into his psyche. It's a smell he'll never forget. He wants to run away, leave the deer for the vultures, never think about it again, but he can't. His Dad will be back any minute now, with the hacksaw.

This is Joey's initiation into manhood. Death. Hunting is a man's sport. He's ten now, too old to cry, so he wipes the tears away before his father returns. He tries not to think about the deer, but images flood his mind.

~

He sees the deer's graceful silhouette through the scope of his Dad's rifle. He doesn't want to shoot, but his Dad's beside him, coaching.

"Steady," his Dad whispers "hold your breath... Now."

It's not a clean shot. The deer runs, then writhes on the ground, life bleeding out the hole in its side, legs kicking air. The pain squirms in Joey's chest like a pool of eels.

His father hoots, slapping Joey on the back. "Finish him. Shoot 'em in the head."

~

Upon his return, Joey's father begins to carve up the corpse, using the hacksaw on the joints. As he works, he explains the procedure to Joey, who stares blankly, unable to focus. The boy's mind tumbles over itself in a stream of doubt. He wonders if this is what it's supposed to feel like to be a man: being a killer.

The boy grapples with the concepts of right and wrong. The rules are blurred, the edges erased. Thoughts drop like stones in water, sending ripples through-out his consciousness. His father has fallen from grace, no longer a superhero.

Joey's sick to his stomach. He wonders if anyone knows what is right. In church, the Sunday-school teacher had taught the kids not to kill, professing this rule to be God's will, proving it with phrases from the Bible. But later, his father had said that the commandment only applies for Christians. It's OK to kill animals and terrorists, just not the sons and daughters of God.

~

Joey pushes the memory from his mind and looks back to the blank paper on his desk. The question haunts him, "What did you do this summer?" He wants to forget, wants the memory to fade like a bad dream, but he feels that the blood is still fresh on his hands. He looks around the classroom. Nervous excitement hangs in the air as the students settle into the first day of grade five. There's a new kid from the city. He's got dark skin and wears a small hat. Joey thinks he looks cool, different.

The new kid sits alone at lunchtime, eating by himself. Joey plays with him. They play X-men in the patch of trees behind the playground. Joey is Wolverine. Kareem doesn't know the characters, so Joey tells him to be Cyclops. Cyclops is the second coolest after Wolverine, because he can shoot laser beams from his eyes. Together, they battle bad guys and save the world. Once the world is safe, they sit and swing.

Suddenly lost in thought, Joey asks, "Do you think it's OK to kill?"

"No."

"Why?"

"Allah says so."

"Who's Allah?"

"God."

Joey is happy that Kareem believes in God. They are brothers in faith. He asks, "If a deer dies, does it go to heaven?"

Kareem ponders the question for a moment, swinging as he gazes into the blue sky. He squints in the potent Texan sun. "Yeah, I think so."

Joey's relieved. At least the deer is in Heaven. Kareem knows about these things. Being from the city, he knows a lot about the world.

The boys spend each lunch hour together for two weeks. They become best friends, playing basketball, tag, and throwing stones at trees. Every day at the end of lunch hour, Kareem goes to the woods to pray. Joey joins him, curious, never having seen anyone pray outside of the church. Joeys thinks it's funny how Kareem touches his head to the ground when he prays. Joey feels good with Kareem; he forgets about the deer, feels whole, forgiven, thankful for the new friend.

Joey's Mom acts weird when he introduces Kareem to her after school. Her white skin pales and she doesn't shake his hand. She doesn't speak on the drive home. Joey's Dad is furious. He slams his fat hand on the kitchen table, rattling the glasses in the cupboard. Grease from the automotive shop discolors his nails. His shirtless body tightens under his overalls, causing the confederate flag tattooed over his heart to undulate, as if caught in a righteous breeze.

"Ain't no way you gonna be friens wit 'at boy." Spit flies from the man's mouth, his eyes ablaze with hatred.

"But dad—"

"No buts. Kid's trouble. No son a mine is gonna be friens wit a devil worshper."

Confused, Joey says, "He believes in God."

"He ain't no Christian. He's a...," the word burns the man's mouth, tastes foul, "...Muslim." He spits.

"But, we pray together."

This infuriates the man. "Stay 'way from that boy. He'll tempt you 'way from Jesus."

Joey doesn't understand. Kareem is a good kid. He prays every day. He never hurts anyone or calls the younger kids names. Just because he calls God by a different name doesn't make it a different God. The German boy Franz calls a car a 'fahrzueg', but it's still a car.

"Allah is the devil," the father continues. "His followers wanna kill our Christian God. Is that the kinna kid you wanna be friens wit? HUH?"

Joey's Mom stands behind her husband, arms crossed, head nodding in agreement like a good wife. "There's only one God," she acds. "Jesus, his son, is the only way to salvation."

~

Another two weeks go by. Joey grows up fast. He learns about the Holy war, about terrorism, about what it means to hate. His parents fill him with prejudice. At first, all this is difficult to accept. Something inside Joey refuses to believe the appalling accusations on Kareem. But Joey's father shows him pictures of what the Muslims did in New York. He explains how they stone their women. In a grave and serious tone, the man details the Holy War in the Middle East. He describes suicide bombers and the ruthless methods in which they attack Christians. He shows Joey pictures of tortured American journalists. "The Devil comes in sheep's clothing," he warns. "It's God's will that he is stopped. Otherwise, the Devil will take over the world."

Joey certainly doesn't want that to happen.

~

At school, Joey stands with three other boys on the playground. They spit and call Kareem dirty. They tell him to move back to Iraq. But he's not from Iraq, he's from New York.

~

Kareem tries to get away. He hates the new game, Soldiers vs. Terrorist. He runs away, gets hit in the back by a rock.

Alone in the woods, the tears come. He's not a terrorist; he loves his country. Why do the other boys hate him? Is humanity not all one family with one father?

~

The bell rings and Joey watches Kareem walk from the bushes alone. The dark-skinned boy's eyes resemble those of the dying deer, confused and pain-stricken. Joey is a master hunter. He's been hunting many times with his Dad. He understands his place now, the top of the food chain. Shaping his thumb and finger into a circle, he puts his hand to his eye. He imagines seeing his prey though a scope. This time, he doesn't hesitate to pull the trigger.

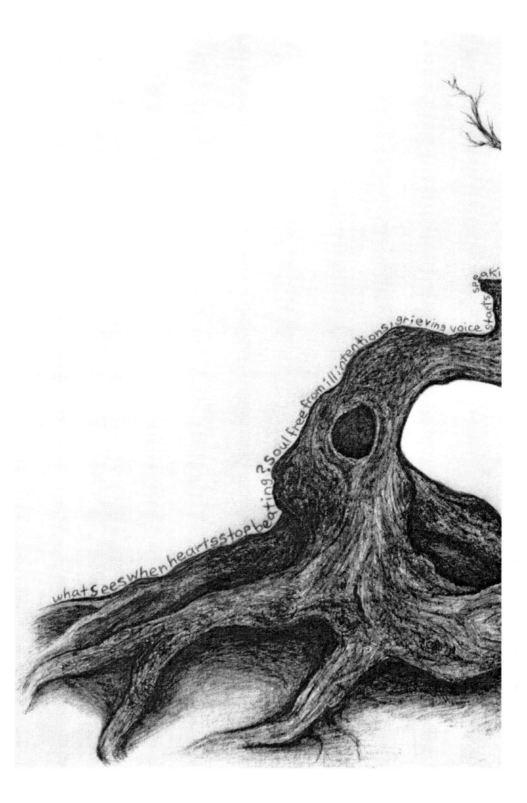

what sees when hearts stop beating? Soul free from ill intentions, grieving voice starts speaki...

19

AS THE APPLE FALLS

"Now that's your type of man." Maxime's mom points to a young muscleman walking shirtless along the harbor. Veins squiggle up his arms like leaches plump with blood. "You'd look so good together."

Fifteen-year-old Maxime shudders at the thought, thinking he looks like a shaved gorilla. He scares her. She doesn't want a man, or even a boy. She just wants her skateboard back. She wants out of these damn heels and too-tight skirt. Her legs are cold. But her mom says Maxime's getting too old for kids toys. Says it's time to become a woman.

"Your dad had a body like that. Used to bench-press every day." Maxime's mom lights a cigarette. "Exercise is important in a partner. You want somebody who keeps it." Maxime doesn't see the point. So what if her dad exercised daily, he still left as soon as a younger woman came along.

A man in a suit walks by, glancing at Maxime's mom. The woman holds his gaze long enough to make her daughter uncomfortable, then boasts, "See how I did that? I used my eyes. My eyes are my best feature. Allure is power. It's our chance to turn the tides on men, wrap them around our little finger." Her mom nods to the muscleman. "Your turn." She nudges her daughter forward. "Think sexy, and chic."

Maxime takes a step. Her ankles wobble.

"Go on," her mom encourages, pleased that her little girl is finally growing up.

20

JIMMY AND THE WITCH

Every day, as Jimmy walked past the toy shop on his way to school, his eyes were drawn to the slingshot in the window. He wanted it more than he had ever wanted anything in his whole life. Before bed each night, he would lay awake fantasizing about what he would do once it was his. He planned to line up his action figures on the porch-railing and blast them off, tape hand-drawn targets to trees, and throw logs into the river, shooting them as they floated by.

During the month leading up to his tenth birthday, every chance he got, Jimmy told his parents how much he wanted the slingshot. When the big day finally arrived, he could no longer contain his impatience. He tore ravenously at every present his parents lovingly laid before him until, finally, he unwrapped the long awaited prize.

Shrieking with delight, he bounded outside, yelling "Thank you" over his shoulder.

As he walked down the street, every object that Jimmy saw became a target. He rolled around gleefully, laughing and shooting rocks at every bush and flower in sight. He transformed into the ultimate slingshot-warrior, destroying hoards of bad guys as they attacked him.

It didn't take long before a stray rock flew across the street, crashing through old Miss Robinson's window. A shrill scream emanated from inside the house, sending shivers up Jimmy's back. He froze in terror. Everyone knew that Miss Robinson was a witch!

As soon as he was able to move again, Jimmy dove behind a bush, trying to be as quiet as possible. Miss Robinson appeared at the window—eyes blazing, hair knotted and tangled in a homely bun, hairy legs jutting out from beneath a ratty bathrobe. Jimmy stared open-mouthed at her weathered face. His whole body recoiled as he spied the moist, pink, flabby tissue of her smoke-tarnished tongue darting in and out, searching for traces of leftover lunch in the gaps between her yellow teeth. *It's true,* he thought, *she really is a witch!*

He shivered as he imagined what her reaction would be if she discovered his crime. She would peel his flesh from his bones and use him to make stew, or turn him into a lizard and lock him in a cage.

Shaking, Jimmy looked at the slingshot in his hand. He had to get rid of the darn thing fast. He hurled it as quietly as he could into some neighboring bushes. In spite of his attempted stealth, Miss Robinson heard the commotion and immediately shot from the door, and made a beeline for the spot where Jimmy was so desperately trying to conceal himself. It took all his strength to stifle the sobs threatening to burst forth. He peered out from the bottom of the bush. As Miss Robinson advanced ever closer to his hiding spot, Jimmy could see the thick gnarled toenails protruding from her calloused feet. Feeling sick to his stomach, he held his breath and tried to lie still.

Miss Robinson called out Jimmy's name. *How does she know my name?!,* Jimmy wondered. His lip quivered and his body trembled. He wanted to run, but he was immobilized by fear's icy grip. When she was so close that he could smell the musty odor spewing forth from her body, his legs suddenly sprang into action, and he made a mad dash for the safety of his house. Jimmy ran faster than he had ever run in his life, but Miss Robinson was right behind him, moving even faster. She grabbed hold of him, scooping him off the ground with one quick movement. He felt her cold hands on his neck, and he whimpered, "I'm sorry. Please don't eat me."

Miss Robinson carried Jimmy back to his house and knocked on the door. Jimmy's father answered. Jimmy stood on the porch, tears streaking down his cheeks and snot bubbling out of his nose.

Jimmy's dad said, "Whoa, calm down. What happened?"

Miss Robinson told him about the rock flying through her window. Jimmy convulsed with fear as he cried out, "Dad, help! She's a witch and she's going to kill me!"

Jimmy's father and Miss Robinson exchanged puzzled glances, and then broke into laughter. Jimmy's father asked, "Where did you get an idea like that?"

Jimmy said, "Tommy told me. Just look at her messy hair and yellow teeth!"

Miss Robinson put her nicotine-stained hand to her mouth, embarrassed.

Jimmy's father exploded, "JIMMY!" and then looked sheepishly at Miss Robinson. "I'm so sorry. He has an overly active imagination."

"It's OK. You know how kids are".

Jimmy's father promised to pay for the damages and assured her that such an incident would not happen again. Miss Robinson thanked him and smiled kindly, walking back towards her house as Jimmy and his father walked into theirs.

Back inside her house, Miss Robinson looked at the broken window, shaking her head. Then, she sighed and walked up the stairs to her kitchen and resumed cooking the large pot of stew that Jimmy's unexpected interruption had taken her away from. She scooped out a bone from the stew and threw it into the cage, where little Billy was tied up. "Eat up sonny," Miss Robinson cackled. "You need to fatten up... my lizards are getting hungry."

at any given moment you could unwittingly be within reach of a **cock**,

grasp **a** flexible perspective, extend the mind to stand erect to belittling beings, and **doodle** a reality where release from misunderstanding tension creates all to fly free.

21

COCK-A-DOODLE

Hugo was scared. Well, scared might be an understatement. To accurately represent the torrent of emotion he was feeling, you'd have to say that he was pummeled by a wave of fear, caught in an undercurrent of anxiety, and dragged along the bottom of an ocean of disgust, while smashing himself on every self-loathing-barnacle covered rock on the way out to a cold, watery abyss. Then, tossed about in the turmoil of the open sea, feeling empty, he was knocked about by the sharks of misfortune waiting to drag him to the depths of hell.

Why, you might ask? The answer is simple. He has a small cock. And that jagged scar over its eye—mere words lack the raw communicative ability it would take to evoke the horror with enough exactitude to fully generate the enormity of its hideousness. If Frankenstein had a love-child with Swamp Thing, it would look like Brad Pitt compared to Hugo's cock. Never in history, since the Big Bang (when some cosmic pepper tickled God Almighty's inner nostril and she sneezed out the cloud of space-debris we call the universe) has anything so horrifically repulsive ever existed. How, Hugo wondered, was he going to win Esmeralda's love with such an ugly cock?

He tried desperately to wrestle hold of his mind. In five minutes, he was scheduled to put his cock to the test for the first time. The most terrifying part of the whole ordeal was that the entire town was going to be there, watching.

He looked at his undersized fowl as it feebly pecked the ground for grain, its only eye turning in circles. In Grimeville, the tradition of Cockfighting was as old as the town itself. For centuries, it had been used to decide matters of law, civil disputes, and land claims. Today's tournament would decide who would win Esmeralda's hand in marriage.

Esmeralda was the town beauty. Her silky black hair, a waterfall of coconut-scented locks, cascaded over her toned shoulders and down the gentle slope of her back. Her olive skin radiated with the luminosity of angels. Her voice was sweet music floating on a minty breeze. And her ass looked like a watermelon had been sliced in two and stuffed into the back of her pants. Nobody cared that she couldn't count to twenty or locate Europe on a map. She had breasts that screamed, 'squeeze me!' and plump lips that glistened with femininity.

Hugo looked down at his small ginger bird and sighed. Being the son of a blacksmith, it was all he could afford. He recoiled at the thought of Gaston's huge black cock, the Annihilator. Since his first day at school, the day Gaston had tied Hugo's hands together and hung the younger boy by the underwear from a tree, Gaston had, time and again, proven himself to be a take-for-himself, pig-headed, bragging, backstabbing, girl-chasing, street-fighting, reckless, tobacco-chewing ape.

~

Hugo stepped into the hall leading to the ring. His small body shivered, even though the heat of summer clung to the air like a naked sweaty back to a leather seat. Drunken cheers from the crowd echoed towards him. Dim lights dangled from wires in the ceiling, illuminating the filthy hall. The dank smell of stale-cigar-smoke mixed with dried blood hung in the humid air. Testosterone permeated the atmosphere, coming alive, pulsating like a feral beast.

The hall's paint had bubbled and peeled, exposing the cement wall. Hugo noticed a patch that looked like the face of Jesus. He touched his forehead, chest, and shoulders in the sign of a cross. "Lord Jesus," he prayed, "please pack my cock with vigor so it can rise to the challenge. Fill my cock with power and grace so that it may strike down all other cocks in defeat, and I may win the hand of the woman I love. Amen."

Carrying his bird in a bamboo cage, Hugo sat on a bench with the other nine contestants. The crowd, a sea of sweaty bodies squirming in anticipation, huddled around the cock-ring, crushing forward to get better views. Nervous excitement filled the room, mingling with the thick smoky air, reek of man, and chicken shit. A balding man in a sweat-stained muscle shirt, and a fedora complete with the red feather of a prized cock, stood in the corner taking bets.

Esmeralda walked by, cleavage bursting from her tight pink halter-top, her breasts threatening escape like a couple of caged animals. Her black, fuck-me boots ended their ascent of her sleek legs at her knees, revealing bare thighs that disappeared into a skirt so short it scarcely covered her watermelon ass. The overhead light gently caressed her meticulously applied spray tan. A teasing flaunt in her step begged the question, 'am I wearing panties?' Her hips swayed suggestively as she blew kisses and batted her eye-lashes at the contestants. They hooted and hollered, desire hanging out like a dog's tongue on a hot day. She smiled, pleased with her sexual prowess.

She was the queen of sexy, the princess of lust, and the goddess of pleasure, self-obsessively ruling over men with an air of egotistical delight. Sitting down, she crossed her legs with the slow, confident seductiveness that comes from knowing you've got more flair than the sun.

A dwarfish man stepped into the cock-ring, taking the microphone in his tattooed hands. He pushed his flat, greasy hair behind his ears, and his voice squealed. "Citizens of Grimeville, are you ready for the tournament to begin?"

The crowd erupted. The MC raised his hands to quiet them. "OK, OK, silence while I draw the names of the first two gladiators." Hugo crossed his fingers as he silently prayed not to be chosen first. The MC pulled a name from the hat. "Gaston." The crowd erupted again.

Gaston stepped into the ring, cock in hand. It was massive, head bobbing up and down as the light glistened off its black feathers. The MC drew another name. "Hugo."

Hugo stood, and the crowd laughed at the sight of his small cock. It looked like a leprosy-infected pigeon.

The two men squared off in opposite corners of the ring. Gaston performed his death stare, eyes bulging as a grimace twisted the corners of his mouth. A thick, handlebar moustache sprouted valiantly around his lips, declaring his manhood with authority. A gold chain hung over his skin-tight white shirt. Flexing, he pointed at Esmeralda. A barbed-wire tattoo twisted up his arm from his wrist to his shoulder. If Esmeralda was the sex queen, Gaston was king of machismo. He called out to Hugo so everyone could hear.

"Nice cock. Looks like mutant road-kill. What are you going to do with that little thing?"

Hugo stared back, burning with rage fueled by a lifetime of ridicule. He wanted to pummel Gaston. He wanted to unleash his cock all over Gaston's angular face, poking out the brute's callous eyes. He yelled back, "It's not about the size of your cock. It's about how it moves. My cock is like lightening, and it's going to dance around that fat turkey."

The bell sounded and the two men released their cocks and stepped out of the ring. The birds flew at each other in fierce combat. Gaston's took the offensive, but Hugo's reacted with swift reflexes. It dodged to the side and caught the big bird on the side of its head with a jab. The cocks raced at each other again, bashing heads. They clawed at each other and beat their wings. Hugo's cock slashed out with its beak, landing two more jabs, opening a cut above the left eye of Gaston's cock. Hugo's hands gripped the side of the ring. The anticipation tore into him like a barbed hook, reeling him in.

In a wild assault, Gaston's cock struck out, plucking out the good eye of the smaller bird. Hugo cried out in horror as the big bird quickly seized its opportunity and tore open the throat of its blinded opponent. The roar of the crowd filled the room, drowning out Hugo's anguished cries. The ugly bird flopped to the ground, writhing as its blood drained from its body. Hugo jumped into the ring, kneeling in the pooling blood.

The young man suddenly realized there had been a distinctive life within his cock—now prematurely ended. His cock would never stand up again. It had been a living breathing being, having its own unique experience of life, and he had subjected it to a form of torture for his own gain. Looking around, Hugo noticed the greedy energy that filled the room. A toothless man stood at the side of the ring yelling curses. In the back corner, a fight had broken out over an unpaid debt. The town pimp, salt-stains yellowing the armpits of his cheap suit, pointed and laughed, eyes filled with the glee elicited by another's misfortune. Noticing the filthy, slave-like conditions of the caged birds, mere objects at the disposal of insatiably selfish men, Hugo was crushed by the shame of what he had just participated in.

Gaston stepped into the ring, arms raised in victory. He stood over Hugo, whose bird lay limp in a puddle of blood. Gaston flexed, then pointed at Esmeralda. "Behold my mighty cock. My cock is king."

She whistled and clapped. Gaston looked down at Hugo. "Get your pathetic excuse of a cock out of my sight, boy. It doesn't deserve to be in the ring with the king. Don't come back until you're a man."

Anger seethed inside Hugo, crawling like fire ants under his skin. It flowed, bubbling up like lava. His body shook as the rage consumed him. Lifelong memories of Gaston's mockery flooded his mind. He hated the brute. The wrath rose, exploding Hugo's psyche in an eruption of volcanic madness.

Hugo stunned the crowd into silence, as he picked up his limp cock and, in a satisfyingly rebellious act of fowl play, used it to smack Gaston in the face. Blood from the cock smeared across the mustachioed grin, oozing into the brute's mouth.

Gaston let out a venomous war cry as he stumbled back, arms raised for battle. Hugo stood motionless, stunned by the uncharacteristic courage of his actions and filled with silent contentment.

Gaston hit Hugo in the stomach with a hard punch, doubling him over. Then the enraged, blood-thirsty savage reached out to grab him, but Hugo quickly rolled to the side and backed into the corner of the ring. The crowd hollered in excitement.

"You're dead," Gaston called out as he approached Hugo, pounding his fists together.

Hugo replied, "You won already. Just take your cock and beat it."

Gaston had no comeback. He was no wordsmith. He may have had the bigger cock, but Hugo had the bigger diction.

The brute stepped threateningly close, filling Hugo's personal space with coffee breath. Hugo swung a right-cross that impotently grazed Gaston's shoulder. Gaston grabbed Hugo's hair, pulling him into a headlock. Hugo twisted to get free, but Gaston was too powerful. The bully rammed his fist into Hugo's forehead.

Not knowing what to do, Hugo grabbed hold of Gaston's pants and yanked them down. Then he shoved the brute backward with all his might. Gaston's ankle-high pants kept his legs from making the step and he tripped, landing on his back.

The crowd burst into laughter at the sight of Gaston lying there, his tiny, peanut sized penis on full display. It looked like a deflated water-balloon, or like the retracted neck of a baby turtle hiding in a patch of black moss. Esmeralda shrieked at the sight, horrified that Gaston might win the tournament.

Gaston scrambled to his feet, pulling up his pants, ready to kill. He looked around but Hugo had already disappeared into the crowd. Enraged, Gaston searched the crowd, wanting revenge.

Outside the building, Hugo started the engine of his rusty Datsun, wondering if men flaunt their cocks because they're compensating for something else. He peeled out of the dirt parking lot and sped down the dusty road that led out of town. He could never set foot in Grimeville again, but he didn't care. He didn't even mind that he would never see Esmeralda again. He was free, on the road, leaving his troubled past behind. The world was in front of him and it was his to explore. He'd finally stood up to his tormentor and become a man. He laughed to himself as he thought about his prior foolishness, finally understanding that there's more to life than having a magnificent cock.

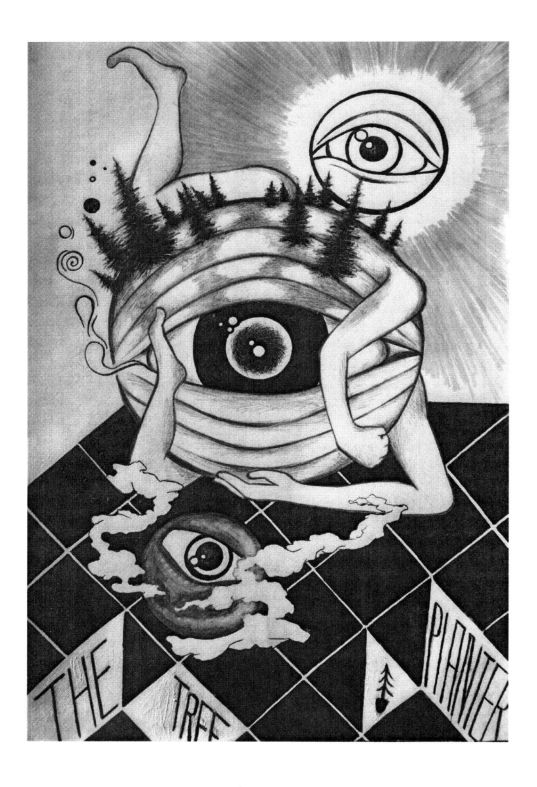

22

THE TREEPLANTER

Long before I stood here, ancient trees towered above, rising into the clouds. Gone now, yet their roots still permeate the earth. I've been sent into the cut-block with 60 pounds of saplings on my back, the city-dweller sent in to complete the cycle of life—the effort of a society with a guilty conscience.

Back sore, muscles burning, legs bleeding, I plant tree after tree. Three thousand a day. Playing God, I design the forest. I am the King of this Mountain. I am the one who chooses where these trees will grow. Yet, like a rattler, I birth my children into the earth and then leave them to fend for themselves.

I'm a thousand miles from home. A primordial impulse courses up my spine, and I feel connected to the earth. A duality exists within me. I am a creature of two worlds, torn between the natural and the material. Mind and soul are split. Empty yet full, alone yet surrounded.

I am here. I pause to grasp this feeling. My body literally comes from this earth, and the pain in my legs reminds me that one day I will return to it. If my trees are not cut down for money, they may live for thousands of years, but even that is only a flash in time.

Across the bare earth, the young forest is reclaiming this mountain. It lacks the awe-inspiring mystery of the old growth. My mind wanders and I wonder what it would be like if all the trees were gone. But then I snap myself back to the task at hand, and begin to plant faster. If I plant enough trees, I'll have enough money to buy a car when I get back to the city.

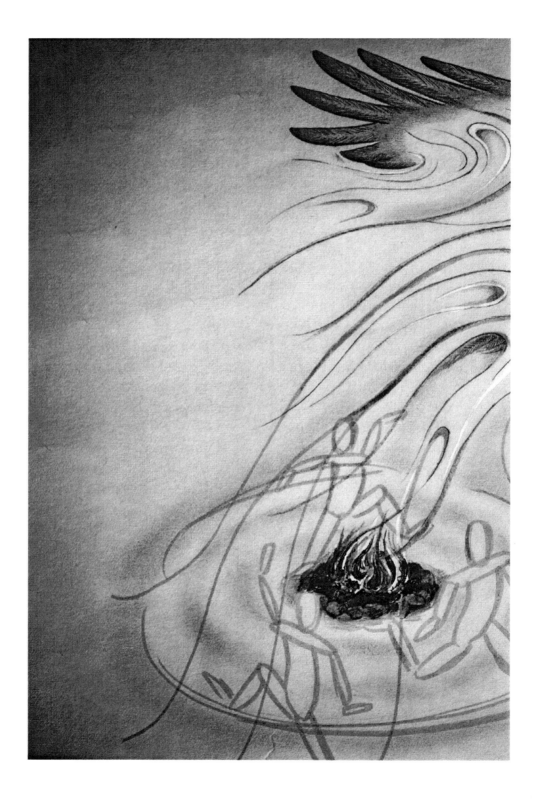

black rock city

23

BLACK ROCK CITY: ANGELS AND HAMSTERS

A hand grabs my shoulder from behind, turning me away from the last morsels of my dinner. Wally stands barefoot, panting, wearing nothing but board shorts, eyes blazing with excitement. "Brah, the driver of that dragon has mescaline." I follow his gaze to a mechanical beast retreating down the street, threatening to vanish into the mayhem of Burning Man that stretches for miles in every direction.

I abandon my place in the circle of lawn chairs and sprint out of the freedom community, past the Winnebago, and onto the street. Wally is right behind me as I jump onto the dragon's tail and climb to its back, which is a crowded dance floor. We shuffle to the front of the dragon, squeezing through sweaty bodies, both costumed and naked. The driver, who's clad in an elfin cloak and tribal, glow-in-the-dark face paint, stands on the beast's head, steering it. The elf turns the wheel and the giant steel head of the dragon pivots, angling the beast onto another bustling dirt road. He pulls a chain and a blast of fire shoots from the dragon's mouth. Smoke seeps from its nostrils, unfurling into the night air, swirling upward and smelling of petrol.

A nervous voice inside my head tells me to be careful. I ignore it and tap the elf on the shoulder, "Do you know where to find mescaline? I have this bottle of Jack to trade." I hold up the half emptied bottle to the light, swirling the liquid. The elf's eyes narrow under his hood as he analyzes me.

"Don't worry. There's no cops around," I encourage.

I haven't personally seen any cops. But according to the rumor-train, this festival is crawling with Five-O. The rumors circulate, increasing the paranoia, making finding drugs more difficult than finding life on Mars. The cops could burst forth from undercover at any moment and ruin your life. According to a warning I got from a half-naked man in a tutu, "one minute you're hanging with a couple naked babes, the next thing ya know the girls got ya in handcuffs, just for pulling out some MDMA and trying to up the party to the next level." Wolves in sheep's clothing, that's what those bitches are. What do they expect when sixty-five-thousand of the world's freaki-est people travel out to the desert for a week long party?

"I got whiskey at my camp," the elf replies. "Can you sweeten the deal?" He steps closer, looks into my eyes. "How 'bout a kiss?"

Damn it. Why a kiss? Wally and I exchange glances. I've never kissed a man before. It's a border I'm not anxious to cross, but mescaline is a precious commodity, a rare substance that comes along only once every few years. Fuck it. I've always said you should try everything once.

I grab the elf by the sides of the face and plant my lips on his. His stubble rubs mine, feeling unnatural, invasive, wrong. A piece of my innocence dies, replaced by painful self-awareness. I break away, forcing a smile to cover the fact that I want to spit.

The elf laughs, "Don't know who told ya I got mescaline, but I don't."

I feel the words like a jump-kick to the chest, a KO to my spirit. I deflate, violated. Then the elf laughs and reaches deep into his cloak, pulling out a couple of yellow granules that look like candy Nerds. He stealthily drops them into my hand in exchange for the whiskey.

Jackpot.

"Thanks, brah." I say, and smile in appreciation.

Wally and I swallow the granules, then jump off the dragon, quickly getting off the road to avoid an oncoming UFO. Two green aliens control it from inside a florescent glass dome. They wave at us.

We walk toward the freedom community to get bikes and recruit some friends to come party downtown. A pair of giant inflatable legs lay parted on the side of the street, exposing the red flaps of a glistening, four-foot-tall vagina. As we look into it, a naked man slithers through, re-birthed. A crowd cheers. Then, the fully-grown-baby stands, and proceeds to suckle from one of the topless women.

Wally smacks my shoulder. His bald head gleams in the newly-risen moonlight as he nods towards the scene. "Got milk?" His thick lips twist in a smile. We howl as if it's the funniest thing in the world, because in that moment it is.

Back at our RV, Jason stands on the roof next to our surfboards, dramatically recounting the story of the wave that almost smashed him into the cliff at Santa Cruz the week before. The moonlight reflects off his toned body, emphasizing his washboard abs, entrancing a couple of the girls. Max, the disco-Vampire, tries to rally the crowd, getting them ready for a mission. His black Afro shakes with every move as he dances in excited loops, waving his arms. The distant thud from the stages calls us—a primal drum message, boom pada boom bat, come party.

I fill a Gatorade bottle with vodka and juice.

~

I find myself alone and in the throes of a mescaline trip while wandering through the dreamlike desert. Parties in the distance sound like twisted staccato bass bombs. Blasts of light ascend into space. I swim through a sea of cartoon colors. I am color, light refracting into my kaleidoscopic self. My body melts. I walk—leave little puddles of myself in the sand. Lights in the distance attract me, turning me into a moth. I fly in erratic circles, rebellious wings flicking and flapping. Laughter erupts... a couple rides past on bicycles... I wave... they don't see me... maybe I'm invisible.

Time bends, wily and elastic... How long has it been? Look at the lights. A spaceship goes by. The world appears grainy, all pixels. A robot man clanks by. It's definitely the future... the year 6000? So many Lasers. Unicorn. Another spaceship. Bicycles everywhere. Fur seats look comfy. Then a giant mechanical octopus appears, blasting fire skyward from each of its legs. The heat on my face has a sobering effect. I have a moment of clarity. Time stands still. Then I'm sucked though a worm hole and dropped back to the desert, finding myself on the edge of a lively street.

I walk as if underwater. Coming across a painting exhibit, I gather my wits and wander into the gallery, admiring the art while trying to look like I belong. A DJ in the corner spins futuristic music full of clicks and beeps—the type of music I imagine robots will have sex to three hundred years from now. A lizard-man stands, elegantly poised with a martini in his hand, speaking to Cat Woman. The couple oozes the type of urban sophistication that reeks of egotism. I eavesdrop on the conversation as the lizard says, "I just adore the way the artist's surrealist style toys with existential musings."

Cat Woman takes a long drag from a thin cigarette. Smoke drifts from her mouth as she answers, "Fabulous. And all while fusing urban graffiti into the mix. Ya?" She points her cigarette toward a painting of a brick wall tagged with the words *Real eyes, Realize, Real lies.*

Wanting to sound intelligent, I say, "And the clor mix bright jump." A little drool escapes through my lips and stretches down my chin. I quickly wipe it away. The couple turns away, noses up, walking to the bar in the corner. *Is this what I've been reduced to?* I wonder— *a slobbering fool, lost, and wacked out on psychedelics?* I suddenly feel like a swamp creature. Eying the crowd, I creep to the edge of the room, imagining swamp-weeds hanging from my scaly limbs. My body is heavy and I drag my foot.

I give Cat Woman a hard look as I walk, but she doesn't outwardly notice. I laugh as I contort my face and blend into the shadows, turning my attention to a painting of a monkey wearing a business suit on Wall Street. The monkey is trying to buy shares of Exxon, but his only currency is his soul. Next to it, there's a painting of a man at a fork in the road. Down one path is a goddess, the other, one-hundred whores. Next to that is a painting of Jesus, Buddha, and Mohammed looking down from a cloud in Heaven. Tears streak each of their faces as they observe a religious war on the earth below.

Outside the exhibit, the large mechanical octopus goes by again, blasting fire above a crowd. I follow it for a while, then board a pirate ship on wheels sailing across the playa towards the larger parties on the far side of the city. Inside the ship, Captain Jack Sparrow spins Dub-Step.

~

The Temple of Boom rises out of the desert like a musical oasis, sending shock waves of bass through the throng of dancers. The speakers stand four stories tall, pulsating with energy. The crowd bounces and undulates under a canopy of lasers—an ocean of bodies rolling to the rhythms. The mescaline has mellowed to a functional level. On the outskirts of the party, fire-dancers flirt with nature's wildest element, swinging the flames around their nearly-naked bodies. As I stare into the flaming orbs, I begin to understand the significance of fire. Water, earth, and air belong to all the creatures of the world, but fire is man's alone. It is a gift from the gods, sent down to earth in a thundering jolt. It elevates man from beast, allowing him to hold the power of the gods in his hands. To dance with this primal element is to risk one's flesh in communion with something both primeval and supernatural.

Inspired by the music, I join the chaos. The bass stretches and oscillates, massaging my body, filling me with awe, sending me spinning in bolder and bolder circles throughout the crowd. Rhythms— bursting, primordial, subterranean, ancient yet modern— reverberate, hitting me in the chest and penetrating to my core. The sound explodes in my mind like a love grenade, blowing my consciousness in a million fiery directions. Energy builds inside me, seething, rising to immeasurable proportions. I feel it surging through me, pouring out of me, flowing freely, connecting me to the crowd. We are all one, all here for the same purpose—life-changing, mind-expanding fun!

The sensations within my body swell with the music's heaving pulse, propelling me forward in a feverish dance-frenzy. I become the sound's physical manifestation—music in movement—twirling, jumping, laughing. Bodies rub against mine, furry bodies, naked bodies, sweaty bodies, all sending jolts of ecstasy through me. A hand grabs my ass, but when I turn no one claims the action. I dance, not stopping until the DJ finishes his set and another takes the stage.

Suddenly, the urge to sit claims me. My legs are stiff and heavy, as if they are made of wood. I look over the crowd, wishing there was a seat to rest on, but seeing none. Turning to search for a place to relax, I trip over a couch. Shocked, I sit, wondering if it had been there the entire time, or if I had just manifested it. My powers of manifestation seem to be growing exponentially as the festival continues. The previous night I had been caught in the grip of hunger and was considering making the trek back to the freedom community in search of food. Then, out of the dark, the popcorn palace had driven up, appearing like a mirage on wheels, and gifting me two bags of popcorn—fuel enough to sustain my body until the sun came up. Hallelujah.

After a few minutes, the DJ drops a bass line so thick it could knock a man over, and I spring from the seat, once again possessed by the demons of dance. I circle the perimeter of the dance floor in a fury of new-found energy. Every inch of my skin vibrates with life, caressed by the cool night air.

Feeling myself in a warm embrace, I turn to find a topless, horned-out angel. She slaps my ass and gives me a flirtatious look. Her jaw grinds and her eyes are all pupil. Thick blonde hair cascades down her back past her wings. Taut legs rise from her Jesus sandals, meeting at a leaf bikini so scanty it barely covers her crotch. Her hand grabs the waist of my patch pants and pulls me close, then begins to trace my abs. Leaves brush against my thigh.

I'm far too deep into my mescaline journey to respond. Sex seems foreign—the mechanics of it impossibly hard, absurd even. But the longer I'm in the presence of this angel, the more I want it—her touch—soft flesh, succulent and silky; shoulders, thighs, breasts. I want her alone, her heat, her plump lips. I want to trace her body, embark on an expedition of the flesh, delve in, and howl at the moon together. But I can't. I have a girl at home, waiting for me. She would never know, but I would.

I'm on a slippery slope, standing on the edge of a precipice. I step back. This angel is just another girl I have to walk away from. It hurts every time. The truth is I want every girl. Not their flesh—that I could take or leave. I want them to know me, to love me, to lust after me. I just do. Jason says it's a man thing, inherent in our genes or some shit.

I walk away, resentful of the leash that binds me from over a thousand kilometers away. Somehow it makes me feel less of a man—like I don't get to make my own choices—like I'm somebody else's property. I crave freedom. Maybe I'm a wolf masquerading as a dog.

In the end, deep down, I walk away not because I love my girl, though I do. I walk away because it's more important to me to be a man of honor than a ladies' man. It's really a selfish decision, one full of ego. *I* don't cheat because *I'm* not a cheater. *I'm* above that, too good for it. Maybe it's all a bunch of pretentious horseshit. I don't know. Who am I?—just a ragged surf kid from Tofino, off his head on mescaline at the world's wildest party.

The unmistakable mothball scent of DMT wafts by, filling my nostrils with a biting blast of bitter. I turn to investigate the source, incredulous that someone could smoke such a powerful psychedelic in this setting. What a weirdo. I want some.

A submarine pulls up to the side of the crowd, releasing a swarm of bikini-clad women with snorkels. The girls' perfect bodies glisten in the lights.

At this point the music becomes grimy, grinding as it glitches out. The sound is like a hammer to my temple. It claws at my skull from the inside, and I feel that this is the type of music to go insane to. Lighting a joint, I dance off in the direction of a giant pyramid.

~

I find myself on my knees. All around me, people melt with love and grief and wonder and peace and synchronization. Many hold hands. The temple embraces us all, rising from the sand in a brilliant testament to the ingenuity of the human mind. Every inch of the enormous wooden structure is intricately carved with sacred geometry. Warm light illuminates it all. Poetry adorns the walls. There are pictures of lost loved ones with heartfelt messages. I hear sobbing from the crowd as someone grapples with their inner pain. They've come to feel this hurt and allow it to pass through them. The temple's beauty rivals any building I have ever seen. Thousands upon thousands of hours have gone into building it. And yet it will be burnt during the closing ceremony. A fiery letting go. A shedding of the old to make room for the new.

On my knees, in awe of this creation, mind shattered and restructured by the creativity displayed throughout this festival, a sudden realization penetrates to the innermost layer of my soul. The idea of God as a grey haired benevolent man in the sky is absurd. That is humanity creating God in our image, not the other way around. God is the creative force flowing through the entire universe, springing forth life and beauty and love and matter and motion and evolution and everything. So if we are created in God's image, we too are that creative force. We are all little pieces of God—seven billion hands of an infinite creator, all experiencing and participating in this grand creation through our own individual lenses.

~

Before the sun rises, I sit in a large dome. The sensation of the mescaline leaving my body feels like honey coating my insides, pleasantly dripping out through my fingers and toes. I lick my finger, expecting sweet, but all I taste is the pungent sting of the alkaline desert. It brings with it the memory of rolling on the playa, rubbing dirt over every inch of my body, the mother hippie chanting "welcome home" as she spins in naked circles, her thick grey hair flowing to her still firm behind—the most vibrant sixty year old I've ever met. Is it weird for a twenty-eight year old to find a sixty year old sexy?

At the edge of the dome, a man plays the didgeridoo, accompanied by a violin player, percussionist, and DJ. Psychedelic images of a desert boy on a vision quest project onto the ceiling and walls. I lay on a bean-bag chair, listening as the music and images carry me on a voyage through time and space. Tears streak my face, and I feel as if I am hovering three feet above the ground. When the band stops and the lights come on, I look around, dazed. There's a crumpled piece of paper in my hand. I open it. Staring up at me is a poem in my own writing, but I can't remember writing it. I wonder how I wrote it without a pen. Sitting back, I read it:

Endless race

I awake,
pick a body
from the wardrobe,
pull it haphazardly over my soul.

Following instructions,
I go outside and join the race,
run frantically
on the hamster wheel—
eyes glued to distractions,
chasing a happiness
forever out of reach.

Faster, I run
getting nowhere—
not understanding
it's not about the millions of steps
I take on the wheel,
but the one it takes to get off.

~

Walking back to the freedom community, the comedown from the mescaline envelopes me like the embrace of an estranged lover. It kisses me goodbye. The empty numbness in my chest comforts me. The trip was worth it—will bring future happiness in the form of memories. The sun peaks over the horizon, ready to start its daily ascent.

A naked man emerges from the shadows. He's small, creepy, and bald, reminding me of Gollum. My eyes are uncontrollably drawn to his erect cock. It curves upward in vascular rebellion, staring me in the eyes. I shudder. Why do we look at things we don't want in our consciousness? He staggers towards me, the purple head of his stubby sausage leading the way. His eyes point in different directions and I wonder if he even knows where he is. He's getting closer as I continue down the path. The light falls across his face, makes him look possessed. As I pass him, he makes a peculiar hissing sound like a vampire in the sunlight. He's walking faster now, following me, too close for comfort, and I'm struck by a sudden fear that he's going to touch me with his penis. The thought encourages me to flee. As I run, the man lets out a squealing cackle that reverberates down the path behind me, wrapping me in a seedy embrace. I quiver with shame.

Near my camp, there's a giant fish with a dance floor in its stomach. I stand at its mouth and look in. It's empty except for a few strung-out stragglers. The pulse of down-tempo beats tempts me to join, but I decide to continue to the love-filled nest that is the freedom community. The sky is getting light and I need to save some energy. I'm taking a Tantric, chakra-healing, yoga workshop in the morning. And besides, tomorrow we burn the Man.

the mind

the climb

the world

our temple

24

THE CLIMB

Frustrated, legs burning, a young man pauses on a stump. Why did the Guru choose the top of the mountain to reveal his wisdom? Perhaps to deter those lacking perseverance.

Finally at the peak, the man bows at the Holy Man's feet. "Please, Great Sage, reveal to me life's mysteries."

To this, the Guru replies, "Any man claiming to know the answers to the mysteries of life has misunderstood the question."

Bewildered, the man descends.

Years later, when the man has grown old, long after the Guru's death, he climbs the mountain again. This time, he has no expectations other than enjoying the mountain's beauty. He climbs slowly, happy to simply be on the mountain.

Reaching the summit, he suddenly realizes why the Guru had chosen the mountaintop as a classroom. Enlightenment is not found in knowledge alone, but also in life's journey—and in the acceptance of its mystery. He finally understands that not everything is meant to be understood; some things can only be lived—felt—experienced.

As the old man sits, looking across the horizon at the curvature of the earth, pondering the organic relationship between himself and life, a young man staggers to the apex, haggard and breathless. His sweat stung eyes turn towards the old man. With awe, the young man drags himself to the elder's feet and bows.

"Please, Wise Teacher, why did you choose the highest mountain?"

Upon hearing this, the old man smiles, "I am no teacher. Who am I?—Just an old man admiring the view. But the mountain must be climbed because it is the journey that teaches us. And," gesturing with his hands, "the whole world is the temple."

25

THE VIOLINIST

Thirty six years I been living here, stomping out my territory on these streets. I seen a lot things change, boy. It ain't been easy. Some a these cats up here are crazy. And I ain't mean, *I think the president is an alien,* crazy. I'm talking, *I'll slit your throat while you sleep for a hit a crack,* crazy. And that crazy's a whole lot more dangerous. But they know me, boy. They know me. They know I ain't got nothin they can sell for a hit a crack. So they just walk on by while I sleep. No point rousing the broke-ass old tramp. I don't need no trouble while I be sleepin. That's why I don't sleep with Bernadette, my violin. Now, technically she ain't even my violin. The lady from the church lets me play in the subway. It's how I earn my liv'n. I call Bernadette my violin cuz I think an instrument belongs to the one who breathes life into it. An instrument is just a piece of wood or metal. It can't make no music on its own. It just sits there lifeless until a musician picks it up and makes it sing. And even though that old nun owns the violin, I be the one mak'n her come alive.

I ain't homeless though, boy. Don't go gett'n an idea like that in your head. I got myself a home. Sure, it be a simple home, but I built it myself. Architected it and everything. Over off Commercial Street in one a those abandoned buildings. Been liv'n there alone since Harvey died. Been hard, boy.

People ain't always good to ya when you work on the streets. Some are. Darlene the baker stops and listens to me in the subway every day on her way to work. And every night I know there's gonna be a fresh loaf of bread waitin for me behind the dumpster. That woman is an angel, boy. An angel. But there are demons walk'n these streets too. Demons that will tear you apart. Demons that will eat your soul, devour your humanity, and bring the devil out in you. I've lost too many friends to these demons over the years. They almost got me too, boy, many a time. But I'm still here, cuz the angels and the violin saved my life.

People are always talking 'bout people like, "oh, look at him, he's a doctor. He's so successful." But I reckon that's all a load a bullshit. Doctor or not don't make you a good man. Boy, I known many a doctor that'd be put'n money before people. There be a lot a rich demons out there. Better believe that, boy. Way I see it, doctor or janitor—ain't neither make you a better man. What counts is whether you be a angel or a demon. Cuz how we treat people is what makes this world heaven or hell.

Take this demon just the other day. I was at the grocery store gett'n some grub from the dumpster around back, and I seen a man hunched over a bin, eating like a feral animal. He's eatin strawberries straight over the bin, drooling and tossing the remains back in. Bad form, boy, bad form. So I says to him, "Anything left in there?" I'm only really want'n to dig in one of those other bins for broccoli or corn or somethin to roast, cuz I feel like making a fire later. And this guy turns and starts throwing produce at me. He's spitt'n and yell'n for me to get the fuck outta there. He'd rather waste the food by throwing it at me than share. Even though I been going to that dumpster for years, and it's the first time I seen him there. And there's plenty enough to feed a whole football team. But life's turned this guy so greedy that he feels he's gotta stamp his claim on the dumpster and chase away the competition. He can't see no farther than his own immediate self. That's what I mean by demon, boy. We got our angels and our demons, and together they shape this world.

My girl's an angel. A ray of pure beauty lighting up this city. Seeing her smile gets me through most days. Amen to that, boy. Camisha's her name. Camisha Jackson. Just say'n it makes me feel good. I go see her after I finish in the subway with my violin. Been seeing her two years now. Every day's the same. I get a muffin and a coffee. And I always tip her from my violin money. Even if I didn't make much that day. I watch her with the customers. Always smiling, always happy. I like it when there's a long line, cuz I get to be spend'n more time up close. She does this thing when she gets excited, where she goes on her tiptoes when she smiles. And she smiles with every muscle in her body. Cutest thing ever, boy. Let me tell ya. After I buy my muffin, I watch her from the park bench. I ain't be loitering inside no coffee shop. I ain't wanna be giv'n her no heebie jeebies or nothing.

Sometimes I follow her home, at a distance. Just to make sure she be making it safe. In case she needs protection from a demon. She don't know it though. She don't know me apart from being the grey-haired man who buys a blueberry muffin every afternoon.

One day, boy. One day she'll know her effect on me. I been writing this poem. I'm gonna give it to her when it's done. So she knows. She's gotta know. It ain't right for her not to know. The poem's not just about her though. It's about all angels. It ain't done, but for now it goes like this:

As I lay dying,
in the grip of this cruel world,
it was you who saved me.

You who I've never met,
who gave me the savage faith
that lifted me from the darkness

It wasn't always like this though, boy. No. I used to have an apartment on the edge of the park. Used to have girlfriends. I was in the newspaper; the orphan who won a scholarship to the country's finest music school. They paid for me to move up here from Louisiana and everything. I was lead violin in the orchestra. I had a whole bright future laid out ahead a me. I played in lots a bands. All kinds a music. I played jazz in the nightclubs in Harlem. Rubbed shoulders with the greats. People loved me. They cheered and bought me drinks. It was heaven, until I got into the dope.

At first, I thought it gave my playing soul. I'd hit it after every show. All us musicians were hitt'n it. Like it was some kinda magic serum that made us superhero players. I thought we were gonna make it rich. Of course, life taught me different. I got sucked into an abyss of fear and hate and greed and self-loathing and anger and all kinds a depression. My hands started shakin. I couldn't play no more. I lost all my gigs, all my respect, all my friends. Traded my violin for dope. Ended up sleep'n in the park, begg'n for change just to get the next hit. Woke up in an alley ten years later with a needle hanging outta my arm, barely enough flesh on my bones to stay alive, and not one person in the world who cared. I'd become what I hated, a demon. I knew then that if something didn't change I would be dead in days.

Then an angel saved me. A young street boy. He sat next me and cried with me. Just knowing he saw me and he cared meant everything in that moment. I vowed to clean myself up. For him. I knew then that if I could clean myself up, this boy had a chance too. I needed the boy to give my struggle meaning. I couldn't stop just for myself, I ain't strong enough, but the boy made kick'n dope about more than just me. And I never touched the shit since. It wasn't easy. Hardest thing I ever done. Ain't nothing as tough as kick'n dope, struggling to turn yourself from a demon to an angel. I tore my flesh, pounded my fists into brick till my hands broke. I wandered the streets like a ghost, winter-air freezing the snot and drool in my beard until I couldn't take no more. I grew desperate, fiending for dope so bad I couldn't think a nothing else.

One day I was standing in front of the liquor store, fixing to rob the place, when I heard the sound of the violin coming from the church. I wandered in. A nun was playing. An angel. She wasn't that good a player, but the music was medicine for my soul. She gave me a bed and some food. Helped me through the withdrawal. I'll never forget her. Sister Marie—died some years back. Left me her violin but it got stolen. I almost relapsed when that happened. But I don't want to talk 'bout that no more. No. Past is past. Better to leave it there.

Now I focus on the good. Like Harvey. He was an angel, boy. Let me tell ya. Twelve years he was by my side. He was there for me when I needed him, loyalty runnin deep through every fiber of his being. Saved my life, that boy did. Helped me through many a craving. Ain't nothin as powerful as knowing you got a friend there for ya, thick or thin. I thought 'bout gett'n another dog after he died, but I just can't do it. Not yet anyway. Even though I think we all gotta have love. Love for us is like water and sunshine for trees.

For now, I have Bernadette. It's enough. Making that violin sing in the subway gets me though the days. I don't mean the money. Some days I make good money in the subway, but I don't care 'bout that, boy. No, money seems to get me in trouble anyway. I'm talking 'bout the pure joy I get from playing. That's my gift to the world. My light to shine onto the lives of others. When somebody stops in the subway, a complete stranger, and just listens. When I see it in their eyes that my music has brightened their day, then it's all worth it—this life with its ups and downs and angels and demons—the love and hate people throw at each other. In that moment, when I'm lost in music, everything else melts away.

I feel my purpose, like a flowing river or a crashing wave. I feel myself as part of this earth, doing what I been made for, doing what be making me come alive. And to know that my passion touches others makes everything else bearable: the flack I get from hoods and cops, the sneering looks from suits, the hunger, the demons, the cold. The instant my bow touches the strings and Bernadette begins to sing, I know that all them demons are wrong, that I've reached something their minds can't understand. I know that I'm an angel, and that I'm here to fight the demons. That my violin is my weapon. And that to channel my experience and passion through it, to fill the air with music, is my purpose. It is my gift.

But I don't blame them demons for being demons. The world turned em that way. You look at children, you ain't never find no demons. But ya can't blame the world neither. Nor society. No. Things just is what they is. Angels and demons. I reckon we need both. The soul needs to be exposed to both, so it can choose for itself. The soul needs to be able to choose in order to be free. It's in the bible, right there in the beginning when Eve eats from the Tree of Knowledge.

God knew what he was doing when he put that tree there. He knows people need to be able to choose for themselves. That's the whole purpose behind this world and this life. So we can choose for ourselves. Eve ain't done nothin wrong when she ate that apple. No, sir. She was always supposed to eat it. It was all part of the plan. That's why God put Earth right smack dab in the middle between Heaven and Hell. So the path be the same distance no matter which way you walk. And you know what the path is made of, boy? Our deepest rooted desires. Yessir. Desire. Cuz our desires come from the root of us, boy. Desires generate thoughts. Thoughts lead to actions, and actions shape our lives. Way I see it, this life and this planet is a gift. And we make it whatever we choose. But we choose it. Every day we choose it, boy. Every moment of every day, boy, you better believe that.

RYAN POWER

Ryan Power is a storytelling samurai, wielding a pen like a sword and cutting to the heart. For over a decade he has traveled the world—a pupil of life, gaining the experience that fills these pages: living with yogis in India, with Rastafarians in Africa, trekking the Himalayas, teaching English in Taiwan, and surfing throughout Central America, Indonesia, Morocco, California, and Canada. As a multi-instrumentalist he has played in various bands, playing at beach parties and bars around the globe. He has partied at some of the world's top festivals, danced naked, laughed until he cried, cried until he laughed, made love in the rain—loved, lost, risen, fallen, and risen again. He has planted over one million trees, surfed next to sharks, stared down a bear, eaten a tarantula, flipped a truck and trailer at 100 Km/h, woken up hung-over in unknown places, danced until his feet bled, broken 7 bones, lost 30 pounds to Dengue Fever, spoken to God, and made peace with the Devil. For work he crew bosses a posse of ruggedly powerful tree-planters. He is an eternal student of the human condition, and holds a BA in creative writing from Vancouver Island University.

COVER ARTIST

She's a gentle badass, a pacifist with a bite, a tattooed beauty. Her hand-knit wool toques adorn heads across the globe. Her art appears in multiple Hollywood blockbusters. Her delicious vegetarian creations tantalize the senses. Her element is nature, where you'll find her shredding slopes in the winter and trekking in the summer with her dog, Whiskey. She's a Computer Graphics artist by trade and a woodland fairy in spirit. She'll melt you with her smile, then mesmerize you with her creativity. She is Danielle Kantola.

INTERIOR ARTIST

Imagine a gypsy forever crushing life on the open road, rolling in his live-in-art-van aptly named Snugzzz Vansion. He is a creator, turning everything he touches into a piece of art. His super power is love, which he harnesses from the cosmos and channels into everyone around him. His name is Court Dheensaw and he plants trees, beats drums, wrestles with water, builds, gives, dances like a drunken jester, and continually surrenders himself to the ever evolving winds of creation. Out of both the goodness of his heart and his love of creating, he armed himself with pen and brush, and designed 25 title pages for his good friend's first literary project, Bottomless Dreams, which he enthusiastically hypes as "the literary landscape where dare dreamers play."

CPSIA information can be obtained at www.ICGtesting.com
Printed in the USA
LVOW11*2335020215

425416LV00001B/2/P

9 781460 259252